Praise for *Dead If I Don't*:

'A lean and mean, modern-day noir western filled with complex characters and situations ... surely a candidate for best crime book of 2013' *New York Journal of Books*

'Waite follows his acclaimed first novel, 2011's *The Terror of Living*, with another searing western noir. Three people face terrifying moral choices as they each wish for what they can't have' *Publishers Weekly*

'A Pandora's box of chain reactions that wreaks havoc on a small southwestern town, havoc that is described in such graphically poetic prose that it occasionally makes the hair on even a cynical noir fan's head stand on end' *Booklist*

'[An] amazing novel ... Like the best of James M. Cain, Jim Thompson, or Cormac McCarthy ... Effortlessly entertaining, thought provoking, and deeply moving'
Alan Heathcock, author of *Volt*

'Waite writes with grace and poignancy and keen comprehension of hard men in hard circumstances ... [The] narrative rages as a perfect torrent of violence flooding toward its inevitable conclusion. Fierce and lyrical' *Kirkus Reviews*

'A disquieting novel that will appeal to fans of Cormac McCarthy' *Library Journal*

'Clearly, Waite has great work ahead of him. After reading this, I found it impossible to deny that his skill grows more sophisticated every year. His latest work explores a nuanced ~~~~ f emotion without sacrificing any ~~~~ made his first book so ~~~~'

fails to survive, these characters all deserve to be mourned' *New York Times*

'A breathtaking debut from a 30-year-old who writes as if he's been working at it for decades. This is a chase, a thriller, a western and a character study that combines everything in beautiful poetic prose that owes a bit to writers such as James Lee Burke and Cormac McCarthy . . . Save this one for a weekend' *Globe and Mail*

'Formidable . . . unfolds in short and all too memorably violent sequences, yet the author also allows his characters room to wrestle with private demons as the intense, often gruesome tale races towards its satisfying resolution' *Wall Street Journal*

'A superbly written chase novel . . . A cat-and-mouse pursuit, gut-clenching violence, loyalties sundered – all come with the genre. What is rarer is the finely honed literary sensibility of the writer, who conveys the sensory reality of his settings with evocative exactitude . . . Waite's considerable talent in general serves him well' *Houston Chronicle*

'Urban Waite never eases the throttle, but even at high speed, it's the interplay between the characters that gives the novel its power. An outstanding debut' *Booklist*

'Sharply written, swiftly paced scenes . . . The meticulously calibrated prose, rushing narrative and sympathetic protagonists mark Waite as a rewarding, promising writer' *Kirkus*

'Remarkable . . . Full of character and bleakness and written with vim and intelligence [that] will linger in the reader's mind long after the book is laid aside' *Library Journal*

DEAD
IF I DON'T

URBAN WAITE

**SIMON &
SCHUSTER**

London · New York · Sydney · Toronto · New Delhi

A CBS COMPANY

First published in Great Britain by Simon & Schuster UK Ltd, 2013
A CBS COMPANY

This paperback edition first published 2013

1 3 5 7 9 10 8 6 4 2

Simon & Schuster UK Ltd
1st Floor
222 Gray's Inn Road
London WC1X 8HB

www.simonandschuster.co.uk

Simon & Schuster Australia, Sydney
Simon & Schuster India, New Delhi

A CIP catalogue record for this book
is available from the British Library

Paperback ISBN 978-1-84983-135-2
Ebook ISBN 978-1-84737-971-9

Typeset by M Rules
Printed and bound by CPI Group (UK) Ltd, Croydon, CR0 4YY

For my mother,
who showed me at a young age
how to pick morels from the ashes.

I wish that road had bent another way.

Daniel Woodrell, *Tomato Red*

How terrible for a person to know what he could have been. How he could have gone on. But instead having to live along being nothing, and know he is just going to die and that's the end of it.

Oakley Hall, *Warlock*

DEAD
IF I DON'T

New Mexico

EARLY 1990S

DAY 1

THE PHONE WOKE RAY AROUND THREE THIRTY in the morning. He lay there, eyes open. The neighboring trailer lights casting a soft orange glow through the overhead curtains and the smell of the night desert outside, ancient and scraped away, through the sliding glass window.

Running a hand down his face, he could hear the phone still. Wasn't this what he'd asked for? Wasn't this to be expected? He bit at his lip, tasting the salt of dried sweat on his skin and feeling the pain as he rubbed at his cheeks and tried to bring some life back into his face.

On the bedside table the phone was still ringing and he put his hand out, searching. A series of empty beer cans tumbled to the floor and he heard the soft patter of a can somewhere below that had been half-full.

Too damn early.

He pushed himself up in bed, bringing the phone to his lap, the receiver to his ear. He rested his back on the wall and waited.

"You ready to have some fun?" Memo said.

"Define ready."

Memo's voice cracked and Ray imagined the smirk already

formed on the man's face. "I thought all you old guys woke before the sun came up."

"I'm not one of those 'old guys,'" Ray said.

"Relax," Memo said. "It's a compliment."

"Yeah? Define compliment."

"It's going to be just like the old days," Memo said.

"I hope it isn't."

The line went quiet for a moment, then Memo said, "I called to let you know the kid is on his way. Let's let bygones be bygones."

Ray sounded out the syllables. "*By-gones*."

"Listen," Memo said. "He's my nephew and he looks up to you. He's the future around here so try not to get him killed." Memo's nephew was Jim Sanchez. He was a kid to Ray, just out on parole after five years away. Ray with no real idea what to expect.

"I never said I'd babysit."

"You also said you'd never work for us again."

"Things change."

"Yes, they do," Memo said, then he hung up.

Ray slid over and put the phone back on the bedside table. Life hadn't worked out the way he'd planned it would. The only reason he'd agreed to work for Memo again was because the job was outside Coronado. It was in his hometown, a place where he'd married, had a son, and raised a family. All that more than ten years ago, when he was in his late thirties. His life had changed so much since then, since he'd taken the job with Memo. The round bump just beginning to show on Marianne's belly. No work anywhere in the valley and Ray with a real need to put some money away.

Ten years and Ray hadn't set foot in the place, hadn't even called home in all that time. A twelve-year-old son down there who Ray feared wouldn't even recognize him anymore. All this Ray had thought about when Memo called, offering him the job, offering Ray a reason to go home, even if Ray's own reasons these last ten years had never been good enough. He owed Memo that at least. Ray had wanted this for so long and never known how to do it, something so simple, a visit to see his son, a new life away from the violence of the last ten years. Memo at the source of it all.

Memo had been a young man when Ray first met him. Thin and muscular with the square Mexican features that later, after his father's death, began to round and cause Memo to appear as solid as a kitchen appliance, his head now bald along the top and shaved clean as metal around the sides and back.

Ray had liked the father more than he liked the son, but it was Memo who had recognized the skill in Ray, and as Memo was promoted up, so too was Ray. Ray was good at what he did, hurting people who stood in the way of what Memo wanted. Enforcing the power of Memo's family and making sure the drugs they imported always reached their destination.

But Ray was careful, too, and he'd survived a long time by picking and choosing the jobs that came his way.

Dark skinned, Ray had a shock of gray hair near each of his temples and the round Mexican head that had been passed down from his mother's side, and that he'd grown used to seeing on his mother's cousins and brothers as he'd grown up. With his hair cut short the definition of his jaw was more apparent, his features more pronounced where the coarse hair at his chin came through in a patchy beard.

He raised his eyes to take in what he could of the room, small and clogged with cast-off clothing. The back of his throat raw with pain and tasting pure and simple as cleaning alcohol. The chalk-dry mouth that went along with his drinking. Seven little dwarves climbing around in the back of his head, ready to go to work, and just like that they did, rock chipping. Miniature picks raised overhead, pounding away at the back of his skull in unison, one after the other.

From the nightstand he took a bottle of Tylenol. Cupped three of the pills in his hand and swallowed them dry, chasing them with an antacid, followed a second later by one of the ten-milligram pills the doctor at the VA had told him to take twice a day. The seven dwarves still chipping away at the back of his skull, singing a child's song he could only now draw up out of memory, but that he'd once sung for his son. "Heigh-ho, heigh-ho, it's off to work we go."

Ray ran the water in the sink. The single bathroom light of

a wall sconce shone yellow over his features. The mirror grown heavy with steam, obscuring the round face that looked back at him.

He held a hand under the water, feeling the heat, and then he brought the water to his face, letting it drip off his chin into the sink basin. The throbbing in the back of his head receding, flowing back into him little by little, medicine working, as if the men in there had gone exploring down his brain stem.

He'd decided as soon as Memo had told him about the job that it would be the last he would do. He was going home to Coronado. He was going home to see his son. The money he'd saved would get him through the first few years. He'd need to look for employment after that, perhaps even roughneck in the oil fields again, but until then it would be enough. This last job would help him with anything extra he needed.

In the years he'd been away he'd kept himself thin, working away on the fat that appeared from time to time at the waist of his pants or in the thighs of his jeans. Rigorously testing his muscles till the sweat beaded and dampened his clothing. Still he'd gained weight over the years since he'd left Coronado. What remained of the lean muscle appeared in the lines of his brow and the slip of his mouth as he worked his jaw in front of the mirror, lathering his face with shaving cream.

He was careful with the razor. Each pull of the blade revealing the thin muddy brown of his skin, a mix of his father's pink tones and the darker skin of his mother. The deep cast of his face swept away with the freshly shaven hair and his father's thin, hawklike nose more prominent.

Memo had said it was a shame what happened. Ray didn't know what to say about it. Nothing he could say would make the past go away, bring Marianne back or cure his son, Billy. There wasn't one thing Memo could do, Ray knew this, knew how it worked, how the past didn't change but the future could.

Far out in the trailer park Ray heard a dog begin to bark and then he heard the sound of gravel under tires. He checked his watch. He went to the kitchen window in time to see the man he assumed was Memo's nephew, Sanchez, pull past in a Ford Bronco, brake lights coming on, dyeing the kitchen blinds red as desert grit.

From the cabinet over the fridge he searched for the cracker box with his gun hidden inside. The cabinet high enough that he couldn't see more than a few inches within and was forced to feel around in the darkness above, bringing out box after box and then shoving them aside. Little mementos of his former life hidden all over the trailer, tucked in beneath the bench seat in the living room, shoved beneath the bathroom sink, out of sight behind half-empty bottles of shampoo. All of them just small things—just what he'd thought he could take with him, what he thought he might want sometime down the road, but that he wanted nothing of now.

He stood looking at a box of Billy's playthings, knowing each and every item inside: a small plush toy, a plastic action figure, a rubber bathtub duck. Everything inside, and even the smooth worn feel of the box in his hand, a reminder of every reason he wanted out of this business and hoped he'd never have to do it again.

This job was just a talk, Memo had said. Though Ray knew it would be more. It would always be more. And he knew, too, that he was out of time, and outside Memo's nephew was waiting for him, waiting for him to come out of the trailer and do this job.

Ray slid the toys back up into the cabinet. Finding the box of Ritz, Ray removed the clear plastic bag with the stale orange crackers inside and brought up the Ruger. The gun a dull metallic black, unreflective under the kitchen lights, pieced back together and cleaned after every use. He wrapped the pistol in his jacket before he heard the knock at the door.

Sanchez stood there at the base of the trailer stairs, his breath clouded around him in the air. Ray pushed the door aside and walked out into the cold. He felt the air first, a dry forty degrees. Behind Sanchez in the trailer park half-light, the Bronco sat with the driver's door left open and the thin drift of a Spanish music channel carried on the air. The only other constants the bark of the dog far off toward the park entrance and the shadowed bodies of the trailers like cast-off building blocks, scattered all down the slim gravel road. Not a one of them the same, scraped and dented from tenants that had come and gone and left their mark. Ray's own trailer, an old Dalton, rented out from the park for fifty dollars a week, rested there behind him on wheels and cement blocks.

Ray watched how the kid moved, looking up at Ray's trailer like it was the first time he'd seen one and could hardly believe it. Like Memo, he was Mexican, a few inches taller than Ray, young and thickly muscled with his head shaved to the skin and a chin strap of black hair from one ear to the other. Wearing a hooded sweatshirt, and white tennis shoes.

"You the new blood?" Ray asked.

The boy stared up at him, a smile sneaking across his face. "You the old?"

A FEW HOURS LATER RAY LEANED BACK IN THE Bronco's seat. The darkness of the locust thicket wrapped all around, shadowing the shape of their vehicle from the dirt road in front of them. The drive down from Las Cruces on the interstate had been quiet. Twenty miles out Sanchez pulled over and let Ray drive. They headed south toward the Mexican border, down a road Ray hadn't been on for ten years. Hardtop, cracked and filled with tar. Frozen in the high desert night and then warmed through again in the day. Hundred-foot cement sections bouncing steady as a heart beneath the springs. Scent of night flowers and dust in the cool desert air.

Sitting there, Ray knew his life had been sliding away from under him for a long time and today seemed like it would be no exception. They'd driven almost two hours. At the end of it, after they'd pulled up off the valley highway and found the dirt road running high on the bluff, they sat watching as the sky slowly lightened in the east. No part of him wanting to be here and only the solitary hope he held on to that the job would be done soon enough, and with it the life he had followed for so long, for which there seemed no cure.

There was a plan and he tried to think on this now. He'd grown up working for his father in the Coronado oil fields, his shoulders and arms carved from a daily routine that he continued still, doing push-ups on the floor till his heart ached and his lungs pumped a fluid heat through his blood-stream.

"My uncle told me you retired," Sanchez said. The slow tick of the engine in the morning air.

"I stopped working for Memo," Ray said. He watched Sanchez where he sat. The close cut of his hair outlining his thick eyebrows and muscled Mexican face. "I didn't retire, I just don't work for your uncle anymore."

"You're working for him now, though, aren't you?"

"I have my own reasons," Ray said.

The Bronco had been stolen off a lot the night before and

fitted with a flasher box, wired directly into the headlights. A spotlight bolted on just above the driver's-side mirror, with a thin metal handle that reached through a rubber glove into the interior of the cab. Sanchez coming to get Ray in the night, before the sun ever crested the horizon. The younger man wearing only a baggy set of jeans and a black sweatshirt against the cold, the smell of tobacco and axle grease hanging thick around him.

Ray in the waxed canvas jacket he always wore. The jacket padded to keep him warm. He wore a flannel shirt beneath, buttoned almost to the collar, and an old worn pair of jeans, stained from other jobs and other troubles, but worn regardless. The smell of sage and desert grit now floating up through the vents as they sat talking, their eyes held forward on the murk of the coming day. "I plan to move out of Las Cruces on this money," Ray said.

"Where?" Sanchez laughed. "Florida? You're not that old and you should know you don't retire from this line of work." He brought out a small bag of tobacco and some papers.

"This line of work?" Ray said.

"You know what I'm talking about."

Ray told him he did. He knew a lot about what Sanchez was talking about. Perhaps he knew too much. All he really wanted was a way out, and he'd had it ten years before. Only he hadn't taken it the way he knew he should have. "You've been lucky," Sanchez said, packing a cigarette.

"I have," Ray said, agreeing. "I've tried not to make mistakes."

"The way I hear it from my uncle it was an accident. But still, mistakes were made."

"Mistakes?" Ray said.

"Your cousin," Sanchez said. "He lost his job, didn't he? He was the sheriff and he lost his job over what happened down here. Killing that cartel woman just because you wouldn't leave it alone."

Ray sat trying to remember exactly what he'd told his cousin Tom. What had he said? How had he put it to him? Ray's wife, Marianne, dead and his son in there at the table with them, sitting in his high chair, while Ray and Tom sat talking to each other. Tom in his old cop browns, his hat thrown out on the table next to the half rack of beer Ray was drinking from. One after the other, like the coming day would never arrive and he didn't want to remember what he was telling Tom to do.

"You should have been the one down there," Sanchez said. He finished rolling his cigarette and placed it on the dash, dipping his fingers back into the bag and beginning another almost in the same motion.

"At the time I was trying not to shit in my own backyard. Coronado had its own problems; it didn't need mine, too."

"Memo always said it ruined you, he said you started doing things your own way. Said you were in your prime."

"Is that how he put it?" Ray said. "That I was in my prime?"

"Memo said you killed the Alvarez brothers in '82."

"That was a long time ago," Ray said.

"I heard about what you did in Deming a few years later," Sanchez went on. "I heard about what happened outside Las Cruces, about the farmhouse north of town. My uncle said you were—"

"I'm not that man anymore," Ray interrupted. He turned and looked at the half-finished cigarette in Sanchez's hands, and then he looked up. "How old are you?"

"Twenty-six."

"And you heard all this when?"

"I picked it up over time. I heard it from the family. I heard you did a lot of the work in the seventies, and that you went pro in the eighties."

"You hear I was married too, you hear about my baby boy?"

Ray watched Sanchez. The younger man wouldn't meet Ray's eyes—Sanchez just looking at the window now, at his own reflection. "I heard about that," Sanchez said.

"Mistakes," Ray said. He put his window down and watched his breath curl in the early-morning cold. It was one thing to do a job with the idea that it was business and nothing more. It was another thing altogether to take it into someone's home, into the kitchen where they ate their dinners, where their wives cooked their meals and their children roamed the floors on hands and knees.

"But you dealt with it," Sanchez said. "You handled it."

"I'm not that man anymore, you understand?" Ray said, his eyes scanning the darkened landscape, searching back over a history he'd run from ten years before, and thought that he'd left far behind. "I gave it all up."

"And my uncle had it all cleaned up for you?"

"He was good about that sort of thing," Ray said, "taking care of things."

"I'm sorry about your family," Sanchez said, finally. "But still, it doesn't change anything, you should know that."

"I'm not that man anymore."

"Whatever you are or aren't," Sanchez said, "you were given a call because you know this country, and you'll play your part just like you always have."

"That's all?"

"That's all we're asking."

"You think this guy will just stop for us?"

"Sitting in this thing with the flashers going, he'll think you're a cop. If he tries to run it's probable cause for a search, and he won't want that. All you have to do is go up there and ask him for his license and registration. Play your part, shine your flashlight in his window, and take the load from beneath the bench."

Ray drew himself up in the seat. He was looking out on the road still, listening to Sanchez. Behind him in the dark of the Bronco, Ray knew there was a long-range hunting rifle. He knew, too, that it was a lot of rifle for a talk on the side of the road. "You going up there with me?" Ray asked. His own Ruger nine-millimeter tucked into the pocket of the padded canvas jacket he wore.

A shotgun rested against the side of the door where Sanchez could reach it, and as they'd driven down, Sanchez had flipped the safety off, then on, repeating it every ten seconds or so, the metallic click of the metal counting out the time. "You wouldn't want that," Sanchez said. "Before I went away on a charge a few years back I worked with this man pretty regular. He'll know why I'm here and, more importantly, he'll know you aren't a cop." Sanchez looked over at the shotgun, pausing to reach a hand out and flick the safety from on to off. "If I get out it will mean something altogether different."

"You really think he's just going to let me take the dope?"

"Keep the flashlight on him, don't let him see your face or mine," Sanchez said. "You play it right, take the dope and let him off with a warning, he can't do anything about it. He's not going to come after a cop, and he's not going to go back to Coronado looking for a resupply. He's stuck."

"Who are these people?" Ray asked.

"The truck we're waiting on comes up from Coronado once a month. They take the drugs up from the border and they move it north to Deming, then east on Interstate 10 to Las Cruces or west to Tucson. All this through a man named Dario Campo, who has a bar in town."

DEAD IF I DON'T

"So that's what this is, a shakedown?"

Sanchez swept the line of cigarettes off the dash into the envelope of his hand. "This used to be our territory," Sanchez said.

"I thought it was still your territory," Ray said. "Isn't that what all this is about? Isn't that why my cousin lost his job and shot that woman, because Memo was trying to play everyone against everyone else?"

"I don't know what you heard, but the cartel is taking over everything these days. Our territory is half what it used to be."

"You ever think maybe there's a good reason it's not yours anymore?"

Sanchez put his finished cigarettes in with the loose tobacco and began work on another, Ray just watching. After a time Sanchez said, "You've been out of the loop. I'll give you that. You think you know how things are down here, but you don't know shit. You're going to need to be careful when you walk up there, when you take the dope. Don't get cocky because you think you've been around longer than me." Sanchez paused, admiring the half-finished cigarette in his hand. "Be careful with anyone who works for Dario. Dario is a real piece of work. Don't leave him with anything. Don't show your face when you take the dope. Just do your job and we'll both be fine."

"I've been doing this for a long time," Ray said.

"That's true. My uncle says you're the best. He told me there was no one better. But I think you should know that Dario is no one to feel comfortable with. He's out of Juarez and he's cartel. The last guy who tried to pull what we're about to pull had both hands skinned wrist to fingertips. They say Dario keeps them in his desk and wears them around like gloves when the weather turns cold."

"Sounds like Memo has been tucking you in at night." Ray laughed. "What is that? One of your favorite bedtime stories?"

Sanchez wouldn't look over at him; he just sat there shaking his head, tightening the cigarette in his fingers.

"Did Memo tell you that?" Ray said. "Did he think that would keep you in line?"

But Ray knew that sometime in the last few minutes everything had slowed. Cartel, Ray thought. There wasn't anything entertaining about this lifestyle anymore. Not like it used to be.

Before his eyes the light had grown grainy and pink as the red dirt road took form out of the shadows. "This guy better be along soon," Ray said.

"He'll be along," Sanchez muttered, fitting the last of the tobacco onto the paper and then sealing it with his tongue.

"We'll see," Ray said, looking out at the thicket and marking where the dirt road ran perpendicular to his vision. "I'm not interested in making more of a mess out of this thing than I'm willing to clean up."

"There's not going to be any mess."

Through the window Ray heard the early-morning birdcalls,

the wind pushing through the locust, and the hollow clack of the branches as they met, then bounced apart. Government BLM land and the smell of cows and dust—all there was now of this place, his father's old oil property only a few miles to the south, closer than he'd been in years, and most of the land now rented out as grazing range to the surrounding cattle farms.

With his arm out the window, Ray let his hand dangle there near the mirror. The whole thing made him nervous. This close to his former life and a family he'd never been completely honest with.

He leaned forward and played with the spotlight, wanting to get it right, wanting it to look official. If he could just get this right he'd be free at least until the money ran out, and if he was smart, maybe longer.

He went on adjusting the spotlight and watching the road until the old Chevy pickup went by about fifty feet in front of them with just its parking lights on.

It took them only a minute to chase the truck down, Ray driving and Sanchez sitting shotgun as the pale flash of their headlights alternated in front of them, highlighting the back of the truck bed. Ray had the spot turned on and through the back pane of glass he saw a man wearing a wide-brimmed hat. His skin pale beneath the spotlight. Another man beside him that neither Ray nor Sanchez had been counting on, but the man was there regardless.

Ray thumbed the Ruger's safety off. "You know something

about this?" Ray asked. He leaned forward and slid the pistol beneath his belt, watching the old Chevy where it sat a hundred feet in front of them, the faint outline of the parking lights visible through the early-morning haze.

"Doesn't matter," Sanchez said. "It's the same as it was before."

With his forearm, Ray leaned into the door and pushed it open. He was carrying in his left hand a flashlight, hitting it in rhythm against his leg. The thick light of the spot falling everywhere and the shadow he cast before him, into which he stepped, deep and dark as an abyss.

Nothing out there except the smell of desert flowers, dirt, and cow dung. A slim line of yellow tree tobacco growing like a weed along the side of the road, barely visible in the coming dawn. He clicked the flashlight on, holding it over his shoulder as he came to the truck. Ray knew men like this could be jumpy when it came to police.

He was near even with the cab now. The light raised as he came forward. Ray knew this man. His name was Jacob Burnham and he'd been working this land since Ray had been a kid. And in a rush, he knew, too, why Memo had been so insistent on having Ray work this job.

Ray had known Burnham all his life. They'd run drugs together when Ray was just getting into the business. The first meeting he'd ever had with Memo's family had been set up by Burnham, twenty years Ray's senior, pale skinned, with his veins showing blue beneath his flesh and his hair silver as mercury even all those years before.

Burnham was the local guy. The one who had been in Coronado all along, moving the dope up across the border. He was the one Ray would hear stories about as a boy, whispered to him as Burnham turned a corner a block up and fell out of sight. Now Ray worked in the same business as this man. Had for more years than he cared to admit. Doing the same type of work, the same profession, and he knew those same people down in Coronado probably still whispered Ray's name, just like they had all those years before with Burnham.

He never let his eyes drift away from Burnham, who sat waiting in the driver's seat. The beam of the flashlight held up to the driver's-side window, blinding the old man. When he was satisfied Burnham wasn't holding anything, he rapped on the glass with his knuckle and waited while the window came down.

"Morning, Officer."

"You have any identification on you?" Ray said, flattening his voice till it was unrecognizable as anything Burnham might remember.

The man dug around in his back pocket. The beige cowboy hat he wore shifted to the side, wide brimmed and flat in a style Ray couldn't remember seeing on any other man outside Coronado. Burnham pulled up his wallet, thumbed out the driver's license, and handed it over to Ray.

"Jacob Burnham," Ray said. He ran a thumb over the ID, looking at the picture of the man on the card. Stone white and skin wrinkled, with gray-silver hair combed to the right and cut at odd angles like he'd done it himself. "And who's in the passenger seat over there?" Ray saw Burnham's eyes dart toward the other man, then come back to rest on Ray.

"His name's Gil Suarez," Burnham said.

"Is that right?" He handed back the man's ID. "Would the both of you mind just stepping out of the vehicle?" Ray said, still holding the light over his shoulder.

Burnham hesitated. His eyes turned up on Ray and his breath moved steady through the beam of the flashlight before falling away again into the darkness. "You're not dressed like any sheriff's deputy I've seen."

"I'm not any ordinary sheriff's deputy," Ray said. The old man squinted out past the light, trying to figure Ray, but looking to the side where the light wasn't as strong. "Sorry," Ray said, "you just don't know these days who's traveling around on these roads. I'd rather have you out here where I can see you and I don't need to go guessing what you have in your hand or under your seat."

The old man sighed, letting his breath out in a long whistle like he was about to take a high fall into a cold lake. "We weren't doing anything illegal," Burnham said. "And we're within our rights just to stay here."

"I know what your rights are," Ray said. He shifted his eyes to where Gil Suarez sat in the passenger seat, judging whether the younger man was going to be a risk, then he ran them back over to Burnham. He watched the old man and when he moved to get out, Ray already had his hand resting close over his hip. "I'm just checking to make sure about something," he said.

Burnham was halfway out the door when Gil Suarez made a run for it, the gun up out of Ray's belt as he came around the cab looking for a clear shot. Gil keeping low, angling toward the protection of the locust thicket at the side of the road. Burnham up out of the cab now, his arms outstretched and going for the pistol in Ray's hand. Ray shoved the old man to the ground and came forward along the truck looking for his shot. Gil almost at the thicket. There wasn't anything else to do, Ray squeezed down on the trigger and the muzzle flash lit the truck cab up like a yellow flare, the bullet ricocheting off the metal roof and caroming into the early-morning gray.

At the sound of the shot, Gil ducked and kept running. Ray was aiming too low. He didn't know if Gil had a gun, or what he might be carrying. Burnham now up out of the dirt and making his own escape around the back of the pickup, keeping low in his stride as he tried for the thicket. Ray fixed his sight on the old man and came around the side of the truck.

He didn't want to shoot Burnham, but he knew he would if Burnham didn't stop. Ray was almost around the edge of the truck when the big boom of the shotgun caught Burnham midstride. He saw the old man fly sideways and disappear over the edge of the road. When he turned he saw Sanchez, up out of the Bronco, pump the twelve-gauge once and then fire again toward the running figure of Gil. Gil fell in the dirt ten feet out from the road. Splatter of buckshot all through the dirt where he'd tripped.

Lucky son of a bitch, Ray thought.

Sanchez pumped the shotgun a second time as the kid got up and ran forward across the sandy wash between the road and the wall of brush, half falling as he disappeared into the thicket of green-brown locust.

Ray stood there with the Ruger pointed into the bushes. The sound of the shotgun fading away down the valley as the wind clattered through the dense roadside growth all around them.

He turned and looked to where Sanchez stood next to the Bronco. "Get that rifle out of the back," Ray said. He sheathed the Ruger in his belt, turning to mark the place the kid had gone from sight. Trying his best to discern a path through the locust. He waited with his hand held out for the rifle.

Sanchez leaned back into the Bronco and came out with the hunting rifle. He was holding the rifle and he one-handed the shotgun to Ray over the open passenger door. "I'll take the younger one," Sanchez said.

Ray held the shotgun in his hands. He'd caught it high on the barrel and he could feel the hot metal on his skin, the sulfur scent of gunfire fresh in the air. "You hit him anywhere?" Ray asked.

"Not that I saw."

Ray stood looking at the place Gil had gone into the thicket. He didn't think the kid would get far, knew he would run out of cover in the lowlands after a few hundred meters, where the highway cut north along the valley floor. Still, it was nothing but shadow in there and dense brush. Light seeped up off the horizon to the east and bled into the sky. Everything above a gray-blue haze and their own shadows stretched away long and skinny to the west. "If he gets out of the bush, he'll see the valley highway."

"Nowhere to hide on that bottomland." Sanchez held the rifle in one hand and with the other he dug out three shotgun shells from his pocket. Cupping them in his hand, he gave them over to Ray.

Sanchez pushed the bolt back on the rifle, looked into the chamber, and then pushed the bolt forward again. The rifle took .308s, almost two inches in length and shaped like miniature missiles. Each of them big enough to take down a four-hundred-pound mule deer, and powerful enough to rip through skin and muscle and snap bone. "Did you see me wing the old man?"

"I saw it," Ray said.

Sanchez took a few steps toward the ditch where Burnham had fallen and the soft gurgle of his breath could be heard. "He's still alive."

"I can see that, too," Ray said, following Sanchez to where Burnham lay.

Sanchez turned around, looking for approval. "Pretty good, eh?"

"You better get going. That kid's just out there running and you've got less than a thousand meters on that scope," Ray said. He was holding the spare shotgun shells in his palm, and he started to feed them down into his pocket, waiting to see what Sanchez would do. "Memo wanted me on this job because he wanted Burnham to recognize me, didn't he?"

Sanchez nodded. He was looking toward Burnham where he lay in the dust.

"I told you it was going to be a mess," Ray said.

"No mess," Sanchez said. The flash of a smile and the brief pride Ray hated to see on the younger man's face. "My uncle set this up pretty good, didn't he?"

Ray paused, letting that sink in.

"There's a shovel in the back of the Bronco."

"Why would there be a shovel?" Ray said, refusing to believe what he was hearing.

Sanchez didn't seem to register what Ray had said. He was already moving away toward the edge of the road and the high thicket of locust, with the rifle in his hand.

Ray raised his voice; loud enough that Sanchez couldn't ignore him. "Why would there be a shovel in the back of the Bronco?"

"For messes," Sanchez said over his shoulder, taking the bank feet first, sliding down till he came out on the wash.

The truth was that as soon as he'd seen Burnham, Ray had known this would be the way it would go. There never was going to be a talk on the side of the road. He'd pushed that all away now. He'd pushed it deep down inside of him along with everything else.

All Memo's talk had been just an excuse, a way of getting him here so that he could do what he did best, what he hated to do, and what he'd thought he was done with. They weren't there for a simple shakedown. They were there to get rid of the competition. Now he watched Sanchez go, disappear into the brush with the rifle held out in front of him like some sort of divining rod, chasing down Gil's path.

Ray turned and looked at Burnham's truck. Both doors hung open and the light from the flashers pulsed over everything. The old man lying in the shadows at the edge of the road. His body thrown out along the ditch, turned over on his back, the air in his chest barely moving his lungs, still alive. Blood pooling slowly beneath him in the dirt. It's a terrible way to die, Ray thought, buckshot like that.

Ray knew this man. He'd known him almost his whole life and he crouched next to Burnham and watched the old man's wet eyes begin to cloud over. The slow labor of Burnham's breath ticking away at Ray's feet as the focus went out of his face. Ray shifted to one knee, watching Burnham where he'd landed after being blown a yard off his feet, little gurgling sounds coming up out of his throat. Buckshot all down the right side, he held one of his hands tight to his body, trying to hold back the blood. And with the other he gripped the earth near his hip as if he might lose his hold and spin loose.

The old man must have been nearing his seventies. Blood showing on his face where the wound in his cheek leaked a deep ruby color into the white of his beard, his face tight with the pain as he tried to move and the skin of his forehead drawn white and clean as fresh paper.

Burnham closed his wet eyes and then opened them again in a slow blink. "Times have changed," the old man said, blood on his lips where he'd put them together to speak.

"Times are the same, *viejo*, it's just you that has changed."

Burnham looked up and found a focus. Ray knew the man recognized him, knew it just as surely as he knew his own face in the mirror. They were kin in some strange way, connected by who they were and what they did, and it was a sickening realization. Somehow through all this, years before, Ray had thought perhaps their relationship would end just the way it was now. There were no surprises and nothing to spare Ray from the future he had imagined all those years before.

Ray didn't know how long the old man had been working this area, but it was over now. From the pocket of his shirt Ray removed his pack of antacids. Resting his weight on the one knee, he chewed at the bitter pill while the old man lay dying on the ground.

"Times have changed," the man said again. "You think they haven't, but they have. You're old enough. You should know it."

Ray didn't want to be like this man, not at all. He stood, trying to put some space between them, but watching the old man the whole while. In his hand he held the shotgun loose in his palm, the chalk taste of the antacid in his mouth. With one hand on the stock of the gun, he fished the spare shells from his jeans pocket and began to load them into the belly.

"All this used to be open country," Burnham said. "Just like you can still find some places down south. Now it's all parceled up and sold off and you can't go anywhere without someone knowing." Burnham leaned his head to the left and spat blood into the dirt, then turned his head back up so he could see Ray. The ball of shot that had caught him in the cheek looked deep and dark as a well in the man's face. "I used to ride all over this land with my family, with my brother and my father, but that's all gone now, you understand?"

The pool of blood beneath the man, an outline in the dirt, was gradually expanding. His eyes drooped once, then again. Ray let him speak, let him get it out. It was what Ray knew he'd want when the time came for him, when he had his final say and tried to make right with the world. When he tried to tell how he'd gotten down this path, and how he regretted it every day, but didn't know how to turn back.

The old man coughed and blood erupted out the side of his cheek. He leaned his head to the side and spat again. Then turned back and fixed Ray like the conversation was ongoing and the man had merely paused to allow Ray the chance to speak. "We used to rustle cattle when the land was open and you could run them all the way down to Mexico and not see a soul." His wet eyes closed and then opened. "I suppose I put myself in this mess." He paused again, looking up at Ray. "I recognize you, you know? Gus's kid. I always wondered where you'd gone and I guess now I know. You still work for Memo, don't you?"

"Yes."

"You know he's playing crooked with all of us? I worked for his father, too. A long time ago, before you even came around, but Memo is something different. He doesn't respect the old ways—doesn't respect anything anymore." He stopped to gather his breath before going on again, pink spittle showing in the corners of his mouth. "There used to be rules for this sort of thing. Memo's father knew them, but it's not like it used to be, not anymore."

"Is that why you went over?" Ray said. "Is that why you started working for the southerners?" Ray stood there looking down. The shotgun waiting and ready at his side. He knew this man, but it didn't matter. None of it did anymore. He would do the job no matter what the man said. It didn't matter.

"Things have changed," Burnham said. "Go on, I'm ready. I've been ready a long time and just not known it. Go on now."

Ray raised the shotgun a few inches from where it hung in his hand. He put the barrel to the man's heart. "*Viejo*," he said, "they don't make them like you anymore." And then he pulled the trigger.

Ray looked up from the dead man at his feet and watched the wind come down through the branches and then go away again. The lights on the Bronco still on, still flashing, leaving a pale indentation over the land, skewing the fall of the morning light, letting it spread thin over everything in a ghostly shade not of this world.

When he looked down at the man laid out beneath him, he knew that it might well have been him. What Burnham had said was probably true: the rules had changed—there were no more rules. He could see that now. Perhaps he'd known it all along. Perhaps he'd been the one to change them. It wasn't hard to see. It had been a mistake to take the job. He'd never wanted this again, not this.

He turned from the man and went to the door Gil had left standing open. Burnham's hat sitting there on the dust-stained floor. The dope somewhere beneath the seat, nothing left to do but get it up out of the bench and take it to Memo. The thought in his head that he was done with this business, that—standing there with the dead man behind him and another on the run—he was exposed once again, just as he'd been ten years before.

He brought out a knife from his back pocket. Leaning into the cab he stuck the tip into the bench and ran it across the fabric. Tufts of white padding came forward through the cut. Beneath, he saw a red and black gym bag with the shape of the bricks visible through the fabric. Inside he knew he would find the brown kilos of heroin.

He put the knife aside and pulled the bag up out of the bench cushion, and set it on the seat. With the zipper undone he saw there were twelve bricks of heroin, all of them the color of molasses.

In the ten years since he'd lost Marianne, he'd tried to get out of this business more times than he could remember, painting houses in the summers or filling in on a construction crew when there was work. None of it paying anything close to what Memo would pay him for this job. But it had been safe. And no one would die for twelve bricks of heroin.

He was burying the old man when he heard the rifle shot far off in the valley like distant artillery. Ray knew one way or another it was done now, and that the younger man who had been riding shotgun with Burnham was dead, and that the job he and Sanchez had set out to do would soon be over.

THE AMBULANCE CAME UP OVER THE RISE behind them. The dog spinning around on the seat as Tomás Herrera pulled his truck to the side of the highway. The sound of the siren flowing by in one complete sweep, followed only seconds later by one of the county cruisers doing about eighty on the narrow double lane. Both gone down the road as swift as they'd come up behind, leaving his truck rocking lightly on its springs. The flat desert the only thing to be seen out the cab windows, the dirt wash off to the side of the pavement where the rains came a handful of times a year, and the dried-up arroyos farther on toward the wind-scraped peaks of the Hermanos Range. The ambulance and cruiser gone by now, far enough along the highway that they were distinguished from all around as only a muted pulsing of light in the distance. His dog, Jeanie, stood stiff pawed on the bench seat, barking after the two emergency vehicles as they went north up the highway.

Pulling back onto the road, he felt his foot a little heavier on the pedal. The old truck engine laboring with the speed, clucking after the ambulance and cruiser like a bird in heat, a trail of smoke behind them—visible in the rearview as the truck burned through oil and gas, going on down the road.

Up ahead, a mile farther along, the accident came into view, a big-bodied pickup truck turned partway across the centerline. The ambulance pulled in beside it and the wavering flicker of lights from three county cruisers parked alongside. Deputy Pete Hastings—a man Tom had trained fifteen years before—shuttling cars around a blocked-off section of road.

He hadn't said much to any of these old colleagues in the years since he'd left the department, not more than to pass a few words of conversation on the street. Every time he ran into any of them, whether he was in town to pick up feed for his hogs or running errands for the Deacon family, Tom acted polite enough, trying as best he could to get himself away as soon as possible, feigning some urgent appointment. All the while fearing they saw right through him, felt the hollowness inside him as he shook their hands.

Tom was a big man, he'd always been bigger than most, six foot four with wide shoulders. That hollowness inside him too much at times to bear, while at other times, in the early years when he'd first left the department, it had been shame that had filled him, compacted with guilt, layered one on top of the other all the way up through him to the thick black hair he wore close around his oblong head. He'd known people to call him handsome before but he'd never truly believed them. His jaw rounded all the way from ear to ear, hung low like a newborn's fat-featured face. No matter how skinny Tom ever got he always maintained the same jaw, covered now with a peppering of black and white hair he could no longer stop from showing.

People had liked him. They'd always liked him and it was

the reason he thought, at times, he'd been elected for a job he'd never truly believed he'd receive. Mexican as he was in a town filled up with white oil barons and Texans brought west to work the oil fields, he was a bit of a loner. It was the reason he still felt uncomfortable walking the streets of Coronado and the reason he'd eventually thrown in with his own family, or gone up against his own kind—depending how one saw it—in a bid for the town's approval. Only it hadn't gone the way he'd hoped and he'd lost his job, as well as a piece of himself, in the process.

He waited now in the line of traffic built up around the accident. A big-bodied truck he could only partially see, blocking half the road. His eyes resting on it for a long time, stirring up some recognition as he waited his turn for the deputy to wave him past.

Straightening up in the seat, anticipating his turn, he checked himself in the mirror. On his face the two-day growth of his beard, coarse along his cheeks, showed the slow untangling of his former self. A little more weight in his belly now, and the feeling that he was living a life that he'd never expected.

The deputy waved his hand and Tom moved forward. Almost the same height as Tom but twice as thin, Deputy Hastings was blond with a hard round belly and the sallow skin of an inpatient waiting on some vital transfusion. A distant cousin of Sheriff Kelly's, he was the oldest in the department now, one of the few left after the layoffs had come down from the mayor's office.

Tom slowed the truck and, with his arm out the window, asked the deputy what happened.

"Can't say," Hastings said.

"What do you mean?"

"I mean, 'Can't say.'"

"Really, Pete?"

"On this one, Tom, I can't."

Up ahead, Tom saw the ambulance parked near a blue Ford Super Duty, the bubble lights over the ambulance still flashing. Through the small side windows he watched the two paramedics working on someone inside. He looked back at the big Ford and knew for certain now that it was the same truck he saw every day at his work. "Clint Deacon get into some sort of accident?"

Deacon's truck sat at an angle across the road, no glass on the cement, not much of anything. "He's a friend of mine," Tom said. "A neighbor." He'd worked for Deacon for two years now, staking fence posts and herding cattle. Tom's father, Luis, putting him on when the money had run out of Tom's hog business. But still he preferred to call Deacon a neighbor rather than his boss. Something shameful now attached to this distinction, that Tom had once been the county sheriff, then a successful farmer himself, but now was just another laborer like his father.

A car honked behind Tom. Looking over his shoulder he recognized one of the roughnecks he saw from time to time when he went for drinks with his father. The man honked again and Hastings waved him past.

Tom waited for the oil worker to pull around and then went on, "Look, Pete, that ambulance went by me in a hurry. I'm just asking."

"I can't, Tom."

A hundred feet up the road, Tom saw Sheriff Edna Kelly walk out from behind one of the cruisers, remove her hat, and wipe the sweat from her forehead with a small white handkerchief.

Ignoring the deputy, Tom raised his hand and hollered a greeting. Kelly looked up, and when she recognized Tom, she motioned for Hastings to let him through.

More than ten years his junior, Kelly had once been his deputy. She was athletic in build with a runner's thighs and the broad, rounded shoulders of a girl who had grown up doing farm work.

"Tomás Herrera," Kelly said after he'd drawn his truck up next to where she stood. His name pulled long in mock disbelief. "You know you can't be here."

Tom shrugged. "I was just driving by."

Jeanie moved over across the bench seat and put her head out the window, looking for a hand from Kelly. The old mutt a gift from Kelly all those years before when Tom had been asked to step down from his position as sheriff so that Kelly could take over.

Kelly let Jeanie get her scent before petting her. "What are you really doing here?" Kelly asked, standing beside his truck looking in, a nervous edge to her voice that carried with it the slightest hint of warning.

Tom pulled the dog back from the window, feeling the old girl fight him for only a moment before settling in on her side of the bench. "Nothing, Edna. Just passing through on my way north."

Kelly waited a moment, perhaps wanting him to say more, and when nothing came, she said, "I can't have you here. Not after everything." The words were hard, but the voice was soft. A lot of history between the two of them and Tom wanted to believe it counted for something. He wanted to believe that maybe Kelly didn't mind his being here as much as she was saying.

Still, Tom felt scolded. At thirty-six, she was more than a decade younger than him, wearing the star he used to wear. The blond hair he'd always felt an attraction for when she'd been his deputy now kept up under her hat in a ponytail. All of her seemed new to him, like she'd never been the person he'd known before. The stress and pressures of the job showing on her face where new seams had formed in the skin, intensified now by whatever she'd just walked away from.

"I'm not here to step on any toes," Tom said, reassuring her.

"You know I'm helping out Deacon these days, trying to make a little extra money to get my hog farm back on the level. I saw the truck. I just thought—"

"Clint is fine," Kelly said, cutting in. She gave a sideways look toward Deacon's Ford. "You can see him up there in Pierce's car."

Tom put a hand over his eyes to shade them from the sun. Up the road Clint Deacon was sitting in the back of one of the cruisers with the door open. The young deputy Tom had seen around town recently standing just beyond taking a statement from him. "I didn't mean to press you," he said, trying to be apologetic.

"I know," Kelly said. "I'm just worried is all. I haven't had much experience with this sort of thing."

"This sort of thing?"

Kelly gave the truck another sidelong glance, but didn't say anything more.

"What are we talking about here?" Tom asked.

"We're not talking about anything, Tom," Kelly said, stepping close as the ambulance's reverse lights came on, and the driver brought the big square body around toward Coronado. "We just need to hold Deacon's truck a little longer."

Tom watched the ambulance go by, rising up, but was unable to see who was inside. "For what?"

Kelly took the handkerchief from her pocket and wiped her forehead again. Down the road the midseason heat played in waves across the asphalt, and under Kelly's arms there were two dark crescents of perspiration. "You're not the sheriff anymore, Tom."

"I know that. Believe me, I do." Tom looked over at his dog, ashamed by Kelly's bluntness. Kelly and he had had a regular meal every Thursday for years but it had slowly gotten away from them. Now, looking at the dog she'd given him, Tom remembered all those Thursday night meals in his living room, eating in front of the television with the then puppy biting on Kelly's fingers with her pinprick teeth.

"I've got the next two days off," Tom said, trying to ease the mood. "I was just going up the road on my way to see my goddaughter. I see this up ahead and I think maybe someone is hurt, maybe I can help." Tom nodded toward Deacon's truck. The tires had left marks on the asphalt. "What happened up there?"

Kelly shook her head and grinned. Looking away from Tom for a time, she turned back to him, her face now sober. "Sometimes I don't know about this job," she said.

Tom mumbled his agreement. He'd felt the same all through that last year he'd been with the department. Ray's wife, Marianne, dead from a hit-and-run accident, and Ray saying it wasn't an accident, it was the cartel. The pressures mounting for Tom to do something about Angela Lopez. A woman rumored to be working for the cartel. Tom wondering all the while if any of it was even worth it. Pissed off about the whole thing. He knew he'd taken it too far, taken the job too seriously. He'd let his cousin Ray talk him into a place too deep for even Tom to go.

Again, Tom mumbled a reply. Kelly on the verge of telling him something she wasn't supposed to, but that Tom was desperate to know. All of his past now crushed up behind him like a stack of freight come loose from its tracks. All of him feeling that longing for his former job, for the weight of the star on his chest, and the purpose that went along with it.

"I don't want this to come back on me," Kelly said, finally.

"Okay," he said, fearing if he said anything more she might hold back.

"Okay," Kelly said. "You were never here."

Tom nodded.

"There was a man, a kid really. Mexican. He came up onto the road. Shot so bad he looked whiter than me."

"Dead?"

"I don't know. Got the ambulance out here as soon as we could, but I don't know."

"You think a coyote decided to turn him loose?" Tom asked, feeling the possibilities begin to churn, the outcomes and story lines that might have brought this boy up onto the road with a bullet through him.

"Don't know anything yet, but it didn't feel right."

"Why's that?"

"The clothes, he didn't look like someone who would be out

here, you know? He didn't look like someone who'd spent the last couple days crossing."

"Drugs then?" Tom said. "He could be one of Dario's boys. Maybe Dario was trying to settle something."

"Don't even say that," Kelly said. "We don't need that kind of talk around here."

"Well, why not?"

"You know why not," Kelly said.

"You have to at least consider it."

"Does this look like something Dario would have done? In the two or three years since he showed up he's been quiet. Why this? Why now? We might throw his name around from time to time, but he's more careful than this."

"Edna," Tom said, offering up a stern face. "You know what they've been saying about him in town."

"I know the rumors."

"He's cartel, or as close as we've had to it since Angela Lopez."

"I don't want to believe it," Kelly said. "I can't afford to go around making accusations without merit. You should know that. It just doesn't go that way around here anymore."

"Well, what then?"

"Deacon just said the kid came up out of the desert, just ran right onto the road," Kelly said. "That's all I have right now."

"Nothing else around?"

"Only a couple out from California, tourists wanting to see

the desert. Came along after Deacon stopped his truck. The woman in the car was a nurse out of Los Angeles. She helped Deacon with the kid. He had to use his own shirt to stop the bleeding."

"And the bullet?"

"Something high powered, it went all the way through. Once we get this road cleaned up I can get the deputies searching for it with the metal detector."

Tom looked up to the west where the hills flowed down from the Hermanos Range like a long, smooth blade bent on its side. Hillsides branched with arroyos showed green where the locust grew up out of the high desert in thickets. "Whoever shot this boy could just be sitting up there watching. You need to send someone now, you understand," Tom said, trying to check himself. He wasn't the sheriff anymore.

"You know what I'm working with here, Tom. We're not trained for this. We can do a traffic stop, chase a rattler off someone's porch, but this is a whole other kind of situation."

"What about the state police?"

"The mayor wants this handled in-house—"

The breath burst from Tom's nostrils before he had time to stop it.

"He doesn't want any outside attention," Kelly finished. "You know how things are around here. Oil's gone. Nothing's keeping them here, and the mayor knows it."

Tom couldn't help it. He was thinking about the Lopez

woman he'd shot ten years before, how he and Kelly had come through the door looking for evidence to convict her, to send her back down to Mexico. Nothing there and Angela Lopez running to protect her infant daughter, Tom making the split-second decision he would never be able to take back. No drugs on her at all, nothing to say she was guilty of anything. "If this thing turns out to be drug related it could get complicated."

Kelly took a moment with her words, thinking it through. "Yes," she said, wiping at her forehead again. "I know that."

Tom knew just by being there he was putting Kelly at risk. He wanted to apologize for the things he'd said, for trying to give Kelly orders he no longer had the right to give.

"Look," Kelly said after a time had passed. "You can't repeat any of this."

"I know. I was just passing by on my way up to see my god-daughter."

"That's good of you," Kelly said. "But maybe now you should be going. I don't want this getting back to Eli."

"The mayor?" Tom said, disappointment any time he heard the man's name.

"If this thing does turn out to be a murder—and it looks like it will—I don't need him questioning how you happened on us."

Tom said he understood. There had been a hearing after Angela Lopez had died. The mayor, Eli Stone, pushing for the judge to punish Tom. He'd been looking for jail time. The judge called it a freak accident. The woman, out of Nogales, had ties to the south. She was known to hold drugs. She was dangerous. Sheriff Herrera had just been doing his job. The only other officer on the scene, Deputy Edna Kelly, had given her statement at the hearing, agreeing with everything Tom had said.

There was no excuse, and Tom knew it. There never would be. Not for any of it. He glanced up and caught Kelly's eyes on him.

"All these years and you still go up to visit that kid?" Kelly said.

"Sometimes I don't know why I take the time. Why I think to even do it. Someday I know they'll tell Elena all about me and I worry about how that will seem, how I will look after all these years. Sometimes I think it's best to just leave it alone," Tom said. He was looking up the road now, planning his course.

When he turned back he saw the shift that had come over Kelly's face, showing the disappointment at what he'd just said. He knew she saw what had happened to the Lopez woman differently—all of it. Everything was different for her. His cousin Ray wasn't Kelly's cousin, it wasn't as personal for Kelly, none of it ever was, and he knew she'd never understand—not fully—all that had come before and led them to that house where Elena sat on the floor as a baby and her mother rushed to protect her.

Kelly shook her head in that slow way she did sometimes, the way she had always done when she thought she knew something better than Tom. The way she did when she saw everything in a brighter light than Tom could see, that he wouldn't permit himself to see. And Tom knew all this, knew he couldn't see any of it because he wouldn't let himself. So he said again, just to nail the facts down, "I don't know why I go up there anymore."

The smile cracked on Kelly's face. "You know why you go."

"Yes, I guess I do," he said, knowing it was guilt, knowing there were a million different reasons he needed to go up that road to visit the girl who had once sat, just eighteen months old, on her mother's floor.

"You tell Heather and Mark hello for me."

"I'll do that," Tom said.

"How old is Elena now?"

"She'll be eleven this coming March."

"Give her a kiss for me, too."

"I will." He was about to leave, then stopped and asked, "You going to be okay out here?"

"I'll be fine," she said. "Just get on before the mayor finds out you were up here."

THERE WAS THE FAINT BEGINNING OF A SMILE on Edna Kelly's lips as she walked over to talk with Deputy Hastings. She didn't know how Tom had come across them on the one highway leading north out of the valley. The story about Elena could have been true. The questions he'd been asking were not only on her mind, but probably on the minds of all her deputies as well. Ten years since they'd had a death like this and no saying how it would be treated by the mayor.

All she could hope for was that none of this blew up on her. The boy coming up onto the road, blood all down his shirt and the gaping hole in his chest where the bullet had gone through. She didn't know what to make of it. All of it so close to her own history when she'd been the deputy and Tom the sheriff. Ten long years to dig herself out from under that, to dig herself out from what could have easily been called a murder, but, in the end, wasn't.

Her one real worry was that she'd get thrown in with Tom. She saw the way everyone treated him now. Like he was some sort of troubled kid come in off the street looking for a job. It was a sad way to look at a man who had given his life to a town, and then received nothing in return. All those years and he made one mistake. Kelly hated them for it sometimes. She hated the mayor, the judge, and the people in the town who looked at him that way, like he wasn't worth the trouble anymore.

Kelly knew that whatever Tom did these days, raising hogs or helping out over at the Deacon property, his thoughts were never far from what was going on in town. She didn't blame him for that. She knew he'd been cut loose over what had happened to the Lopez woman, that he had to be let go. As she walked the yellow line of the road to talk with her deputy, it was just that, though, that worried her about Tom. He'd never truly stopped being the sheriff, even though everyone had stopped believing in him.

"Rumor has it Tom has got one of our old radios at his house," Kelly said to Hastings, trying to get him to smile.

Hastings removed his hat and wiped his forehead. "What do you think?"

"I don't know," Kelly said. "He has some amazing timing."

A car approached and Hastings waved it by. "His timing is what got him into trouble."

"Yes," Kelly said. "It did."

She was the sheriff because of Tom. Ten years ago he'd asked her to come with him. Said he'd gotten a tip about Angela Lopez, about something she was up to. Kelly knew the tip had come from Tom's cousin, Ray Lamar. She knew, too, that Tom wouldn't have told her about Ray but she could see it clear as day. Ray had grown up in Coronado just like the rest of them. He was the son of Gus Lamar, one of the original oilmen who owned fields north of town. And, more importantly, she knew

Ray was looking for a way to settle things up without completely going to war.

There wasn't anything wrong with a law officer going over to a woman's house to ask a few questions, to get to the bottom of things, and to check out the tip she was holding drugs for the cartel.

What was wrong about that day, about following that tip, was that Kelly knew that Ray and Tom were looking for someone to blame, had been looking for a long time. The hit-and-run death of Ray's wife was still fresh on everyone's minds in those days.

The news of the accident coming to them one day as they sat in the department office, the phone on Tom's desk ringing, and all of them—six deputies at the time—looking up as they always did, anticipating what trouble might be on the other end of that line.

It had been Kelly who'd eventually gone out to Ray's house, out of town a ways on Perimeter Road, one of a hundred new houses built all in the same fashion to house the oil workers coming west out of Texas, to tell him about the accident, to bring Ray to the hospital where his two-year-old son, Billy, had been taken. The boy surviving only because he'd been thrown free from the car. Ray's wife hadn't been as lucky. Tom himself told Ray that Marianne had died while Ray waited outside the operating room doors.

In the weeks that followed, Ray's business, or the premise

of one, slowly disappeared as he pitched himself against the cartel like a man slamming his fist into a wall, hitting at it till the bones in his hands went to jelly, calling in to the sheriff's office daily.

Perhaps Ray had put his family in disaster's course, led them into the canyon as the shadow closed in above them. Perhaps he'd done that, and perhaps the outcome—what had happened to his family, what had happened to Ray—was all there was left for him. Kelly didn't know. She didn't know anything about it, but she could say without a doubt that afterward Ray didn't let it go, the phone in Tom's office ringing every day as, little by little, Ray began to feed Tom information and Tom's suspicions about the Lopez woman began to grow.

Beside her, Hastings nudged her elbow. Down the same road on which she had watched Tom drive north toward Las Cruces, a news van was now approaching.

"Shit," Kelly said, lifting her hat back up onto her head and feeling the sickening wash of an ocean rolling through her insides. "Eli isn't going to like this."

"No," Hastings said. "I don't think we'll like it much, either."

The two of them stood there watching as the van grew bigger, moving south toward them, the waves of heat playing across the road.

"That true?" Hastings said.

"About what?"

"About Herrera? About the radio?"

"If he has one," Kelly said, "he's obviously not the only one listening in." About a hundred feet in front of her the news van slowed, then pulled off the road onto the shoulder, gravel popping under the tires.

R AY LAMAR SAT ON THE TOP STEP OF THE PORCH watching the desert. The house, two stories in height and constructed of clapboard siding, had been painted yellow at one time but now appeared dirty and wind-worn in its coloring. It was a forgotten place, sun-bleached pale as an Easter egg. A house Ray knew only as the Sullivan house when he'd grown up here, one of the old abandoned homes outside of Coronado, long forgotten after the big oil companies came through, buying up the land. So many of them outside the town that Ray and Sanchez had had their pick, trying as they were to find a place to hide the bag of heroin and Burnham's pickup truck.

Looking out on the land that sat before him, rolling hills populated by creosote and burro bush, the mountains to the east and north scraped clean to their rocky surface, he was aware that he had lived a life complete in itself before this one. And that he was now left here in a sort of afterlife of his own making, which he shared with the memory of his wife, alone.

They had married after they found she was pregnant, Ray working in the fields for his father after he'd come back from Vietnam. Oil the only thing he'd known his whole life and the only skill he had to rely on here in the world he had left and to which he had returned, wanting simply to put those years he'd been away behind him. He was young then, in his early twenties when he'd left, and midway through his twenties when he'd returned.

His relationship with his wife, Marianne, started long before he'd even come back. Before he'd set foot in the States again and taken work with his father. Marianne, small in stature, five foot four at the most, with pale translucent skin and sharp green eyes. In Ray's memories her hair tied, dark and brown, behind her in the day, always hung loose at night for dinner. She was the sister of one of his old buddies from the war. They had stayed in contact after his buddy had passed, writing letters to each other, sending them from one world to the next. Those letters getting Ray through his last few months, writing to her almost as if he were a piece of the brother she had lost, an extension of the same man, with the same fears and shared experiences.

Marianne and his son were the reason he'd started to work for Memo in the first place, wanting to provide for them as the oil went out of his father's property. All of Coronado infused in some way by Marianne. His memory of her drifting by him like a wind, there and then gone again in its wanderings.

Ray ran a hand up through his hair. He sat on the porch looking out at all he'd left and now had returned to. Burnham dead at his feet only hours before and the thought in his head that he hadn't wanted to pull the trigger but that he had all the same because it was his job. It was what he was paid to do and if it came to it, he knew he would do it again like he had done it so many times before.

Behind, he heard the porch door open. Casting a glance over his shoulder, he saw Sanchez standing there, the tips of his white athletic shoes red as desert dust, and the black sweatshirt and jeans a size too large on his frame.

"Done?" Ray asked.

"I found a place for the bag inside one of the walls upstairs."

"Hidden?"

Sanchez smirked, the look young and arrogant on his face. Raising his hand to take in the desert and heat-blurred shape of Coronado farther on, Sanchez said, "This place is falling apart. No one is going to be surprised if there is a little extra plaster on the floor."

Ray's family had been one of the original oil families to populate the valley before all the big oil companies came through. Ray's childhood caught somewhere between the boom and gradual bust. His mother a Mexican cook and his father, Gus, one of the richest private oilmen in the valley at the time.

White haired even at a young age, with a crooked nose and the white skin that always burned too easily in the desert sun.

All Ray could see of Coronado from the porch laid low across the horizon to the south. A town constructed out of memory, barely visible in the midday heat. But a town that Ray knew was there all the same. The wooden church with its black iron steeple, the brick courthouse where he'd been married, and the hospital where he'd been born, all of it in a line off Main, where the road ran south to north with grain and feed shops, restaurants, and bars. All of it, even in the years Ray had lived there, slowly creeping off the edge of the map. In twenty years he doubted it would even exist; a hundred years more and there would be nothing but foundations and a few iron fence posts.

Most of it, even the house Ray and Sanchez had chosen, built during the first good years, when the oil rush had come through, before the larger companies began speculating on all the properties. Ray's father had been one of the first into the area and Ray knew he was out there still, even now after the oil was gone and all those old properties, like those owned by the Sullivans or the Clarks or the Andersons, had been abandoned by the larger oil companies. Leaving carved-out farmhouses to dot the valley floor.

"You going to make the call or should I?" Sanchez said.

Ray stood, swiping the dust from his pants where it had accumulated. Over his top he wore the flannel shirt he'd put on the day before and the padded canvas jacket he had used to keep him warm through the night, waiting by the roadside for Burnham to come along. His short black hair, giving in to his age, showed white at the temples, his skin already worn from years of this work, and the years before when he'd worked oil himself.

Even with the dust coming up off his clothes he knew he needed a washroom if he was going to make the call. He needed to clean himself up and make it look like he hadn't been down in the dirt for an hour, digging a shallow grave. "I'll make the call," Ray said. "It should be me."

"He paged me again just a minute ago."

"Memo? How many times does that make?"

"Six."

"Is he usually like this? Your uncle?"

"I was an independent before this," Sanchez said. "I told you how it is with me and him, he wants me to learn something from you. To see how a real professional works."

"Is that what he said?"

Sanchez smiled, revealing a range of uneven teeth. "In a nut-shell."

Ray knew he didn't belong here. Not like this, not for this type of job again. But he'd taken the job to get home and here he was so close to the place he wanted to be. Ten years since he'd been this close to Coronado. His life here was gone now, his son Billy handicapped by the accident that killed his wife, now twelve years old and living with his grandfather. The car

Marianne had driven that day smashed in on one side like it had been broadsided. Deliberately killed in order to hurt Ray. Nothing else around and the road going on toward the south, the wide double track of a truck tire painted into the cement where it had rammed her car from the road.

Ray hadn't wanted a life like that for his son; handicapped, his mother gone. Ray didn't know how to care for a boy like that. A kid with troubles who'd never speak and had sat mutely in front of Ray for weeks, watching him as he'd made calls to his cousin Tom, hoping every day that he didn't have to look at the boy anymore.

Ten years had passed and Ray had spent that time working the areas around Las Cruces, even doing a few federal jobs out of Albuquerque, but this business with Burnham was something different. It was a grudge killing, working for Memo's family again. The same people who'd gotten him caught up in this line of work to begin with. Only he hadn't worked for them for years and he was starting to see why. The pressure of the job, the lack of preparation, and the stakes that much higher than he was used to this close to a place where people might recognize him.

It was a lot of time for Ray to go missing, to abandon his own blood like that. But at the time he'd seen no other way and he'd run, distancing himself from everyone. Knowing there would be questions, and that those questions still waited for him to answer.

He'd run because he'd set his cousin up. He'd wanted it evened up between him and the cartel, asking Tom to go over there and hurt that woman a little, the only cartel connection Ray could find. The only direct connection he could make to Marianne, the cartel to blame for what had happened to her and Ray filled with a hate there was little he could do to turn. Ray had wanted Tom to scare her, make her think he was going to take everything away from her. And then somehow, in the worst possible way, his cousin had.

In all those years since, Ray had tried as best he could to forget about his own family's place here in the valley, his father, his son, his uncle, his cousin. He'd tried to forget about what had been done to his wife, about his mute and deaf son, about the life they'd been building and the plans he'd had for them. How easily that plan had slipped out from under him. How easy it seemed for his life to slip from one thing into the other.

He knew, too, that in this new life, there was an emptiness to his actions, a hopelessness that had come with his time away, carried along beside him like a parasite in the skin. Never to be satisfied in this world or the next, and that would keep him going until he might fill that hole, bored through from one side to the other. For which he felt, sitting there on the porch looking back at Coronado, he would never find fulfillment. It had made the killing of that old man in the hills outside town all the easier.

The beep of the pager went off again and Sanchez unclipped it from his pocket and looked at the number.

"Number seven," Ray said.

Sanchez slipped the pager backward into his pocket, showing the clip outside his pants. "Like I said, this is all a learning experience."

They'd taken Burnham's truck with them, as well as their own Bronco, both trucks now parked out back of the Sullivan house. The town a thin gray line against the horizon ahead. The high steeple of the church on Main barely visible. Ray turned and fixed Sanchez for a good second or more, letting the younger man know he was serious. "What did I tell you up there on the road, before all of this happened? What did I tell you was the most important thing?"

Sanchez shifted his weight from one foot to the other, his eyes skittering away from Ray like a schoolboy's. "No mistakes," he said.

"Memo has paged us seven times," Ray said. "You shot that boy, didn't you? You saw him take the bullet and fall dead on the ground. That's what you told me, isn't it? Isn't that what you said?"

"I shot him," Sanchez said, the muscles in his jaw held tight beneath the skin.

Tom put down the picture he'd been looking at—an old photo from when Mark worked the wells
outside Coronado, posing in his yellow foreman's hard hat.

"Did you have a good drive?" Heather asked again, her voice
carrying in from the kitchen. "Did you run into any traffic?"

"There was an accident just north of Coronado," Tom said,
moving from the living room into the kitchen, Elena sitting
farther on toward the back of the kitchen, doing her homework
at a small table. "I was able to talk to Edna for a bit and then
it was an easy hour and a half or so to get up here."

"Nothing serious, I hope," Heather said, as she cut chicken
breasts. "Anyone we'd know?" The knife paused in her hand
while she waited for an answer.

Late-afternoon sun came in through the kitchen window as
Tom thought over his response. He didn't know if Mark and
Heather had known the Deacons when they lived in Coronado.
It wasn't a very big place to begin with and he felt ashamed
even after two years to tell Heather that he'd had to take work
raising cattle while his own farm went on hiatus.

At the other end of the kitchen Elena raised her head,
waiting to hear what Tom had to say. Probably wanting to hear
the gory details. The last time the girl had ever really paid
attention to him was when she was seven years old and he'd
bought her a stuffed cow for her birthday, one of those plush
toys with a string dangling out the back. Heather, Mark, and

Tom able to hear her anywhere in the house, pulling the string as a mechanical moo sound groaned out of the animal.

"Nothing serious," Tom said, watching as Elena went back to her homework. "Did you ever meet the Deacons?"

"No," Heather said, shaking her head. "If they weren't in the oil business I don't think we'd know them."

"Cattle," Tom said. "They're old neighbors of mine."

"The people your father started working for after Lamar's oil went dry?"

"Those are the ones," Tom said.

Heather finished with the chicken, scooping it up with the blade of her knife and putting it into a bowl.

"Edna says hi, by the way."

"How is she? We haven't heard from her in a while. She must be busy now that there's only three of them in the department."

"Not her best day," Tom said. "They're all overworked. About five minutes after I left, a news van passed me on the road, heading toward the accident. I'm sure she wasn't too happy about that."

"News van? I thought you said it wasn't anything serious."

"You never know what qualifies as news these days," Tom added, looking again to Elena.

He didn't really know why he even came anymore. Heather and Mark had made him the child's godfather, but he had never wanted it, never thought it was appropriate after all that had happened. Maybe it would have been best for him to stay in Coronado, to never leave, to just keep on going on the course that had been chosen for him. Like Kelly said, he wasn't the sheriff anymore, but there were still things that reminded him he'd been, like some vestigial tail left behind from another era.

Heather asked Tom to get the tortillas out of the fridge. He brought them over and they stood at the counter, rolling the tortillas around the chicken. The silence thick between them till Heather asked Tom about the town, about everything that had changed since she'd seen him last, finally working her way around to asking about the woman he'd been seeing off and on for the past fifteen years or so. A secretary for the mayor's office down at the courthouse, the woman's name was Claire and she'd worked there since before Tom had been the sheriff.

"We stopped seeing each other a month or so ago," Tom said, the second-to-last tortilla in his hands on the scrubbed tile counter.

"You two never could stay together for more than a month at a time." Heather laughed. "She stop seeing you or you stop seeing her?"

"I don't know exactly, it just ended. It always ends this way and I expect it will end this way again. I think we just tired each other out."

"This thing between you two has been going off and on for a while. You didn't think it would slow down for you at some point?"

"Not this way," Tom said. "The mayor caught her ear on

something and instead of letting it go she tried to defend me, only he just wouldn't let up. Claire said it was me or the job."

"That's not right, Tom."

"I know it's not right, but you expect her to quit her job over me, just because the mayor can't keep his mouth shut? Me and Claire never had that solid a relationship to go on as it was."

Heather finished the last enchilada and placed it in the baking pan. "I always thought there was something happening with you and Edna anyway." Heather laughed and shot Tom a sly grin.

"No," Tom said. "Too much history between us at this point, plus you know she got married a few years ago. I'm not that man, not ever."

Heather bumped him with her hip, saying, "Not even on the sly, Tom? Come on now."

He liked Heather a lot just for saying things like that. Just for giving him a hard time, and joking with him the way she did. It was hard to find people in Coronado who'd treat him like that these days. People who would joke around with him the way Kelly sometimes did, or even Claire, when she was talking to him.

His heading north to see Elena had a lot to do with how Heather and Mark treated him. They were good people for Elena, regardless of Tom's history with the girl. And he knew the simplest reason Heather and Mark were now Elena's family was that they were home. After everything, they were the first people on the block to ask about the baby inside, coming out of their own house and taking the baby out of Kelly's hands, keeping her till Protective Services could be called. Those few hours cementing their relationship with the baby, following up on her through the months, checking in with Elena's foster care—asking about her family in Mexico, if anyone had come forward yet to claim the baby—even as they moved north to Las Cruces for Mark's new job. Eventually adopting the little girl when she was almost three years old.

Mark came home about ten minutes later, the sweet corn smell of the enchiladas baking in the oven. It had been a long time since Tom had had a meal like it.

"Will you drive back tonight?" Mark asked after Heather had excused herself to take Elena to one of her friends' houses.

Tom checked the time. It was still early, and the local evening news would come on in ten minutes or so. "Do you mind if I just stay to catch the news and then head out? I'd like to get on the road while there's still some light."

"I don't mind if you stay all night," Mark said. "It's nice to have another adult around. I don't know if you noticed but Elena doesn't exactly like to talk to us anymore."

Tom helped Mark clear the table, and when they were done, Mark brought out a couple beers and they settled in and turned the television on. Heather came home and sat with them as the news started up.

The story about the shooting outside Coronado was the first

one up, Kelly there on the side of the road looking harried and uncomfortable as she did her best to avoid the reporter's questions.

"I thought you said it wasn't anything serious," Heather said after the news cut back to the anchor in the studio.

"It wasn't," Tom said. He was listening as the anchor took up the story, trying to make it into a report about illegals crossing the border.

"What was all that about a boy getting shot then?"

Tom shook his head. "Not a good day for Edna."

The news had switched to the oil war going on all the way across the world, the night sky highlighted by the bright green tinge of bombs going off somewhere in the cityscape. The anchor finished, and then the camera swung over and the sports guy started talking about the local high school games.

Mark let out a low whistle and took a swig from the beer. "It's been a while since I've seen them go to the trouble of sending a news van to Coronado."

Tom leaned back in his chair, still looking at the screen as young high school basketball players ran offense across a wooden floor. "About ten years," Tom said.

"I didn't mean it like that," Mark said.

"I know."

"It just came out."

"Don't worry about it," Tom said. He drained the beer back in one pull and got up to take the bottle into the kitchen.

"Do you think Edna will be okay?" Heather asked.

Tom stood there in the middle of the living room. "You know how it goes, they'll have forgotten about it all by tomorrow. It's not like she was the one to shoot him."

SHERIFF EDNA KELLY PAUSED OVER THE BLOOD, dried and balled in the sand at her feet. Kneeling, she pulled a pen from her pocket and with the tip rolled the bead over once, then stood looking at it. A slight pull felt now in her stomach, hard and tight against the muscle, threatening some unknown danger.

Out on the highway pavement there was a stain of blood where the kid had lain down in front of Deacon's truck, hoping he would stop. Now, hours later, she could see the news vans waiting for her, waiting while she and the deputies followed the blood trail back across the plain. The skewed footfalls of the kid's erratic pace, a bullet already passed through him, and the trail showing where he tried to find his footing, stumbled, fell several times in quick succession, then kept going.

Out on the highway the news vans waited. Three of them altogether, the last arriving only thirty minutes before while many of the others had already come and interviewed her, rushing their stories north up to Las Cruces or Albuquerque. Each of them wanting her to speak the same words into their cameras that she had said too many times already. She looked down at the bead of blood in the sand. Perfect in the way it had been preserved. Somehow standing there in the kid's path like a rough-hewn jewel simply waiting to be retrieved.

She'd never wanted this job. Just twenty-six years old when Angela Lopez died and Eli came to her with the idea of setting her up as the interim sheriff. Only a week after Tom's hearing, after he'd stepped down, and Kelly, whether Eli had his say or not, had started to run the show.

She was thinking this all through, following the trail of blood through the desert lowlands. The footprints going on ahead of her. The gait of the victim pressed into the desert landscape where sand and blood stood fixed behind him as he ran. The occasional touch of the kid's hand as he'd lost balance, teetering onto his fingers to push himself up. A long divot the length of a body where she saw he'd fallen and moved the earth forward.

Each step telling its own story until there was no blood left to follow. Hastings sweeping the sand with a metal detector while Pierce took pictures of the blood splatter. A thick coating of red soaked into the ground at his feet. The news vans and camera crew watching them wherever they went, the portable lights shining a glare over the landscape, creating dark pools of shadow between the dunes.

When they came to the place the kid had been shot, they

saw how he'd rolled, taking the shot at the top of the dune, then spotting the hillside all the way down.

They had come to the edge of the flatlands, the highway a quarter mile behind them and the hills stretching on to the west. Kelly and the new recruit, Pierce, just standing there looking down.

"Strange to think this is human," she said, not knowing why she'd even thought to say something like that. Perhaps just searching for anything to say, to take the edge off and make it seem, against all odds, like some small piece of normality.

Deputy Pierce repositioned himself over the blood splatter, clicked the camera, then advanced the film. The youngest of the three of them and the newest hire, he was underpaid and fresh out of high school. Looking at him, she knew he wasn't going to say anything, not here, not about this. He was just doing his job, and she could tell right now, he wanted his job to be over as soon as possible.

He was still a boy in many ways, but old enough to have the job, taking pictures and helping out the best he could. Hastings still circling with the metal detector and Kelly listening to the low sonar blip of the thing as it sought out what lay beneath the sand.

Hastings was already kneeling when the metal detector gave off a low, long beep. Pierce and Kelly turned toward him, where he knelt close to the ground with a small plastic bag in his gloved hand.

At the age of thirty-eight, Hastings was just two years older than Kelly. They had grown up together throwing rocks at empty beer cans and sketching out intricate games of hide-and-seek throughout the town. During high school they'd drawn apart, separated by age or sex or something else Kelly herself still couldn't quite figure. The aftereffects of those times lasting into their early twenties as Hastings had gone off to tour the western states, working first as a bull rider on the circuits and then a rodeo hand as his back worsened through the years. He returned to Coronado in his late twenties, flecks of gray already shining in his hair.

Now, Kelly watched as he dug around in the earth with a gloved hand, removing something and dropping it into the bag. Kelly standing over him to see what he'd found.

"It looks like a .308," he said, handing the plastic Ziploc up to her.

She took the bag from him and turned it in the palm of her hand. The bullet was almost two inches in length, the metal inside already corroded. Sticky with blood, punched in slightly from the force of the impact. She'd seen a million of these at the shooting range, the back hill built up in sand and the bullets that came out of it looking warped and disfigured. "A hunting round?"

Hastings nodded.

"Doesn't feel right, does it? Not this close to the highway."

"You think this was an accident?"

70

"I hope it was. It's better than the alternative." She gave the bullet back to him and told him to run it north after they were done. "What about a casing?" she asked.

"Still looking."

Kelly walked on, knowing that the news vans were waiting behind. The light from their cameras reaching out toward her. She picked up the boy's track on the other side of the small rise. His gait more controlled there. One foot in front of the other. No bullet in him yet. In her mind she was starting to put it back together. The boy moving up over the rise, running for the road, in the distance the silver flash of a car window and the sound of a semi truck downshifting as it ran on toward the mountains to the north.

Even now, as far as she was from the highway, the sound of sporadic traffic could be heard as a far-off rush of air. All of what she was looking at now, the boy's footfalls, his wobbling uneven steps up one rise and down the other, seeming so out of place.

When she came down over the second rise, the plain came to an abrupt stop at the edge of the hill country. She studied the boy's track for a long time, checking the angle, seeing how deep his shoes had sunk into the soft earth. Something not right about any of it, about how deep and wide the track was, each footfall seeming too big, too pronounced in form, like a man slogging through a field of snow. Now she realized she was looking at not one track, but two. The boy's and then in the same space, following, another track altogether, erasing the boy's as it came.

Whoever had shot this boy had followed him out onto the plain to finish the job. Above, the hillside went on, climbing through the locust on its way up out of sight. Nothing but the green and brown brush all the way up the slope and the call of birds deep within the thicket, so dense she could see no more than a foot within. The boy's trail ending at the bottom, where the hillside met the plain. The ground harder here, mud dried stiff as cement in the small wash fed by the hillside gullies. The dash of two or three motorcycle treads preserved in it from a rain two weeks before, but otherwise nothing. No tracks at all.

R AY PUT HIS HEAD AGAINST THE GLASS. HE WAS standing in the phone booth outside the Lucky Strike Diner, six miles north of town. "The kid's alive?"

"Unless the news was lying to me," came the response from Memo.

Ray didn't have anything to say. He was thinking about Memo sitting there at his desk in Las Cruces, the dark eyebrows that stood out on his shaved head, and the phone held to his ear. The kid was alive. Ray was thinking about what this meant, about all that it could mean and all that would soon result. Memo as hardheaded as they came. But he was smart, too, and Ray had never known a plan of his to go wrong, not if Ray was involved and there was blood to be spilled.

"Where are you?" Memo asked.

"Just outside Coronado."

"Home sweet home," Memo said. His voice slowing into a singsong rhythm, the same Memo who had sweet-talked him into this corner, the same who had sweet-talked him into this life so many years ago, offering him money for what, at the time, seemed only a simple job.

"I did what I was supposed to, I have what you wanted me to get, everything else is extra, you understand?"

"You have a problem," Memo said. "You don't fix this problem, then it becomes mine. I don't want that to happen, and I'm sure you don't."

"You set me up," Ray said. "You knew what would happen to Burnham as soon as I saw him. You knew from that moment he would be dead."

"Yes," Memo said. "But I thought you'd do a better job of it."

"You're telling me to kill this kid."

"I'm telling you to handle this problem."

"It's not on me," Ray said. He ran a hand through his hair, resting his scalp in his palm. It was already late enough in the day that the sun began to stretch the shadows long and thin across the parking lot, constructing a stilted world that teetered toward the point of falling. Inside the Lucky Strike he saw Sanchez talking with a young waitress. "Your nephew is the one who got us into this mess. He's the one with the problem here, he's the one who fucked up, who lied to me about killing that boy. He's the one with the job to finish."

"You think he knows what he's doing? He's down there with you because you're supposed to know how to handle yourself. I know you can't let this go. That boy talks they're going to find you out and it will be just like it was ten years ago. I can't protect you this time, not like I did before when it was your cousin who did the killing for you. This is on you. If that boy in the hospital identifies you, or even comes close to it, there's nothing I can do. They'll come for you and there'll be no stopping them. You should know that."

"They?" Ray said.

"The cartel."

"What's left for them to take from me?" Ray said. He was angry and his voice was beginning to show it. "Besides," Ray said, holding his breath for a moment before going on. "Burnham wasn't cartel. He was just an old white man who'd stayed in the business too long."

"No," Memo said. "Burnham wasn't, and neither was the kid my nephew shot and told you was dead. But that heroin was, the stuff you took out of that seat, that was pure cartel import and they're going to want it back. I suggest you don't leave any witnesses."

Ray was thinking about what Burnham looked like there on the ground, the lingering seep of blood from the wound in his cheek. The old man's words whispered up out of his bloodied mouth.

He wanted to just put the phone down and walk away. He wanted to be done with Memo and his lying nephew. All this, being here, doing this job, had been a way for him to return to Coronado, to set himself up for the years to come. He'd cut himself loose from that past, from his father, from his son, from his cousin and all that he'd left behind, now all he wanted was to go home.

Ray had lied to himself all those years before. He'd lied to Marianne, promising her he would be more than just an oil worker, that he was capable of more. But this wasn't it. Standing in a phone booth outside his hometown, listening to Memo tell him how to solve this problem. No, Ray thought, there was nothing here that would ever make him better, or would ever satisfy his promise to Marianne.

"You want to tell me what's going on here?" Ray said. "You want to tell me how you knew where Burnham and this kid would be and what they would be carrying?"

"Control the town, control the flow," Memo said.

"That's what you're saying? That's how you're explaining this to me—this situation."

"It's not a problem," Memo said.

"Was it Burnham who tipped you off?"

"I'm sorry about the situation we find ourselves in, but you really just need to concentrate your efforts on the present."

"You want me to finish what your nephew started?"

"You're from Coronado. It shouldn't be a problem for you to find your way around."

"I was from here, I'm not anymore," Ray said.

"Easier for you than us."

"I haven't been back in ten years—"

"You're also not like us, not quite," Memo cut in. "You're the son of an oilman who married his Mexican cook. You're half-white. You're not like us at all."

Ray watched a car go past out on the highway on its way into town. A pounding beginning somewhere deep inside his head, the whole world beginning to come off its axis, threatening to roll.

"You didn't think I knew all that?" Memo said, the sound of a laugh lingering at the back of his palate, like Ray had joined in on some joke halfway done in the telling. "You thought we didn't check you out when you first started working for us? That we didn't start asking about you when you got into all that trouble down there? When we kept you hidden and protected you?" Ray heard Memo shift the phone from one ear to the other. He pictured Memo sitting there in the Las Cruces office. The dark wood desk where Memo sat, the chair on the other side of that desk where Ray had received his first job. "And now you think you can come back to us any time you like, pick your jobs, and then move on," Memo said. "That's not how we do things anymore."

Ray leaned forward and rested his head on his forearm, putting his weight onto the glass of the booth. He sucked at the insides of his cheeks until he could feel the flesh between his teeth. He was done with Memo. He knew it now. "I'm staying," Ray said. "I'm not coming back after this. I'll send your nephew north with the dope and I'll do what you're asking, but I'm done after this. I've spent too long hiding from the past. No one will be looking for Burnham's truck if your nephew goes now. If he leaves now it will work and I'll do what you're asking of me and then I want my money and I don't want to hear from you again."

"No," Memo said. "I can't trust my nephew. He's messed too much up already. I need you on this. I need you to finish this for me. Keep my nephew's pager and send him north, but don't send him with the drugs. I can't trust him. I want you to hide the drugs and when you're done with everything I'll send someone to pick them up."

"I can do that," Ray said. "But you hear me on this, I'm not coming back."

"If that's what you want," Memo said. "If that's what you think will solve this problem for you. But you should know it's all on you. If for some reason the drugs aren't where you say they are, it's all on you."

"You'll get your dope," Ray said. "You'd have it today if you let me send it north with Sanchez."

"You know just as well as I do that my nephew isn't right

for this work. His balls are too big. Thinks he'll run the business someday. You're untouched, you've never done a bit of time, and except for ten years ago you've kept yourself clean. You've done a good job for us over the years but staying there isn't going to solve any of this. Coronado will never be the same as it was when your wife was alive. It's simply been too long to go back."

Ray unwrapped an antacid and put it into his mouth. He knew Memo was right, nothing would ever be the same, though he hoped somehow it would. He would send Sanchez north and he would stay.

"Antacids?" Memo asked. "All these years and you still eat those things?"

"Heartburn," Ray said.

"I told you to see a doctor about it."

"I did."

"He tell you to take antacids?"

"He told me a bunch of stuff, only I wasn't listening."

"That's not good," Memo said. "That's never good. You should listen to what doctors tell you."

"Why?"

"They're usually trying to save your life."

Ray looked across the parking lot at Sanchez sitting there in the diner, then looked away, the pumice taste of the antacid still on his tongue. Burnham had been right—everything had changed. None of it was the way it used to be, and now Ray was stuck in this life, one leg thrown over the fence that divided this new world from the old, knowing he should never have come back to Coronado for this job.

"You ready to listen now?" Memo asked.

From his coat pocket Ray took out the small orange prescription bottle with the pills the doctor at the VA had given him. Meant to get him concentrated, to get his mind right and keep him in the present. To keep his mind off all the ghosts that followed him around. Only the pills didn't seem to work, or maybe he'd just grown used to them, because nothing had felt right for a very long time. "Yeah," Ray said. "I'm listening."

IT WAS EARLY STILL WHEN TOM CROSSED THE RIO Grande on his way home, the passenger window open for Jeanie, and the clay smell of the water below as he passed.

Perhaps it had been the accident on the road, perhaps the newscast, perhaps Mark's mention of the trouble years before. Tom didn't know for sure. But there it was, rooted into him, and now spun loose, bobbing around through his insides. All of it heavy in his mind, big as a tree pulled green and full from the bank and strangely alive as it went on down the river.

The drive took him two hours. Not really aware of where he was going until he arrived. Turning off the highway ten miles outside of Coronado, he took the long dirt road west, watching the last of the sunlight close out the cattle fence. The house looked just as it always did, pitched somewhat crooked, with the wide frame of the place lit from within by lamplight. The old staff houses he'd known as a child, off a ways from the main house, melting little by little into the ground—boards rotted through, and the adobe walls crumbling.

His only real reason for coming simply that he didn't want to go home. Tom rang the bell and waited. When the door opened Gus stood there looking him over. "You see the news tonight?" Tom said.

Gus stood there behind the screen door looking out at his nephew. "I saw it. I expect you want to come in and relive the good old days, is that it?" He pushed the screen door open and held it for Tom.

The house had the old familiar smell he'd grown up with—something of cooked meat and talcum powder—all of it bringing Tom back decades. The old green wallpaper, the split-wood furniture, dust-covered lampshades, and sun-stained curtains always pulled a quarter way across the windows.

"My father around?" Tom said, after he'd come in and sat in one of the armchairs in the living room.

"I haven't seen him take off for the bar yet, so I expect he's still out back in his place if you want to go get him," Gus said. He was standing near the middle of the room, close to the fireplace, looking Tom over where he sat.

"No," Tom said. "I just thought I should ask. I see enough of him now at work as it is."

"Coffee?"

"If you have some."

Waiting while Gus moved around in the kitchen, Tom rose and took in the old pictures of Ray up above the mantel. Ray in his army uniform, another of Tom and Ray as children out by one of the steel-framed oil wells up the valley, a picture of Gus and his wife thirty years before. At the end of the mantel, the most recent picture of Gus, Ray, and Marianne, twelve years ago, pregnant then with their boy.

"Where's Billy?" Tom asked.

"Go on into his room, he's back there."

Tom walked to the back hallway leading off the living room and pushed open Billy's door. The room had been Ray's when they were kids and Tom looked in on the same bed and dresser that had always been there and the dioramas that now lined the walls, which Ray's son, Billy, made of exotic places. Shoe boxes everywhere with jungle scenes, tropical islands, and remote villages built from bits of wire, painted newspaper, and construction paper.

Billy was sitting on the bed cutting cardboard with a pair of safety scissors, the half-made model of some new landscape taking shape inside an old shoe box. "It looks good," Tom said, letting the boy read his lips, and then a moment later, using his hands, Tom signed, "You're getting good at these."

"Thanks," Billy signed, and then went back to his cuttings. He was skinny and short for his age. A scar running up through his black hair where the doctors had gone in to relieve the bleeding and the lasting effect of the accident, a pair of hearing aids that Billy almost never wore.

Tom closed the door and went back out into the living room. He took down one of the pictures and looked at his cousin's face. There had been days of discussions over what should be done with Billy, about how Ray couldn't deal with Marianne's being gone. Tom driving over to Ray's house in those weeks after the accident and sitting around at the kitchen table, watching Ray drink. Billy sitting there in his high chair, trying constantly to take the bandage from his head, and the mute musings of a two-year-old boy that the doctors said would never be normal.

"I know it's wrong," Ray said. "But I just can't go on like this anymore." He was on his third beer and he gestured to the medications laid out on the table, some for Billy and some for him. Antidepressants and children's antibiotics. "You know what I'm saying?"

Tom looked back at Billy where he sat, the plump little fists now given up on removing his bandage and gone on to reaching for a roll of medical tape on the table and a box of bandages.

"I want you to do something about this," Ray said. "I need you to do something about this."

"You know I won't." Tom shook his head. Ray always asking

him the same thing every time they talked, wanting Tom to go by and scare that Lopez woman, to chase her off. Tom just sitting there listening to Ray and wanting out of there. The house smelling like antiseptic and rotting garbage. Ray just letting it all go.

"I'm giving Billy up," Ray said. "I'm taking him over to my father's for a little while. I can't keep going on like this."

"Going on like what?" Tom said. "You need to pull it together. You can't just take off."

"The man I work for now offered to help. He says he can help me with what happened to Marianne."

"It's a bad thing that happened to you, Ray. But we don't have anywhere to go with that. I want to help you but I just can't go knocking on the cartel's door, pointing fingers. What happened to Marianne was horrible, but you leaving, giving Billy up, it isn't the answer."

"At one time there was me," Ray said. "And then there was me, but there was a little less of me, you understand? I don't know how to get that piece back."

"Jesus, Ray. It might not seem like it, but people go through this stuff every day."

"'Every day it gets a little easier,'" Ray mimicked, making his voice low and cruel. "I've heard that enough from the doctors."

"They're telling it to you for a reason."

"It doesn't get easier, Tom. Not for me. What happened to

Marianne, that's on me, that's my fault. You understand? I shouldn't have started taking the work with this man, but I did and there's no going back in time. The cartel knows who I am now and I'm just trying to do what's best for everyone. What happened to Billy, that's on me." He finished the beer and put it down on the table, the sound loud in the kitchen but Billy not noticing. Ray picked up the bottle again and put it down hard, again and again, louder and louder. Beside Tom, Billy never looked up and Ray threw the bottle across the room, where it hit the wall and then fell to the floor without shattering. After a time, he said, "I'm fucking losing it, Tom."

"He's a special-needs kid. That's all. He's still yours. He's still the same kid he was."

"They're telling me he's going to need to go to a special school," Ray said. He wouldn't look up at Tom. "He's retarded. He's never going to be normal. You know that, Tom."

Tom shook his head. The things Ray was saying weren't right, they weren't Ray, but it was no good trying to talk to him about it. They sat like that for a long time till Tom picked the bottle off the floor and they went into the living room and watched television. Billy sitting on Tom's lap and Ray drinking another beer.

The next day Tom would go over to Angela Lopez's house and shoot her point-blank. Knowing the whole time—as he went up those stairs to her house—that what he was doing wouldn't solve a thing. His own inability to help Ray with his problems, to bring Marianne back and make everything better. Tom had known it wouldn't get any better, but he'd hoped all the same that it would. So many years gone by now. All that time spent thinking about what had happened and he'd never been able to figure out if he'd done it on purpose or, as everyone said, if it was an accident.

When he called over to Ray's soon after, there was no response, and in the days that followed he'd learn that Ray had left Billy with Gus and gone north.

Holding the picture in his hand now, ten years later, Tom looked down on a face that hadn't changed one bit from when he'd known his cousin all those years before. Before everything that had happened, before the Lamar wells had gone dry and the money had gone out of the family and Ray had left his son in Gus's care.

"You hear anything from Ray lately?" Tom asked, raising his voice a little so it might carry into the kitchen.

"You know the answer to that just as sure as I do," Gus said.

Tom carried the picture over to the kitchen doorway, where he watched Gus fill the pot with water, then walk back over and fill the machine. "You ever feel like you were meant to do something else, Gus?" Tom asked.

Gus waited, watching the coffee begin to percolate, then turned to look at Tom where he stood in the doorway. "I'm too old for you to be asking me something like that," Gus said. "I'm stuck with whatever I've already done. There's no going back."

"I went up and saw Elena today," Tom said.

"Banner day for you, isn't it?"

"I guess you could say that. I've certainly been making my way down memory lane."

"You want to go back?" Gus said, the water in the machine falling dark into the pot. "Is that it? Do it all over again, have yourself investigated again by the DEA because you took some advice from Ray that really didn't pan out. Is that what you want?"

"Honestly? Yes, sometimes I do. Sometimes I think I could have come through this thing all right."

Gus gave Tom a sad smile. "You only got off because the judge went easy on you, Tom. I'm not saying what happened deserved the punishments they were going after you for—I'm not saying that. But I do think you should consider yourself lucky." Gus poured the coffee and led him into the living room again. "We have this conversation every couple years, don't we? Sometimes I think you come over here and you want to talk it out, but other times, like tonight, I think I'm just standing in for Ray because he's not here."

Tom took a sip of the coffee, hot and bitter as it slid past his tongue. "Did I ever tell you I tried to track him down through a friend in the DEA?"

"I didn't think you had any friends left in the DEA."

"I don't really," Tom said. Telling Gus how Agent Tollville was an old acquaintance who'd helped him out with some work in the eighties, but whom he hadn't talked much with since. When Tom called—a month after Tollville had come down to testify at Tom's hearing—Tollville had been more than a little surprised.

"You want me to look into Raymond Lamar?" Tollville had said. Disbelief coated thick through his voice. "You think we haven't already? There's nothing there." What Tollville did have was a roster of tours Ray had done all over Southeast Asia in the late fifties and early sixties, special ops, most of it before the war even officially started. Most just recently declassified. No current address or number for him. The only thing that came up a job working for some land company in Las Cruces that turned out to be bogus.

Gus finished his coffee. He looked over at Tom and waited, but then when nothing came, Gus said, "Your cousin was never a good man. Never was going to be and never will be."

"Harsh words from his father."

"I'm not saying I don't love him, but I think you know he made some bad decisions after the wells went dry." Gus got up from his chair and went into the kitchen. Ray had been gone for ten years now and there'd been nothing from him in all that time. The only things left of Ray his son, Billy, and his wife's grave up the valley under the big oak, a little apart from that of Gus's own wife. A place where Gus, nearly eighty years old, said he'd be buried someday as well. "You done?" Tom heard Gus say from the other room.

"With the coffee?"

"No," Gus said, coming back to look in on Tom where he still sat in Gus's living room chair.

"I'm sorry about this, Gus, I just thought—"

"I can't keep going on with you about this. I just can't. You understand?"

Tom stood and brought his coffee cup into the kitchen and put it in the sink. He sprayed water on his hands and then dried them on his pant legs. "I'll go now," he said. "I suppose it's getting late."

When he got home there were several messages waiting for him on the machine. One was from his father, giving him a start time for the day after next, the other two were from Claire. Tom rewound the tape and listened as Claire's voice came on the machine again. "Tom? You there?" A long pause and then, "Call me when you get this message." He pressed delete and then listened to the most recent message, left only twenty minutes before. "I know you must have seen the story tonight, Tom. They just replayed it on the ten o'clock news," Claire said. "I know we didn't leave things in the best light, but if you want to talk, I'm around."

Tom deleted the message, then walked into the kitchen and took out a beer. He was standing with the door of the fridge open when the phone rang. The message clicked on and he listened for a while to the silence of the machine and then, "I'm getting worried about you, that's all. I've left messages and you're not calling me back. I'm just going to come by and check up on you, Tom. That's all. I'd feel better about it if I did."

Tom stared at the machine. The light of the open fridge on him as he stood in his kitchen, expecting the answering machine to click on any moment and keep talking to him. "Jesus, Claire," he said under his breath, taking another long pull from the beer and then putting it down on the counter. He closed the fridge and then called to Jeanie, "You want to get out of here for a while?" watching the mutt where she lay on the cool tile floor at the far end of the kitchen.

RAY RAISED THE APPLE TO HIS MOUTH AND TOOK a bite. He was sitting in the Bronco, watching the front drive of the hospital. The hospital was three floors in total, built of a beige sandstone composite, with a side entrance for the emergency room and the bright gleam from the front glass emanating all down the block.

The air had turned cold with the night and with the windows up, he could see his own breath as he exhaled, the moisture in the air beginning to condense against the glass.

He set the apple down on the dash and took the white paper napkin out of his jacket pocket. The room number written there in blue ink. Memo had given him all there was to know about the kid up there and the state of their affairs. Ray knew that if the kid lived, he was a liability to them. He didn't need to hear it again from Memo, though Memo had been insistent on telling him.

From where he was parked, three-quarters of the way down the block and one block in from Main, he could see the two county cruisers sitting there in the drive. One had been there most of the day, and the other had appeared just a few minutes before.

At a distance of three or four hundred feet, Ray couldn't be quite sure, but he thought the woman officer who had shown up was the same who had been Tom's deputy all those years before. The one who had responded to his wife's accident, telling Ray the news about his son, and the way the car had rolled after being broadsided.

Ray picked up the apple again. The flesh where he'd taken his first bite already stained brown from the air. It was the first thing he'd eaten since the diner, and he was staring at it like he might figure his future from the thing like a mystic would from a glass ball. He finished the apple and when he was done, took Sanchez's pager off his hip and checked the time. He'd been sitting in the Bronco now for the past five hours, waiting.

The root of the problem, or at least what Ray had been able to get out of Sanchez after they'd gotten back to the Sullivan house from the Lucky Strike Diner, was that Sanchez just wasn't built for the thing. He could talk a good game. He could tell Ray all the things he would do if he was given the chance, but Ray just couldn't believe him.

Sanchez hadn't done what he was supposed to. He hadn't killed the boy and instead of making sure the boy was dead, tracking him down as Ray would have done, he'd simply run off.

"You're telling me you shot him," Ray said. The two of them standing in the living room of the Sullivan house, a broken-down sofa turned halfway out from the wall, and the cracked plaster of the place around them on all sides. "Because I've already heard that, it's all I've heard from you all day and I'm getting tired of you lying to me about it."

Sanchez was leaning against one of the walls, picking at the plaster, his fingers a chalk white and a small mound of detritus developing on the floor at his feet. "I'm telling you I shot him," Sanchez said. "I'm not saying it was perfect, but I shot him and I saw him go down."

"And then what?" Ray said. They'd spent the last hour eating their food in silence at the diner, Ray faced away from the door, hoping he wouldn't run into anyone who might recognize him. Sure at any moment Tom would walk in or worse yet, his father.

"The gun was so loud," Sanchez said. "I wasn't expecting it to be that loud and I got scared. I didn't know what to do. I was looking to where he'd taken the shot and he was just lying there in the sand." Sanchez crossed and recrossed his hands, a white rim of plaster showing under each fingernail. "I walked down and pushed the gun into his back. He was dead. He was dead where I left him and the traffic was going by out on the highway."

Sanchez seemed like he was going to cry and Ray looked away. The sun had gone down out on the desert and there was a pink haze left in its wake, followed above by a dark blue spreading upward into the sky. "But he wasn't dead, was he?"

"I thought he was."

Ray went over and sat on the old sofa. He rubbed his hands over his face and spread his fingers up into his hair. This close to Coronado and he couldn't avoid it, he was thinking about the day he'd come clean to Marianne about who he was, about what he did. It didn't go well. Marianne telling him that he would ruin their marriage, that even then, as they stood close together there in the kitchen of their house, he was ruining their marriage. She wanted them to move. She said if the oil was gone and this was the work he was doing, they should move. If this was their life, then there must be more to it, to their life together. All of that only weeks before she died, before the cartel tracked Ray down and took her from him.

When Ray looked back over at Sanchez, he'd already decided. Ray would do it, but he didn't want anything to do with Sanchez anymore. Ray would go to the hospital because it had to be done. There wasn't anything more to it than that. "Memo doesn't trust you," Ray said, looking up at Sanchez. "He wants you to go north in Burnham's truck tonight. Tomorrow, after the job is done, he'll send someone for the drugs."

Sanchez's face fell. "He didn't say that."

"He said that exactly."

Ray asked for the pager and when it was given, Ray had to wait only a moment before Sanchez went out the door.

Now Ray sat in the Bronco watching the hospital entrance. The white napkin he'd taken from the diner in his lap and the air condensing all around him on the Bronco's windows.

Five hours had passed since he'd driven into town. On his way he passed RV lots where the trailers never moved and broken-down cars sat on deflated tires. He passed houses where he could still remember the names of the families that had lived there twenty years before. He passed areas, too, where lots that had once held two-story clapboard houses now held only the craterlike indentations of cement foundations, damaged with time and standing alone.

After Sanchez left, Ray walked out a ways in the desert with the shotgun he'd killed Burnham with and the bag of heroin. Counting his steps as he went, the shovel in his hand, he made sure that he'd be able to find the spot again if he needed to. Taking his time as he dug the hole, pausing to wipe the gun clean, then burying both the bag and gun. By the time he was done, the sun had set and there was only the pale light to be seen in the west. He walked back to the house and sat on the couch trying to figure a plan.

Out on the street there was nothing moving and Ray pulled himself up on the wheel. Sitting straight-backed in the driver's seat, he pulled at his pants where the jeans had ridden up his crotch and tightened at his waist. He wore the nine-millimeter Ruger at the back of his belt and he brought it out and looked it over, checking the slide on the gun before placing it beneath the seat.

He was dying for a piss. Turning to look into the backseat for a cup or a bottle, he saw the case for the hunting rifle. He'd thought for a moment about burying it along with the shotgun and drugs, but then thought better of it, knowing he still didn't have a plan for the kid up there in the hospital room.

With his bladder beating a constant rhythm against his belt buckle, Ray got down out of the Bronco and urinated against one of the chain-link fences nearby. He kept himself in the shadows, the only thing to tell he was there a steady rising of steam from the piss on the ground at his feet. He zipped up and looked back at the hospital.

It was then, standing there in the cold of the desert night, that he saw the truck go by on the street before the hospital. The reverse lights came on and then the truck backed up to the curb. All of this Ray watched, fascinated after all these years to be back in the same town. His cousin Tom, there before him with his truck door open to the street. Ray watching as Tom clapped the door shut and walked up the drive toward the hospital.

IT WAS PAST MIDNIGHT WHEN KELLY CAME OUT of the hospital and saw Tom Herrera sitting on the hood of her cruiser with his feet on the bumper. "Careful," Kelly said, "you wouldn't want to damage county property."

Tom grinned. "I don't know if the county quite knows how much damage I've already done." He slid off the hood and stood waiting for her. At the bottom of the drive she saw his truck and his mutt, Jeanie, sitting inside with her window rolled down.

"You two are getting to be a regular occurrence, aren't you?" Kelly said.

Tom looked back to where he'd parked his truck, the street all the way down a dark lane of shadow. "I guess we are," Tom said. "I was going to see if you wanted to come out for a beer with me."

"Tomás Herrera," Kelly said, with a lift of her eyebrows. "Are you trying to ask me out on a date?"

"If that's what you want to call it."

"Let me guess," Kelly said, walking around him to her door, "you want to go by Dario's bar and see what the mood is like tonight?"

"I always knew you'd make a fine sheriff," Tom said. He watched her where she stood, waiting for her to say something, and when she didn't, "I guess we could drive separately. I wouldn't want anyone thinking we were becoming a thing."

Kelly smiled at him. She opened her door and got in. She hadn't planned on having a beer or going in to see Dario tonight, but she would if Tom wanted to go with her. Dario's wasn't exactly the type of place she liked to spend her evenings. Low ceilinged, with a central bar that cramped all the tables and chairs close to the wall, the only light in the place from the neon beer signs that hung behind the bar and against the windows.

Down on the street in front of the hospital she saw Tom start up his truck and pull it around toward Main. Following him out she saw the empty parking spots all down both sides of the street, a good collection of cars outside Dario's bar. Dark storefront windows running parallel to her as they came down the block and parked just across the street.

"A lot of cars for a weeknight," Tom said as they crossed the street toward the bar.

"Looks like a roughneck convention might be going on inside."

Tom led as they crossed the street, looking back over his shoulder at her. "I didn't think there were that many oilmen left in this town." He gained the curb and in three quick steps had the door to the bar open. The smell of wet dish towels and spilled liquor leaked out onto the sidewalk, followed close by the thick billow of tobacco smoke from inside.

"Wonderful," Kelly said. But Tom didn't seem to hear as he went in ahead.

Walking into Dario's was like walking into a cave. The streetlamps outside blocked by the tinted windows. The back was lit only by the light of the bathrooms, shining out into the barroom from far down the back hall. The only dependable light in the place from the green and red beer signs along the walls.

"Find us a table. I'll be back with a couple beers," Tom said before disappearing into the crowd of oilmen that surrounded the bar.

Kelly looked around at the place. It was her first time inside since Dario had come into town and taken it over almost three years before. She didn't much care for places like it and until tonight there hadn't been much cause for her to come in. All down the bar now, the men were turning to look at her, one after the other as they noticed her standing close by the door.

To the right of her, someone called her name and turning she saw Luis, Tom's father, sitting at one of the wooden tables close by the window. In front of him he had a tallboy of Coors and an empty shot glass. His eyes already glossed from the alcohol.

"You driving tonight, Luis?" she said, pulling a chair up to the table and then another for Tom.

Luis rolled his head around and gave her a grin. "You going to be a buzz-kill tonight, Edna?"

"Never with you, Luis. You know that."

"Sure," Luis said. He took a sip from his beer. "They laid off thirty men from the Tate Bulger well today." Luis put the beer down. "Seems like a good enough reason to have a few drinks."

Kelly looked around at all the men in the bar. Some were going at it pretty good, while others sat quietly to themselves in the corners of the bar. It was the fifth layoff in about the same amount of months and it wasn't getting to be much of a surprise to Kelly or these men. "You worried at all, Luis? All these young roughnecks out there looking for work, and you at the boyish age of eighty-one."

"Boyish, huh?" Luis smiled over at her. "Buy me a drink before you start sweet-talking."

"You know I love you, Luis, but not in that way."

"Worth a try," Luis said. His eyes shifted away from her as Tom came back with the drinks.

"Here you go, old man," Tom said, sliding a shot of brown liquor across the wood to his father. For himself and Kelly he'd brought two beers in glass bottles. "I guess they laid off a few more," he said after he sat. The three of them circled up to the table, their backs to the window, watching the crowd.

"Your father just mentioned that," Kelly said. "They seem to be doing all right, though." She leaned to the side, looking the men over, trying to see past them toward the bar. Many of the men she knew by name, but about half of them she thought she'd never get to know. "You see Dario anywhere?"

Tom shook his head.

Next to her, Luis put back the shot of liquor and then

finished it with a drink of his tallboy. Kelly watched him till he was done, his Adam's apple beating a constant rhythm beneath his weathered skin. "Kind of hard to tell the mood of the place when there's a party going on," Kelly said.

"More like a wake," Luis added.

Tom smiled across the table at Kelly. "I guess that's one way to look at it." He raised a hand and motioned for the bartender to come over.

The bartender was a thick man named Medina who spoke little English. From what Kelly had been able to put together on him, he knew about thirty words and they all had to do with liquor or beer. "*¿Su jefe?*" Tom asked, Medina standing there, looking from Kelly back to Tom.

Medina wore a liquor-stained white T-shirt with a picture of a buck on the front of it and a pail of icy Milwaukee's Best printed on the back. When he turned to look around for his boss, his wide belly followed a split second later. "*La oficina,*" he said. "You want?"

"No," Kelly said. "We just wanted to see if he was here."

Medina kept staring at her like he didn't understand. His pupils, very big in the dim light of the bar, shone green and bright with the reflection of the beer sign above. Sensing there would be nothing more, he turned back to the bar, where the oil workers were calling him.

"You didn't want to talk with Dario?" Tom asked.

Kelly laughed. "Probably better if he just knows we're here.

Might be nice if he felt a little pressure from us." She tipped her beer back and drank, watching Tom. "Besides, unlike Luis, this isn't what I'd call a usual night."

"Baby steps," Luis said to Tom.

"You're the expert," Tom said to his father. Then to Kelly, "You don't think the talk of the town hasn't been all about that boy you have in the hospital now?"

"I'm sure it has, and now everyone is wondering why I'm in here and why Dario is hiding in the back office on one of his best nights. At least I'm wondering that myself."

"Everything all right with that boy in the hospital?" Tom asked.

"His name is Gil Suarez," Kelly said. "We got the printout on him late this afternoon. He served three months in county on a possession charge when he was nineteen."

"How old is he now?"

"Twenty-one."

Tom sat back in his chair. "Does he have a PO?"

"Up in Albuquerque, but they hadn't heard anything about him in a year till I called up there this evening."

"What are his chances?" Tom asked.

"He hasn't woken up yet. Pete is with him now and then the new kid, Pierce, will take over for the night."

Tom held his beer halfway to his mouth but didn't drink. "What are the chances Gil wakes up and has something to say?"

"According to the doctors, if he keeps going the way he does, things look pretty good. Whether he has something to say is another story altogether."

Tom stayed quiet and they watched the oilmen at the bar for a time and then Tom said, "You think that boy needs to be scared like that? You think he wouldn't want to say anything against anyone, even if we could protect him?"

Luis grunted something under his breath, but Kelly just kept staring at the men by the bar. There was a discussion going on about burning down one of the well trailers to get even with the Tate Bulger bosses. It was drunk talk but still Kelly listened, knowing how easily drunk talk moved from the bar out onto the street. The voices rising for a moment and then dying away as the men drank. She watched and listened, trying to identify those who were the loudest. A big man named Andy Strope seemed to talk the most, his voice carrying above the rest. Mike Shore was also there and Steve Herman, but the rest of the men in the group either stood with their backs to her or she didn't know them. After a while she said to Tom, "You don't have to worry about protecting anyone, Tom."

"Everyone has to make a choice," Tom said, his voice low against the background noise from the bar.

"I know," Kelly said, "but your choice has already been made." She looked at him to see how he'd taken it. She was about ready to call it a night. All she'd meant to do was come by and let Dario know she was still around, that she hadn't forgotten about him, or what he might represent. Whether the boy lived or not, it didn't matter in the bigger scope of things. If Dario was cartel, there was no way a boy like Gil was going to speak out against him.

Tom finished his beer and looked over at his father. "You about ready, old man?" Luis nodded, he put his hand out on the table and steadied himself for the move. "I know you don't need any looking after," Tom said, watching Kelly where she sat, "but I'm looking out for you all the same." He put a hand under Luis's armpit and pulled him up, the old man wobbling a bit as he found the floor.

Kelly nodded to Luis and the old man nodded back. She watched Tom go and then, when the door closed behind them, she finished her beer and brought the bottle over to the bar.

Medina broke away from the group of men and came over. He was looking at the empty beer bottle in her hand. "¿Otra?"

"No, not tonight." Kelly handed him the bottle. Past the group of roughnecks, she saw Dario standing just inside his office door, watching her or the door behind. When she looked over her shoulder and then back at the office, Dario had closed his door.

DAY 2

IT WAS A LITTLE PAST NINE WHEN THE SOUND OF the explosion came to Dario where he sat at the bar drinking his morning coffee. The windows rattled in their casings and he looked toward the street, from which the sound had come, and from where he could see the morning sun falling through the dust-stained glass onto the barroom floor, as if through a diffuse curtain.

At the age of thirty-four he was still alive, even though he'd never expected as much, and he thought constantly of his death and how it would occur. All of it, the bar, the town, the shipments he held and then sent north, like any other place he'd been while working for the cartel. It was all the same to him, the same job, filled with the same thrills and boredom, the same highs and lows. He couldn't have said it any other way, because, as he saw it, there was only this—there was only this life, this present. Though he hoped almost every day for something more.

Sliding from the stool, he went to the window and looked out on the street, where over the buildings, he saw a growing trail of smoke rising into the air. Unlatching the heavy wood door, he went out onto the street where several cars had already stopped in the middle of Main, the drivers out of their vehicles looking to where the black smoke crested the edges of the buildings to the west.

He wore a thin linen suit on his slim frame, and as he turned the corner off Main and came within view of the hospital, his jacket billowed behind him. His shirt open at the neck and a sheen of sweat already showing on his ashen skin. The only thing left of the county cruiser a charred and black body in the hospital drive, still smoldering, the tires and the last of the oil burning away. A crowd grown around the carved-out wreckage as the first group of volunteer firemen made an effort against the flames.

Dario had heard about Gil the night before, waiting as he usually did for the oil workers to come in while the newscaster gave his report on the television overhead. All of it like the news was being reported just for him. Telling him everything he didn't want to know.

On the other side of the bar Medina raised a glass to the light, checking for imperfections. Finding none, he put the glass down on the back bar and grabbed for another. He was working on a third by the time Dario caught the bartender's eye and told him he was going into the office to make the call.

Medina put the glass down. Overhead Dario saw the news had exhausted the local sports and gone on to the national weather. A fat green blob of weather coming in across California and bunching up along the Sierras. No idea who he would call when he reached the office.

"*¿A quién vas a llamar?*" Medina called after him, as if sensing Dario's doubt.

"*Quién te crees,*" Dario said over his shoulder. The certainty he'd felt in his voice fading as he closed the door to his office and saw the phone there on his desk.

With the phone held to his ear, Dario listened to the message repeat itself again and again. The number Memo had given him two weeks before, now disconnected. The deal they'd made now seeming less and less of a deal. The sweat beading at the edge of his hairline as he thought about what this meant, and where he might find himself in a day or more.

How long had it been since they'd talked last? Just two or three days? Dario was having a hard time remembering. A tightness in his lungs creeping up the back of his spine into his throat. What had Memo promised him? A way out, a new life away from the cartel, Dario eager for anything that offered a change, but there wasn't going to be any of that and he cursed himself now for ever believing there might.

All he could do was wait. He tried Memo's number again, thinking perhaps he'd misdialed. But he'd already tried it ten, twelve times, reading the numbers off to himself as he pushed the buttons, and every time the same answer. All Dario had wanted was a way out, an escape from the violence he knew would now soon be coming. Two minutes had passed already and he wasn't going to get through. He wasn't going to get an answer.

A knock came at the office door. Dario sat forward and put the phone in its cradle. He was hunched up at the desk with the phone pulled close toward him by the time Medina came into the office wanting to know if Dario had made contact with their bosses down south in Juarez.

"*¿Nada?*"

Dario shook his head.

Burnham and Gil, neither of them was supposed to die over a thing like this. Memo had told Dario how it would go, a roadside robbery on the bluff overlooking the highway, nothing more. None of this was what it was supposed to be.

He would try Memo later, he would keep trying, and if he never got through he would make the call down to Juarez. It was a call he should have been making that very moment, a call he knew Medina was expecting Dario to make. "*Nada,*" Dario said.

All of it had been adding up as the sheriff came into the bar that night and the oil workers drank away their savings, putting off whatever would come tomorrow. Sitting in his office with the phone, Dario could appreciate that, he could understand it, and if it wasn't for the sheriff out there he might even have joined them.

Now, with the cruiser still burning in the hospital drive, he backed away from the growing crowd, smoke rising still from the charred body of the car, and turned up toward Main, a few coins in his hand, looking for the nearest pay phone. All the time wondering if it was his own men out of Juarez who had come for the boy in the hospital, or if it was some other.

T OM WATCHED KELLY WHERE SHE STOOD LOOK- ing over the burned-out cruiser. He'd gotten the call in the morning and by the time he was on the highway headed south, the dark smoke was rising above the town. He wasn't sure what had changed inside Kelly between telling him to leave it alone last night at the bar, and this morning, but he knew one thing as they stood there looking the cruiser over: Gil Suarez was certainly dead.

From where he stood, only feet away from the blackened hulk of the car, Tom smelled the acrid remnants of the tires. The fire burning so hot that the shotgun, resting upright between the driver and passenger seats, stood up like a long matte black pipe, the pump handle melted all the way down to the floor, where it pooled against the metal. The patrol car a complete loss and the interior paint peeled away in a thousand little black scales. Kelly knelt and ran a hand through the ash. The history of what had happened now stained into the tips of her fingers.

"Road flares and some sort of accelerant," Tom said, as he caught the smell of gasoline and gunpowder. He stood on the driver's side of the car, looking in through the frame of the front windshield to where Kelly knelt on the other side.

Kelly wiped her hands on the knees of her uniform and stood.

"That's the smell," Tom said. "You get that? Something like cordite mixed with a chemical base."

"You ever see anything like this?" she asked.

"I've seen some bad accidents," Tom said. "But never like this. Not arson, not anything at this level."

"Scares you, doesn't it?"

"I don't envy you this one," Tom said. "You called me out here for a reason and I'm happy to help, but I'll need to know what you do. What are you thinking on this?"

"Officially?"

"Unofficially."

"Sometimes you hear of things coming out of Mexico that make you want to move up north, just to be ahead of it," Kelly said.

"You think that's what this is?"

"I don't know."

Tom watched her.

"Sometimes you just have to ask the *who, when,* and *where* of the thing and hope it doesn't turn out to be the *what* you were thinking it was the whole time."

They were in the elevator on the way up to the third floor

and the boy's hospital room, when Tom said, "How bad is it up there?"

"Broke his neck and nearly popped the boy's head right off his shoulders," Kelly replied.

"Scares the shit out of you sometimes, doesn't it?"

"Yes, it does," Kelly said.

R AY DROPPED THE BRONCO DOWN INTO THE wide bottomland before the mountains. As he drove he looked out on the tall blue mountains to the northeast, the crownlike spires of lechuguilla and sotol growing all around him on the gray desert hills. The road winding on and the Sullivan house visible ahead of him with its yellowed wood boards and dull cream trim.

The instructions he'd received from Memo were to stay at the house, lie low, and wait out any attention he might have received on the highway. One more day and Memo would send a man to pick up the drugs. Counting back, Ray estimated he'd been awake nearly thirty-six hours, his eyes feeling sanded over in their sockets. The thought of Tom out there still bothering him just as it had all through the night.

Coming up the drive Ray found Burnham's truck parked outside the house. Pausing, he scanned the road behind. Only the stillness of the broad desert to see before he turned to the house again, the truck still sitting there and Ray knowing it should have been anywhere but here. He brought the Bronco forward till it was parked alongside. Nothing to tell him it was anything but the same truck he had sent Sanchez north in the day before. He opened the Bronco door and went on ahead to the house.

With the Ruger pulled from his belt, he ran a hand along the metal of the hood, feeling the receding warmth of the engine. No idea what the truck was doing back here, but a rising certainty in his mind that Sanchez had been unable or unwilling to do as he'd been told.

It was only after sweeping every room that Ray found Sanchez sitting out back of the house, with a beer in his hand and five more at his feet. "You get lost?" Ray said, shoving the Ruger back down into his belt.

"No," Sanchez said, turning halfway around in the chair to look up at Ray where he stood on the back steps of the house. "But I thought I should see the job through. I thought I'd earn my uncle's trust."

"You're drunk," Ray said, a feeling thick as oil coated to his insides and just as suffocating. "You should have gone north."

Sanchez took a drink from his beer. It looked to Ray like he'd had several more than just the one in his hand, his body loose in the chair and Burnham's wide-brimmed cowboy hat dangling from Sanchez's neck.

"You've been here all night?"

"Personally, I thought you'd be dead by now."

"And if I was, you were going to save the day?"

"Something like that."

"Let's get something straight," Ray said. "Just so you and Memo know, I'm done after this. Memo wants this town, I don't want anything to do with it, and I don't want to be associated with him or you after this."

"My uncle will have this town."

Ray smiled. He couldn't help it. He was angry and exhausted and all he could think about was just lying down for a moment and forgetting about everything Memo had told him yesterday and all Sanchez was saying to him today. "How many of those have you had?"

Sanchez looked at the beer in his hand, dreamy with alcohol and the count going on in his head. "Seven," Sanchez said. "I bought some for us last night and then when you didn't show up, I bought us some more."

"I told you to leave yesterday," Ray said, the hoods of his eyes and the glare from the sun giving his face a weathered, worn-out look.

"No," Sanchez said. "Like I said, I'm surprised you're still alive, and that it worked, whatever you did. I thought maybe you'd need me." He put the hat up over his head and tipped it back, feigning something perhaps he'd once seen in a film.

"What about doing your job? Doing what you were told to do." Ray could feel little cracks beginning to form in his voice and he wondered what exactly might come through. "Your uncle asked me to send you north. Why didn't you go?"

"Coronado."

"I don't care," Ray said. "You shouldn't be here. No one but the cartel wants Coronado." He still hadn't moved off the back stairs and he was wondering how quickly he could get to Sanchez if he needed to. He didn't like that Sanchez was there, that he'd come back.

"Relax," Sanchez said, breaking one of the beers from the plastic and tossing it to Ray. "The job's done. You killed that boy, didn't you?"

Ray ignored him. He stood there with the beer in his hand, looking at the lawn chair on which Sanchez sat.

"Did you do it?" Sanchez asked. He was all the way turned on the seat with his spine bent and the aluminum chair creaking beneath him.

Ray walked over and stood watching the mountains. "It's done," Ray said. "I finished it for you. We'll spend tonight here and you'll leave in the morning."

"Have you talked with my uncle?"

"Yes."

"He knows it's done?"

"He knows."

"Did he ask about me?" Sanchez said. "When you called up

there to tell him about the boy, was he worried about where I was?"

"He didn't say anything about you."

Sanchez took a long sip off his beer and then set it down between his legs. "My uncle told me I'd learn something working with you."

Ray pulled the tab on the beer in his hand, and the aluminum opened with a loud crease of gas and foam. "I guess I should have showed you how to work that rifle," Ray said, drinking the beer and then just cradling the can face-out in front of him like he was assessing its worth. "You certainly didn't learn to listen. Memo would have never told you to go anywhere near Coronado. You buy this beer and that chair at the grocery store?"

Sanchez studied the mountains, not saying anything. He wouldn't look over at Ray. "My uncle told me not to let you do all the work."

"You think not listening, going to the grocery store—showing your face in town—is work? You think that kind of thing helps either of us?"

Sanchez ignored this. He was watching the rolling plain where it met the mountains farther on. "My uncle told me you'd teach me something."

"That what he said I was going to do? Teach you something?"

"Yeah, he said it was going to be just like old times down

here." Sanchez finished his beer. Tipping the can all the way back until the sun was full on his face. The cowboy hat fallen back, lopsided and unnatural, on his head.

"That's a dead man's hat," Ray said.

"I know," Sanchez said. "I figured Burnham wouldn't need it anymore."

"It's not a good look for you," Ray said. "You should take it off."

Sanchez finished the can he'd been drinking and leaned forward to break a new beer from the plastic. "Memo said it would be good fun down here," Sanchez said. It was perhaps the second or third time Ray had heard the phrase from Sanchez since they'd met.

Sanchez opened the beer, waiting on Ray's response. A cold wind rolled past them and Ray heard the grains of sand hitting away on the siding of the house. "You should be happy about what you've done," Sanchez said. "The killing."

"Happy?"

"Burnham and the kid. Cartel boys like that. Thought it would help you," Sanchez said, smiling up at Ray with the beer in his hand, the ropy looseness of alcohol rolling through his voice. "*Salud.*"

"Why would that help me?" Ray asked.

Sanchez retracted the beer, sipped it, the cold bubbling liquid at the corners of his mouth. "Memo told me what you did when you got out of here, after he covered for you and hid you from the cartel and the law. He said you went house to house, making visits, killing anyone you thought was cartel."

"Before this," Ray said, ignoring Sanchez and his silly alcohol-filled grin, "you ever kill anyone?"

"Sure," Sanchez said. "I've killed."

"You have?"

"You saw me yesterday," Sanchez said. "I did all the work. Caught that kid on the run, shot him from about three hundred feet out, right through the crosshairs."

"Should have killed him," Ray said. "You don't finish, and it can end up hurting you."

"I would have finished," Sanchez said. "I should have been the one in that hospital room. It was my kill."

"You ever kill someone up close? With your hands? No gun?"

"I have."

"You have?"

"Sure."

"Lots of men?" Ray asked.

Sanchez looked out on the desert. "Enough," he finally said. "I've killed enough."

Ray finished his beer in one long drink. "You haven't killed anyone," Ray said. "I don't know what you thought you were going to learn down here or what Memo said I was going to teach you."

"Pick someone," Sanchez said in a rush. "Pick someone and we'll see how I do."

"Pick someone?"

"Sure," Sanchez said. "Pick someone for me. I'll show you how it's done. I'll show you how easy I can do what you do."

Ray felt disgusted. Not waiting for Sanchez to offer, he reached down and grabbed another beer from the plastic. He stood there for a few seconds longer. Out on the plain a rain shower was moving across the desert before them in a sweep of gray-blue light. "I'm tired," Ray said. "I can't talk about this anymore." With the beer in his hand he went back inside the house, leaving Sanchez to sit alone in his store-bought chair.

K ELLY LOOKED IN THROUGH THE OPEN DOOR. The kid could have been sleeping. Gil's head turned away toward the window, the crime scene just as it had been found. Sheets pulled up over his chest, his arms resting on either side. The only thing to indicate what had happened a deep bruise on his neck that seemed to grow deeper while she looked in on him.

"He never woke up?" Tom asked, standing beside her and Hastings.

"Not that we know," Hastings said.

"Pierce stepped away from the room for a minute when his cruiser went up. Walked down to the end of the hall to that window," Kelly said, pointing toward the front of the hospital. "He was probably only gone from the room for thirty seconds."

"And the staff?"

"Did just the same," Hastings said.

Down the hall the elevator opened up and Kelly watched the mayor move out through the doors. Halfway up the hall he was already speaking to her. "You had a nineteen-year-old kid guarding the victim," Eli said. "It should have been you or Pete up here, not Pierce." The closer he came the more he slowed, looking behind Kelly to where Tom stood. "What's he doing here?"

"I called him."

"Called him?" Eli's eyes gone small in his large head, a yellow oxford wrinkled up at the waist and the sleeves rolled up to the elbows. "Come here with me a minute." He reached a hand out and took her elbow, leading her away. "What do you think you're doing? That man is not your friend anymore," Eli said in a low hiss. "He could have ended your career just like he did his. You need to be smarter than this. You need to understand there's no good reason to bring him in on this, no matter what you may think."

Kelly nodded. She wasn't even really looking at Eli, so

much history between them and none of it any good. She felt his grip hard on her elbow. "We're not working with much here, Mayor. We're not working with anything, really."

"You have a name, don't you?"

"We have a dead boy with a name, and a record for drug possession," Kelly corrected.

"You tell any of that drug stuff to anyone and we'll have a federal investigation here," Eli continued. His hand wrapped tight to her elbow, he led her farther down the hall, Hastings and Tom still up by the room, watching them both where they stood almost at the elevator. "Yesterday was bad enough," Eli went on. "You understand? That's not what we need. That's not at all what we need around here. News vans, reporters, federal agents.

"You left a kid to do what you and Pete should have been doing and now that boy in the room back there is dead. I don't even want to know what this will mean for our image."

Kelly mumbled an apology. Part of her not even listening, holding her tongue back, knowing it was no use. She felt bad for Pierce, she'd let him down, let him get buffaloed by some unknown force, either Dario or some other, and still she had nothing to go on but the dead boy in the hospital room back there.

"Seventy-five percent," Eli was saying, still going on his tirade, "that's what is left of the population. Layoffs and empty storefronts, that lot at the end of town big enough for a Wal-

Mart, no developers in two years, nothing happening. You tell someone about this boy and his drug charges, about what you or Tom thinks is going on in this town, and it will kill us. You understand me on this, Sheriff?"

"Yes," she said. "I hear you." Kelly knew it was only a matter of time now. She couldn't hope to hide any one of these things from the town, from the people, and especially from the media. One of her patrol cars burned to the metal three floors down, the black smoke of its tires visible for miles around. What the mayor was asking was out of her hands, there was no stopping it, a balloon on the wind, rising skyward.

"Good," he said, releasing her elbow. He stood straight now, almost a foot taller than her. "I don't need any further aggravation. I don't want to see Tom around here anymore, it's bad enough with everything we have going on in this town." He paused, looking up the hall. "You hear they laid off thirty more men yesterday?"

She nodded. "I heard that."

"Just what we need," the mayor said. "There's a meeting tonight and I want you there."

"The union?"

"Whatever they're calling themselves."

"What about Gil Suarez?"

"Who?"

"The victim."

"I thought we understood each other on this," Eli said, his eyes sharpened. "I'll field any questions that might come up on this. I don't want you going down any dead ends. Right now that's not what we need. Business," he said, "that is all we should be worried about now. Business and making sure this town isn't empty by the end of the year. You might as well start looking for a replacement for your deputy while you're at that meeting tonight. There will be a lot of men looking for work." He turned and without saying good-bye walked toward the elevators.

Behind her, sitting just inside the nurse's station, Kelly saw Pierce watching her. "I'm sorry about that," Kelly said. "I'm sorry about what the mayor just said."

Without moving from his seat, Pierce said, "I fucked up. I know that, there's nothing else for me to say. Maybe Gil would still be alive if I was on that door. The mayor's right about me."

"No," Kelly said. "No, he's not. If you had stayed on that door you'd be just as dead as that boy in the room. They were coming for him no matter what, and it was my fault for not seeing it." Up the hall, Hastings and Tom were still waiting for her. She didn't have a clue where to go from this point. She felt scraped raw by the mayor's words, by what he wanted her to do, and all that she knew she was powerless to defend.

DARIO FLICKED THE KNIFE DOWN AND WATCHED it quiver in the wood floor of his office. The steel handle shivering like a tuning fork. He was sitting in his desk chair with the door closed and a .45 semiauto on the desk in front of him. He stretched out his hand toward the gun, wanting it close to him. The skin showing white where it came exposed between his fingers. The knife on the floor still lightly moving.

Juarez was sending men. They had always been planning to send some. But now, with the killing of the boy in the hospital, there would be more of them.

He was examining the gun when Medina came to the door, knocking lightly until Dario responded.

"¿Muerto?" Medina asked, putting a cup of coffee in front of Dario. Through the doorway, behind Medina, the plastic tubs of cherries, limes, and lemons were visible on the bar where he'd been prepping them for the day.

"Si, probablemente," Dario answered.

"¿Y los hombres?"

"En la tarde." Dario put the coffee cup to his lips, thinking about the men who would come in the afternoon and what that would mean for them.

Medina stood in the doorway wringing his hands as if looking for something else he could do. "¿En la tarde?" Medina said. "¿Cuántos?" He looked from Dario to the knife on the floor, and then back to Dario.

"*Bastante*." Medina turned to leave and Dario stopped him. "The knife," he said in English, holding out his hand toward where he'd flung the blade down. Medina pried it off the floor and brought it over. Dario watching him, wondering how much longer they'd be together in this town.

Memo had offered him a way out, but all that was gone now, all that was in the past. And the feeling came onto him in that moment with a strength he hadn't been expecting. He was scared, possibly for the first time in a long time. And he knew he would do anything now, that Memo had put him in a corner, had possibly even meant to from the start. Leaving Dario to dangle in the wind.

Only Memo hadn't counted on how far Dario was willing to take it. He had wanted a way out, a change, but all that wasn't how it could be anymore. He looked at the knife and knew he would gut anyone who came between him and getting the drugs back. He would slice the lips right off a man who said a thing about him. He would reach down and take the tongue right off the back of a man's throat and leave him drowning in the blood. It was that simple.

He was tired of it all. He was tired of all that his life had become and all that was expected of him. Now, he thought, he would do what he knew he should have done from the start, he would do what needed to be done to preserve himself that little bit longer. The thought of death still circling him, as it always did, high up like a vulture on the wind.

TOM SAT IN THE CHILDREN'S SWING OUTSIDE Kelly's house. He pumped his legs and let the momentum take him up, the chain links grating against each other as the swing moved. Inside, he could see Kelly's husband, Drew, at the kitchen window. Kelly's place a quarter mile away from the center of town. The swing set left there after the family before had moved out and Kelly had moved in.

He pumped his legs again, feeling the metal pole above bend with his weight. The door to Kelly's house opened as Kelly came out, carrying a couple beers.

"Your husband all right with you taking a late-afternoon swing with another man?" Tom asked, pointing to the second seat there beside him. His own legs dug now, toes first, into the dirt at his feet as he teetered forward on the rusted chains.

Kelly smiled, giving one of the beers over to Tom and looking behind her at the house, where Drew was still hard at work on what was left of the dishes. "I doubt he'd mind it just this once."

She sat, the metal beam above their heads bowing with her added weight. Tom had offered her a ride home, waiting while she'd finished up at Coronado Memorial, then going into the department office to help her with the paperwork. Inside the kitchen, Drew looked out at them and waved. He was a big man, over six foot, with short-cropped wavy brown hair.

"He loves you," Tom said. "It's easy to see, you know."

Kelly took another drink from her beer, pumping her legs, her feet dragging against the ground with the backswing. "My gentle giant," she said. "Sometimes I wish there was a little more excitement to our lives, but you know when it comes down to it we're happy here."

"A normal life."

"Something like that," Kelly said.

Tom took a drink from his beer. "Thanks for this," he said.

"Dinner?"

"Just this." He circled his hand to encompass the ground, the house, the world, all of it together. "I had a good time today. It brought me back to old times."

"It was worth it just to see Eli's face when he saw you," Kelly said. "If you want a little more of this life, running around keeping order, you'll come with me to the union meeting tonight."

"I thought the mayor told you to stop palling around with me."

"If he cared enough about this he'd be at the meeting himself."

"No," Tom said. "I think I've had enough, I certainly don't miss sitting in on those meetings, listening to everyone bicker."

"Cattle keep to themselves, don't they?" Kelly smiled, making sure he knew she was only joking. "Tomorrow it's back to the usual?"

"Who would have known," Tom said. "Me as a cowboy."

"I would have. Not much difference from your job to mine," Kelly said. "One way or another, we're always going to be wranglers. The best thing about your job is that you actually know what you're going after. Me, I don't have a clue." Kelly put her heels to the ground, dragging them till the chains stopped their swinging. "What do you think this is all about?"

"Gil?"

"Yes," Kelly said. "I hate that we didn't protect him. Whatever he was into, he deserved better than this."

Tom took a sip of the beer. He felt just like her, but he knew she felt that guilt worse than he ever could. Gil had been hers to protect, though Tom had never really thought someone would take it to that level, burning the cruiser like that and killing the boy in his sleep. "Don't do that," he said. "Don't blame yourself for something you couldn't have done anything about. You said it yourself when you talked to Pierce: they were coming for that boy no matter what."

"I'm trying to figure it and I just can't."

"What is there to figure?" Tom said. "It just comes back to the usual suspects, drugs or money."

"How much?"

"Enough to try and kill that boy one day, then come back and finish him off the next."

"*That* much," Kelly said.

"I'd estimate it was *even more* than that," Tom said. He kicked his legs out and swung till he could get his feet fully under him, leaning back now against the seat of the swing to stand.

"What's your view on all this?" Kelly asked.

"I don't have one," Tom said. "I wish I did, but the truth of it is that people do crazy things for far less than drugs or money."

"There it is," Kelly said, trying to stifle a laugh.

"There what is?"

"The optimist I love from the old days."

"Pessimist, you mean."

"Exactly."

T HE MEN CAME UP FROM THE SOUTH IN THE afternoon. There were six of them. Coming into the bar, it seemed to Dario, all at once. Not there, then there. Six dark figures, blocking the light from the front window, big and menacing as anything he'd seen in recent years.

The six figures just waiting there, letting their eyes adjust to the gloom. Medina paused in his work at the bar to look back at them.

Dario stood slowly and drew their attention. He knew half

of them by sight, the two brothers, Ernesto and Felíx, as well as the big Oaxacan, Lalo.

Dario introduced them to Medina. Asking for their names and while they told him, committing each of them to memory, Hector, César, and Carlos. He asked each man in turn if he wanted anything—a beer, a Coke, a water—and began to tell them what little there was to know about Gil Suarez, Jake Burnham, Coronado, and the twelve kilos of missing heroin.

T OM MADE IT HOME JUST BEFORE THE RAIN began to fall. With what little daylight remained, he stood in the stables grooming the two big bays, their coats dusted in white hair like an old dog's muzzle. Both startled and showing the white bulge of their eyes as the rain began to ping on the tin roof.

Jeanie, resting at Tom's feet, didn't even bother to raise her head from her paws as the rain came on. The pellets hitting hard as stones, then rolling off and falling in ropy streams to the ground. A small carved line of earth where the rain fell and dug up the land.

He put a hand out, feeling the drops hitting on his palm. Above, the sky had grown dark and flat as river stones. The events of the day somehow faded into memory. Kelly and him walking out of the hospital hours before, nothing but the thin purple bruise along the kid's neck to say anyone had ever been in the room with him at all.

He brought his hand back in and put it wet to the horse closest to him, its eyes not as big and white as before. His hand moving down its neck, feeling the smooth, almost waxen, touch of its coat. A gust of wind and the splatter of rain falling now in sheets.

Outside, through the falling water, he saw where a small part of the southern fence needed mending. What remained of his herd—twenty-some pigs in all—crowded up under the particleboard shelter. Farther on, his own house a dull gray against the rain, the windows the only points of light. Inside he'd kept it just the way it had been before all his trouble; before he'd shot Angela Lopez, before he'd lost his job and his life had changed in that most definite of ways.

From where he stood, he could just make out the cars going past on the highway. A slate-blue coloring to everything around him and the lights of the traffic moving up the highway, first there, then gone in the rain, only to reappear, floating again across the wide bottomland of the valley floor like lightning bugs over a darkening background.

He'd been expecting her when she came, the headlights turning up off the highway and traveling on up his drive toward the house. Claire's face in profile to his own as she pulled her Volkswagen in beside his truck.

Watching her for a time as she stood in front of his place, the rain falling everywhere, he came to the door of the stables and waved her over. It was a hundred feet at most and by the time she made it she was soaked through. "I didn't think you'd be here," she said. A cold, straight cut to her face, the rain all over her skin and falling from her chin. The dimples now seen in her cheeks as she looked up to him and her skin marked in places by small moles and other minor imperfections.

Tom turned and went back to the stalls. "Why'd you come then?"

Claire stared back at him. He knew he'd said the wrong thing but he wasn't in the mood for her tonight. The dimples in her cheeks gone and her lips downturned where she stood just inside the stables, her long brown hair black with water as it hung against her back. She was ten years younger than him. They'd known each other for a long time now, and there was little Tom felt he could say to her that she hadn't already heard.

"Don't be like that," Claire said, walking over to where he stood next to the horses. The same two he'd bought three years before when he'd had the money. One for Claire and one for him, but the romantic idea of riding them every day never quite their reality. "I came by last night and you weren't here. I got worried, that's all."

"I'm fine, you can see that, can't you?"

"Fine?"

"Yes," he said. He finished grooming the horse and then went over and brought the blankets and leathers back farther in from the rain, the water splashing up off the ground and speckling the stable floor.

"You pissed off Eli pretty good today," Claire said, leaning back against the stall, watching him.

Tom tried not to let the smile show, but it was there all the same. "Yeah?"

"After coming back from the hospital he was furious. He didn't understand what Kelly was doing, letting you up there like that," Claire said. "I didn't really understand, either. But I liked to see him angry about it, and for once he didn't stack it all against me."

"Kelly probably shouldn't have brought me in on this, but I'm glad she did," Tom said. He was watching her, wondering if it would ever work between them again, or if it was working right now and he just didn't know it.

"He doesn't like you very much," Claire said with a smile.

"No, he never has. Even when I was employed and he was just doing his first term."

"The newsmen showed up again and he talked to them about the boy. I don't think he wanted Kelly doing it."

"I saw some of the vans on my way through town. It looked like they were going to stick it out for the night."

She shivered a bit where she stood and Tom looked away

toward his truck and her small Volkswagen sitting out there in the rain. He was trying not to invite her in, knowing where all of it would lead, just as it always did between them. "You ever hear of the rule of three?" Tom said, turning back to her. "They're using a tried-and-true method of newscasting, waiting around for the next big event. Something's bound to happen."

"Yeah," Claire said, "if they wait long enough. In this town it might take years."

He'd run out of things to do, the bridles and reins now put back from the open stable doors, the blankets over the stall gates and the horses fed. No idea what he was doing anymore, what he was putting off. Something inside of him nervous as a little boy about to ask a girl out on his first date. "I was going to wait the rain out here, but it looks like you could use a towel," he said.

"You'll probably need one, too, by the time we get inside." She was grinning now, looking at him in that way he knew there was no returning from.

Outside the stable doors he saw the rain falling against the bent wire fence. All the things that needed fixing in his life, and nothing ever seeming to get fixed. In the morning he'd go over and see about Deacon's cattle. And it would be back to a life that—even for the shortest time—he'd allowed himself to forget.

A BOVE, THE NIGHT HAD GONE COLD. THE SKY flat and low across the valley as Kelly drove down from her house on her way into town for the meeting. Lights on in many of the windows now and the rain falling, gray, from an oyster-colored sky. She wasn't looking forward to the meeting. No reason really for her to be there except that Eli had ordered her.

Pulling up in front of the church, she saw the basement lights on through the rain and heard the sounds of the men inside. The conversations carrying through the falling water, the door pushed brightly open a hundred feet in front of her, shining light out onto the parking lot, where it glistened like silver on the puddles.

The meeting hadn't started yet when she walked in. Streamers hanging down the paneled room from a wedding a week or so before, highlighted in places by a rainbow of crepe flowers taped here and there along the wall. All down the hall, chairs had been set up and many of the oil workers sat waiting in them, while still more milled around a fold-out table where grocery store pastries and coffee were laid out.

"The mayor must be thinking we're going to storm the courthouse," a voice nearby said.

Kelly looked to the last row of chairs where the voice had come from and found Tom's uncle, Gus Lamar, turned with his arm raised over the back of the chair beside him.

"Investing in our futures," Kelly said, walking over to stand behind Gus. "We're always wondering when the oil companies will buy up the state government offices here in town."

"The mayor told you to come?"

"Eli is just looking out for our futures," she said, the sarcasm heavy in her voice as she came around and sat next to him.

Gus smiled and looked up toward the front of the hall, where the heads of the union were taking their seats. "You must have forgotten where you are," Gus said, turning back to her. "This is a union meeting, we don't give a damn what the oil companies do. As long as they keep paying a fair wage and stop laying men off every month."

In the ten years she'd been sheriff she'd attended four meetings, always at the request of the mayor, and only if he thought there might be trouble. "I thought you retired, Gus. What's all this us-against-them stuff?"

"I've been sitting in for a year or so now. I'd sit in on the corporate meetings over in Houston if I could, but I never made it into the billionaires' club and my wells went dry a long time before the big guys came through and bought everyone out. I figure I'd just like to know what we're in for in this town."

"You looking out for our futures, just like the mayor?"

"Looking out for Billy's future," Gus said. "He's going to need a job soon enough. I'm not getting any younger."

"I just saw Tom, so I'm guessing you have Luis sober enough to watch Billy for the night."

"Billy is most likely watching Luis," Gus said. "He was too drunk to drive home last night and he left his truck in town."

Kelly smiled, but didn't say anything as she thought about Luis and what he'd said the other night, drunk on whiskey and tallboys. All of it a mess and Kelly sitting in on some meeting she didn't have any desire to be part of.

One of the union reps was standing now, asking everyone to sit. Kelly recognized a few of the men she'd seen at the bar the night before, Andy Strope a head above the rest of them as he sat four rows up. "Last night I caught them talking about burning down a trailer over at the Tate Bulger," Kelly said.

"Who said that?"

"Strope and some others."

Gus shook his head like the whole thing was funny to him. "Andy doesn't even work for the Tate Bulger. He's just trying to get the rest of them all fired up."

"Isn't that why this meeting was called?"

"I don't know about that," Gus said. "What good would setting a fire do? They're mad, but no one thinks if they lash out they'll get their jobs back. It would never happen and all the union reps know it. I'd guess they're going to talk strike, if they talk anything at all."

Kelly looked up toward the front of the hall, where the

union rep had raised his hands for quiet. She watched Andy Strope, four rows up, turn and whisper something to the man beside him. The union rep beginning to speak about the lay-offs and what they meant for the union.

Beside her Gus sat up a little in his chair. Nearly eighty years old, he was still taller than most in the room and well built from the years he'd spent working his property. His had been a family operation at one time, but she knew that his son had fallen in with the wrong people many years before. The death of Gus's daughter-in-law outside of town in a hit-and-run accident was still considered by many to be some sort of retribution for something Ray Lamar had done against the cartel.

Up in front a man stood to speak and then was shouted down, several in the audience, including those around Strope, standing up to protest whatever the man had been about to say.

Gus leaned toward her. "He was going to tell them he thought a strike wouldn't do them any good and that they should just be grateful that those remaining still have jobs."

"Really?" Kelly whispered. "You read minds now?"

"There was a big discussion over it before you came in. To tell you the truth, I think he's right. The way things are going I doubt there's much more than a year before the whole place goes dry."

For a while Kelly tried to pay attention to the discussion,

but most of it she couldn't follow, the conversation going back and forth with the oil workers and the union reps as they tried to establish the basis for what they would do. A low chant arising from the crowd as the head of the union stood to speak. "What are they saying?" she asked Gus.

"Fire."

"I thought you said it wouldn't come to that."

Gus shook his head. "It won't. A few of the men that were laid off spent the day drinking in their trailers. They're just spouting off, wasting their time. They should have been looking for work."

"I certainly don't need any of this right now," Kelly said.

"I heard," Gus said. "Tom stopped by on his way down from Las Cruces last night. He told me he'd seen you on the highway earlier."

"Well, as you probably know, it didn't get much better today."

"Heard that, too," Gus said, half listening to her and half watching something that was going on up front. "I'm sorry," Gus said out of the side of his mouth, "this is a waste of your time."

Kelly turned back to the front just in time to see Strope stand and let one of the store-bought pastries fly toward the union head where he stood at the table. The pastry caught the union man square in the chest and slipped off his shirt with the thick weight of its icing. "Jesus, Strope," Kelly said, as she got to her feet, speaking low in the silence that followed. "You can't really be this dumb, can you?" She took her time walking around toward him, making sure she was between Andy Strope and the door as she went forward up the row, one hand outstretched to keep the other men back, while the other clutched at the cuffs on her belt.

The whole time, Strope, square jawed and big as he was, just standing there looking at her with that same dull blaze in his eyes Kelly had seen the night before at the bar. "You can't take me in for this," he kept saying. "What's the charge? I threw a donut at a man, and you're going to take me in?"

Kelly didn't let her stare drop away from Strope. She was aware of everyone watching her, the oil workers sitting and waiting to see what she would do as she forced her way up the row trying to get to Strope. "How about public drunkenness," she said. "I can smell it on you from here."

As big as he was, he went pretty easily, perhaps knowing it wasn't going to do him any good to bullshit her. She'd been in the bar last night, she'd heard just about all he was going to say to her, and now she was just tired of the whole thing. Tired that this was getting to be her normal night in this town, oil workers pissed off and blowing off steam.

There was a dead kid in the morgue, and she was stuck doing work like this. It didn't matter to her, and she had half a mind just to let him go on throwing pastries at the union heads. She sort of wanted to do it herself, but she didn't, not even bothering to cuff Strope as she led him outside to the patrol car, where he'd get locked in the rear cage.

When she came back in, Gus was waiting for her at the door, looking out at the rain, the meeting already started back up again. "Now I'll be spending the next couple hours babysitting a drunk till Hastings comes on for the night shift," she said, looking to Gus. "Any other enemies of the state I should be watching out for?"

"I'd say you got public enemy number one, right there," Gus said. "At least you know in this rain no one is going to light anything on fire. They'd have to light the wells if they lit anything, and even Strope isn't that dumb."

"Thanks," Kelly said. "Please don't mention that to the mayor, I might end up on a stakeout with more pastries." She laughed and looked away to the patrol car, where Strope was leaning his forehead against the rear pane of the window.

"Good luck with him," Gus said, exchanging a smile with Kelly before she turned away and went out to her cruiser, shielding her face from the rain with her hand.

R AY WOKE IN THE DARK TO THE SOUND OF A hard rain falling on the roof. Stiff from sleeping on the floor in the upstairs bedroom, he rolled over and pushed himself up. He couldn't remember if he'd been dreaming. For years after his service he'd taken pills to help him sleep. Years traveling through jungle hills could do that. The unease he'd felt after returning to the quiet of the desert cityscape following all those years away, hiking through foreign forests before the war had even been official. The wooden stocks of their guns warped from the humidity. Every shot he took in those first months off by a centimeter or two, as he struggled to calibrate his rifle.

All of it only a moment in his life, a small blip along his timeline that kept replaying itself nightly in his dreams. The doctors even using the term recalibrate in his first months back as they gave him the pills, talking to him about his homecoming, talking to him like he was a rifle with a centimeter-or-two leftward pull.

The rain had woken him and he felt for a moment lost in the sound. How many hours had he been asleep? He'd let himself be pulled down into the black abyss. It had been too easy and he knew it. He should never have closed his eyes.

After he'd lost Marianne and given up his son he'd replaced the pills with alcohol, drinking himself to sleep. But since deciding to come home, he was back on them again, blending alcohol and medication every night in order to get his sleep. The pills helping him concentrate, a whole bottle to help him keep his mind from wandering. The empty beer cans there on the floor, taken from Sanchez, not enough to get him through the night. And the feeling of those pills mixed with the alcohol like a soft snow, coated heavy on his skin.

He stood in the dark of the second-floor bedroom, working his hands over his eyes. Through the window he saw the rain out there in the desert falling straight and hard from the sky, hard as ice and just as loud.

Taking a blanket he'd found in the back of the Bronco, he'd gone to sleep in his boxers and when he walked to the window, he felt the cold draft that had come with the rainstorm. The moon shrouded in clouds. Outside, everything a dark gray movement of rain and wind. The storm over the plain looking like some ancient picture show, speckled with flecks of dust, eaten away with time, crackling with age.

He'd felt uneasy standing there in the backyard with Sanchez, looking up at the mountains he'd once known. Talking about how to kill a man, how to put your two hands to his throat and pop the vertebrae apart like chicken bones. It wasn't how he'd remembered it, how he'd thought killing would always be for him, it was cold-blooded and murderous, the boy never waking, just the body fighting it, subconsciously aware.

A growing unease moved through Ray now. Sanchez boasting about the things he hadn't done. Each word seeming to close in tighter around them. A vision of Jacob Burnham in the dirt at Ray's feet. The barrel of that shotgun to the old man's heart and Ray's finger bent down around the trigger.

Sanchez was just a kid, half Ray's age, and kids did stupid things. They didn't listen. They went to town when they weren't supposed to. Ray had gone upstairs thinking it through, thinking how good it would be to get clear of all this, of Memo, of Sanchez, of the whole damn business. He was done with this thing, he knew it now, knew he didn't have it in him, knew if he carried on with this life he'd be dead soon. He didn't care. There wasn't anything left and he stared out the window thinking about Burnham's final words, and how if Ray had listened maybe he wouldn't be here now.

Out on the rain-swept plain Ray saw headlights break over a far-off hill, nothing else around. The headlights dipping back beneath the earth, into the ground, then rising up again over the next hill, gradually coming closer.

He backed away from the window and took the Ruger from beneath his folded jacket, there on the floor. He saw the car fully now, metal body streaked in rain, moving across the plain with its two bright lights leading the way. He dressed and waited at the window. Watching, he saw the headlights slow and move up the drive toward the house.

He recognized it now as the Bronco. From the upstairs window, he saw Sanchez push open the Bronco door. Stand up into the rain, then run for the house in five long steps, trying as best he could to avoid the puddles.

The boy scared Ray. Not in a hurtful way, but in a reckless, broken way that carried with it no forgiveness. Ray didn't know how well he'd handled the boasts Sanchez was making, trying to build himself up in Ray's eyes. Perhaps he'd been too hasty in dismissing the boy, too ready to not believe.

Ray's attention turned again to the dark desert landscape as two more cars materialized from the rain—brought up out of some deep crack in the earth—no headlights on. Just following along in the same rain-swollen ruts Sanchez had taken over the small rise a mile out, then dipping back beneath the earth, then rising once again.

Ray gripped the gun, the metal as solid and dangerous beneath his skin as those two darkened ghosts traveling in a line across the desert toward them. His first thought that they were Memo's men come to get the heroin, but the reality sinking into him that it was too early and they were not Memo's men at all. Watching, Ray knew Sanchez would never listen, would never stick to what he had been told, and that it was a mistake for Ray to have thought he could have trusted him.

FROM THE LEAD CAR, DARIO WATCHED THE MAN who'd been in his bar that night—too drunk to know they'd been following him—close the house door behind him. Medina was driving and they sat at the bottom of the drive with their lights off and the wipers pushing water across the windshield at a steady pace. Dario nodded his head toward the house. There in front of it was Burnham's pickup truck. The same truck he'd loaded the heroin into only a couple days before.

Without needing to be told, Medina eased the car forward up the slight incline. Water everywhere on the drive and flowing down toward the road like a river. The man had come into the bar two hours before, already smelling of alcohol, speaking to Medina like he was underwater.

"All these people," the man said under his breath, Dario sitting at the bar, three stools down. "They don't know me, they don't know what I'm about." He threw up his arms, raising the tempo of his voice, trying for attention. "I've been to prison. I put my time in, earned my place here at this bar, in this town, running things for my uncle."

He ordered a drink from the bar and sat mumbling to himself. After a while he turned and spoke to Lalo and the other men, sitting off a ways at one of the wooden tables. All of them watching him since he'd entered, following his movements from door to bar stool. The man trying to give back that same cold look, but his eyes drifting again toward the bar and then the drink before him.

Dario watched him drink two more whiskeys, doubles both. The night had been slow and Dario sat smiling over his cup of lukewarm coffee, watching this man, a few years younger than him, sinking deeper and deeper toward the bar.

Dario waved Medina over and told him to give the man one more double, on the house. There were no well workers in the place tonight, all of them staying away after the blowout they'd had the night before. Many, Dario thought, probably already gone back up north to look for work, heading for the interstate, Texas, and probably farther.

That the man was looking for someone to talk to was obvious, he would talk to anyone at this point. The cowboy hat he had been wearing cast out on the bar before him and Dario moving over on the stool as Medina brought the whiskey. "You should go," Dario told him. "You should take off and get away from here. The police have been looking for someone like you."

The man turned away from the whiskey to look at Dario with his linen suit, clean-faced from his shave that morning.

"I was listening to you," Dario said. "I think you're the man they've all been looking for."

"Who's been looking for me?"

"The sheriff," Dario said. "She came in last night looking for you, she was looking all over the place, asking if we'd seen you." Dario watched the man's eyes drop once, then again, the hoods working and the lashes bobbing on his face with the alcohol. "Friend," Dario said, addressing the man. "What were you saying you were in the business of?"

The man wobbled off the stool with one hand held out on

the bar for balance. Dario just watching, not getting up, but watching, only his coffee cup on the bar before him.

"I think I've had too much."

"Your hat," Dario said, looking at the worn threads of felt there on the bar, the familiar look of the thing he was sure he recognized now.

"It's not mine," he finally said, the focus in the man's eyes drifting. "Never was."

"Yes," Dario said. "Perhaps it isn't." Dario picked the hat up off the bar and examined it under the overhead light. "Maybe a friend of mine left it here."

Both of them standing now beside the bar, the hat in Dario's hands as the man searched the room with his eyes, panic now apparent on his face. The words that eventually surfaced a train wreck of bent metal. "It's time . . ."

"It's time you were going," Dario finished.

Behind, there was the hard squeal of a chair. Lalo stood from the table, looking to Dario for direction.

"Perhaps we can help you out with a ride?" Dario asked.

"No," the man said, holding out a cautious hand, speaking to both men now. "I'll be fine."

He stumbled toward the door without turning to look behind him. Dario watched him go, and when the bar door closed, they were already moving to the back, where their own cars sat.

WHEN THE DOOR SHATTERED INWARD WITH the big booming sound of a shotgun fired at close range, Ray was already moving down the stairs. A big Mexican came through what was left of the door frame with a Mossberg pump raised on his shoulder in a sweep of the room. The door lay turned over on the floor, both hinges blown out of the jamb, a fine dust of plaster from the walls in the air, and splintered pieces of wood all across the floor. The Mexican turned at the sight of Ray and raised the shotgun toward the stairs. Ray put one bullet in the man's chest from about twenty feet out, then, still moving down the stairs, before the man had even fallen, Ray put another bullet in his head.

A strange quiet filled the room for a half second. The big Mexican lay there on the floor, his arms played back in a pose suggesting he had tried to catch the bullet with his hands. Ray carried the Ruger, holding it on the door and the night beyond. His pants pulled roughly up on his hips. Barefoot, he took the stairs two at a time, switching the Ruger to his off hand in order to scoop the Mexican's shotgun up. Then almost in the same moment flattening his body to the floor as the guns opened up on him from outside the house.

For a minute there was nothing but gunfire. The sound of it so close it seemed to inhabit the room. Glass broke from the windows and fell crackling to the floor, plaster walls took bullets and broke apart, exposing the fine ribbings of wood beneath. The overhead light fixture rocked back and forth on its wiring, spewing a haze of ceiling dust before crashing to the floor. The sound of it all, like the rough fill of gravel down a metal sink. The mildewed, time-worn smell of plaster dust everywhere in the air.

Across the room, Ray saw Sanchez's legs splayed out flat on the kitchen floor, his back hidden behind the small wooden island. Everything in the kitchen, cabinets, empty beer cans, tiling, bit up and dancing as the bullets went past and either shattered them or thudded into the plaster and framing behind.

They were being fired on by what sounded like submachine guns, the bullets hitting rapidly and in distinguishable lines across the walls, as if the gunmen meant to sweep through the house one room at a time. Hazed in dust, the downstairs rooms hung suspended in a plaster fog when the firing stopped.

Ray pulled himself across the floor toward the kitchen, parting glass with his forearms, the Ruger tucked down in his back pocket and the shotgun held in his right hand, dragging himself forward through the chaos. No sound now except the rain.

"Are you hurt?" Ray asked, pushing himself up next to Sanchez, both men now hidden behind the small kitchen island that separated them from the living room. The smell of alcohol on Sanchez's skin like a generous pouring of cologne.

"No," he said. The hunting rifle in his hands, a collection of unused bullets on his lap. "You?"

"No." A sheen of sweat appeared all along Sanchez's skin, the scent of him in that room, sour as moonshine. And Ray watching him, trying to decide if the boy was sober enough for any of this. The cold seep of reality now seen working away as the sobriety came into his face. It didn't matter, it couldn't, ready or not they were going to have to do something.

Ray pulled the shotgun around and shucked the bullets. There were three more casings in the pump. He put them, one at a time, back into the body of the gun and leaned against the island next to Sanchez.

The two of them sat there breathing in the thick air. Adrenaline going. No lights on and Ray—with his back pressed uncomfortably into one of the island cabinets—looked onto the desert behind the house through what remained of the shattered kitchen door.

Car high beams came on brilliant white in front of the house and created a mirror from what remained of the glass in the windows and door. The two of them reflected in the panes, covered in plaster, white as painted aboriginals.

"We've got to go," Ray said. He put his head up over the island and looked into the living room. Beams of light entering through every hole in the wall, looking somehow like stars in the darkness, like galaxies suspended milky through the room.

"The dope," Sanchez said.

Ray swore. "It's hidden," Ray said. "Buried twenty paces from the back stairs." He looked around behind again at the galaxy of holes in the front wall, and then he looked toward the back door and the night out there, knowing they'd never find the dope in the darkness.

"We can take them," Sanchez said, repeating it several times until Ray responded.

"No," Ray said, realizing for the first time that he didn't have his jacket or even his shoes. "We can't."

Sanchez moved to get up. "No," Ray said again, pulling him down. He could feel Sanchez panting beside him. His sweatshirt still gripped in Ray's hand. "I'm sorry about what I said earlier. About doubting you, but now isn't the time."

Ray swiveled out to see what he could make of the situation, knowing that even if they escaped it was going to be rough going. "Who's out there?" Ray asked, speaking to Sanchez, the light everywhere and the room feeling infinitely smaller.

"The cartel," Sanchez said, his voice cracking at the edges.

"Dario?"

Sanchez told him yes, he was clutching the rifle to his chest, the collection of bullets scattered across his lap. "I wasn't sure earlier, but I'm sure of it now and for what it matters, I'm sorry."

Ray nodded, acknowledging the fear he heard in Sanchez, the insecurity in the boy's voice. He turned and spoke to

Sanchez. "Run out the back," Ray said. "Go straight on for thirty steps, then lie flat, I'll find you."

Ray kept his eyes focused on the living room, on the light coming in through the little holes, through the window, and through the empty doorway. He brought up the Ruger and braced it along the island, watching for movement. "Now," he said. "You have to go now." Ray turned and looked at Sanchez, trying to make him understand.

"Fuck," Sanchez said. "We can take them." But they were empty words. Ray knew Sanchez would go, that whatever liquid courage he'd filled himself up on had faded and that he was scared now, as he should have been.

Ray heard the wet slopping sound of the rainstorm outside. Sanchez eased the door open, and somehow, even with much of the door gone, the storm seemed louder than it had been before. The heavy drip of water falling off the eaves and collecting in streams along the ground. Sanchez paused to look back at Ray.

"Go," Ray said. He watched Sanchez for a second longer, crouched there at the kitchen door with the hunting rifle in his hand. Giving Ray one last look before he slipped through the door and the shadow of rain swallowed him up whole.

Ray focused his attention on the front of the house. He waited, counting the seconds. Ten seconds passed like ten minutes. A shadow moved across the holes, blotting the light from the room and outlining the figure of a man bent double at the waist. Ray traced the figure of the man as he moved along the porch toward the empty doorway. The figure stopped just outside, and Ray fired three shots into the living room wall, raking the gun upward along the door frame. The man fell out across the opening of the door and lay still on the porch. The guns opened up immediately.

He had known he would get one man coming through the door, but they wouldn't try it again. They knew someone was still alive. Someone with a gun, and they'd try for the back next, or come in through one of the side windows. They would spread out or stick together, but they wouldn't go back to trying the front door again till they knew whoever had fired those shots was dead.

The only thing Ray heard as he went out the back door was the whisper of bullets parting air, singing through molecules as they cut the fabric of the night. He felt the rain cold on his skin. He felt it in his hair and on his face. There was no stopping it. No adjusting. No time. He counted out the steps as he took them, feeling bullets whizzing by in the night air.

DARIO WAITED FOR THE GUNFIRE TO STOP. LALO, the big Oaxacan, was dead. One of the new men, too, possibly Hector. No idea really, and no clue where the two brothers had gotten to. Dario just sitting there in the rain, his back to Burnham's truck, feeling the water pelt down everywhere.

Under his suit he wore a bulletproof vest he'd taken from his office. In his hand a Walther MPK he'd been given, the same model he'd seen the military using in the streets around Juarez, and he kept checking the slide like he didn't believe it would ever work. Holding this type of gun was not something he was used to anymore and he kept checking the band of his pants where he kept his .45, watching the sides of the house, hoping for any kind of movement.

He'd had big hopes for his time in Coronado. Thought that by being up out of Juarez and away from all the troubles down there he'd be infinitely safer. That he could avoid the reputation he'd made for himself down there and that he'd hoped hadn't followed him north.

He bent over into the mud and crawled to the edge of the truck. His suit clumped with the wet earth. If he saw someone he would stand his ground, he would try to take them apart piece by piece, shooting the fingers from hands if that's what it came to. Breaking whoever was inside apart, bullet by bullet. He waited. Staring out at the house. His eyes just beneath the front fender looking up to where the light of their high beams flooded the rain-washed siding.

Nothing moved. The feel of the cold desert mud under his palms, slipping up through his fingers. Sand and grit, little pieces of pebble, and that deep smell of earth that always came with desert rainstorms.

He eased back around and pushed himself up on the tire, keeping his head hidden behind the body of the truck. Wet all the way through. His linen suit caked in mud. He couldn't see a thing around him. The night out there and the sound of the rain coming at him like a wave cresting in a black ocean. He didn't know where any of his men were and he was tempted to just run straight on toward the house with the Walther switched on full automatic.

RAY LAY THERE IN THE MUD NEXT TO SANCHEZ. Both watching the back door of the house. Quiet all around, broken only by the constant fall of the rain. Neither daring to say anything.

The house—caught up in the high beams—emanated an aura of light from every side like some celestial house of worship. His face so close into the earth that Ray could smell the turned dirt leavings of worms. All around him he knew the insects of the desert were trying for escape, tarantulas and scorpions flooded up from their burrows and now forced to crawl the surface like the rest of them.

He didn't have a plan, but he knew they had to get out of

there. Killing all the men just wasn't a possibility. He could see getting one of them, but the moment he fired, the sound of the gunshot would give them away, and in the open, the remaining men would get them easily.

He forced Sanchez to a low crouch, brought him up by his elbow, the two of them hunched over in the rain, caked in mud and a fine layer of desert sand, watching the house.

"Now what?" Sanchez said.

"We run."

"You could take them," Sanchez said. His voice sounding stronger than it had in the house. Rain sobering him, sinking cold into his skin, and bringing him back from whatever place he'd disappeared to.

"I don't think so," Ray said.

"Then what?"

"We need a car. If we went on foot, we wouldn't get far enough away."

"We could run for the town."

"We'd be halfway there when the light comes over the mountains. Anyone with a pair of binoculars could pick us off the plain."

Sanchez didn't say anything. He seemed to be weighing the options, only there weren't any, and he stood there with rain dripping from his nose and chin, holding the rifle in his hands.

"Take this," Ray said, giving the shotgun to Sanchez. "It'll spray enough of a space that even if you miss it will hit something." Ray took the rifle and strapped it over his shoulder. He still held the Ruger in his other hand.

From the window he'd watched the two cars drive silently up toward the house. He knew who these men were. Their faces clear, reflecting the red tinge of Sanchez's brake lights for only a moment. Burnham's pickup and the Bronco parked in front of the house, beneath where he stood looking out of the upstairs window. The Bronco was closer. If they could get around the house without being seen they'd have a chance.

Ray asked Sanchez for the keys and as soon as he had them, they went circling low and wide around the house, straight out from the back about fifty yards, then circling around to the west. The rain fell harder, the earth saturated, their skin wrinkled and sopping with water, their clothes soaked through. High beams from the cars still focused up onto the house. No sound except for the continuing rain.

They circled wide through the desert, the front of the house now visible. The man Ray had shot through the wall lay out on the porch, dead. The light from the high beams the only thing telling him the cars existed at all.

One of the men had positioned himself on the driver's side of the Bronco with his gun braced over the hood, covering the house. A veneer of light—reflected off the white clapboards— fell like a shroud over the puddles in the earth and the metal of the Bronco.

Sanchez and Ray lay flat on the ground, just outside the reflected light, watching the car. Goose bumps on their skin, the rain falling, and shivers moving through their bodies in electric waves. "It's going to be fast," Ray said. He talked with the Ruger held forward on the man in front of them, ready at any time for the man to turn.

"I don't see anyone else," Sanchez said.

"It doesn't matter," Ray said. "When I get to him you just open up with the shotgun. If we can't see them in this, they can't see us."

"I won't even know what direction to shoot."

"It doesn't matter," Ray said. "Just try and aim away from me."

"Okay," Sanchez said.

"You ready?"

"Yes."

Ray pushed himself up off the ground and ran as fast as he could through the rain, hearing only the slap of his bare feet as they hit the puddles. The man hiding behind the Bronco turned and for a moment all Ray could see was the black outline of his body, backlit by the tall face of the house. He was yelling something, his mouth open, the beginnings of a syllable on his lips when Ray shot him twice in quick succession. His body pushed back against the truck with the force of the bullets. He bounced off the front fender, then fell face-first onto the ground and lay still.

"Where is everyone?" Sanchez yelled over the noise of the rain.

"Shoot," Ray yelled, already pulling the Bronco door open.

Ray threw the rifle in ahead of him and then pulled himself inside, fumbling out the keys as he went. Twisting the key in the ignition, the motor rumbled on just as Sanchez opened up with the shotgun.

For a moment the interior of the Bronco was awash in explosive noise and light. Ray reached over and pushed the passenger door open. Sanchez rounded the hood, blasting nothing and everything all at the same time. Sanchez ducked his head and as soon as he was halfway through the open door, Ray gunned the engine and they went spinning through the mud toward the road.

"I think I got someone," Sanchez yelled, his eyes chasing whatever point in the night he thought he'd hit.

From the surrounding desert, muzzle flash opened up on them in pockets of light. Ray heard the bullets skitter across the metal, thud into the body of the truck, and go crashing through windows, the night pouring in after them. His foot already pressed hard against the gas pedal, the Bronco went scraping past one of the cars at the base of the drive, fishtailing in the mud, then finding purchase and pulling forward up the road.

DARIO LAY IN THE MUD. THE COLD SEEP OF IT up into his clothes from the ground beneath. The Walther still in his hands. The front fender speckled with buck from the shotgun. He didn't know how he was alive, how he had managed to avoid getting shot. The man holding the shotgun, their eyes meeting—the same man from the bar, the same they'd followed to the house—and then the shotgun going off, Dario half turned with his finger on the trigger. Somehow, though, Dario was alive. Lying in the mud, feeling the sore intake of air into his lungs.

Running a hand along his chest, he felt where the balls of shot had struck the metal plate beneath. With one hand he undid the Velcro straps from his shoulders and pulled the vest off. Two distinct impacts in the chest plate, one beneath the heart, the other at his navel.

Nearby he knew one of their own was dead. The strangled call Dario had heard as one of the brothers—Felíx—yelled for help just before Dario heard the double pistol shot.

Dario forced himself up on his hands. The Bronco gone now and everywhere the falling rain. Twenty feet away the open, unmoving stare of Felíx's eyes. Two deep chasms of blood printed on his forehead.

Three of Dario's men were dead and the life Dario had made for himself in this town was already changing. The cartel's place in Coronado no longer what it had been just days before.

He heard running now, the scuffle of soles across wet earth. Medina coming out of the darkness. "*¿Estás herido?*"

"No," he said, checking his shirt again for blood. "No." The Walther submachine gun in his hand, clutched so tight his fingers ached with it. The dented plate of the vest at his feet and a change coming over him that went rattling up through his bloodstream. Inside he felt something slide from one side to the other and he didn't want it to go back.

Across the yard, Dario saw Medina's eyes had turned away from him and looked toward the body in the mud. The light, off to the side away from where the headlights fell, a grainy black as gray and indistinct as newsprint.

"*Está muerto,*" Medina said.

"*¿Quién es?*" Dario asked, even though he already knew the answer.

"*Uno de los hermanos.*"

"*¿Quién?*"

"Felíx."

Dario pulled himself up and rested against the side panel of Burnham's truck. He should have been just as dead as Felíx. The puckered indent of the breastplate at his feet. The man wheeling around on him with the shotgun, the discharge of the barrel just bright enough for Dario to make out the face of the other man.

Out in the darkness, the sound of gunfire opened up again,

followed closely by the race of the Bronco engine fading away
through the night.

R AY DIDN'T DARE TURN ON THE BRONCO'S
headlights. Rocks caught in the tires and went skittering around through the undercarriage. The dull white hands
of the speedometer read fifty-six miles per hour, the night road
coming at them out of the rain in twenty-foot sections.

Something wasn't right with the engine. He could feel it,
the temperature gauge hitting the red and the smell of burning oil coming through the vents. He didn't know if they
would make the town.

Checking his rearview, he saw a blaze of headlights turn
away from the house, then follow up the road. He had about
a half mile on them. The only thing visible in the rain-swept
darkness the sight of those two pairs of headlights behind.

Using the emergency brake to avoid the sight of his brake
lights, he turned the wheel hard to the right and they
bounced off the road. With the speed now at twenty miles per
hour, he could make out the rocks and bushes before he came
to them and he headed due north across the plain toward Las
Cruces, though he knew they would never make it.

TOM WOKE TO THE SOUND OF THE RAIN WASH-ing against his bedroom window. The wind strong from the west and the window casings thumping together like two wooden boats in a storm. He turned over in bed and put his feet to the floor, wiping his hand down along his eyes. The room slow to come into focus. Behind him he heard Claire turn away in her sleep, pulling the bedding from where he sat. She lay facing the far wall with her back half exposed and the sheets bunched at her waist.

Quietly he dressed in an old T-shirt and a set of baggy cotton pants. The feel of the material falling and then straightening on his legs as he rose and walked to the window to pull back the shades. Thunder had woken him, but now there was only the night out there. Nothing but the rain moving around in the darkness. A brief flash of lightning far off over the mountains but no thunder.

What Claire was doing wasn't right, leaving him one day and then showing up again, as if she hadn't left him in the first place. Or perhaps it was his fault for letting her do this to him. He was starting not to care, that was the trouble with it. He never thought he'd become a person like that, but looking back toward the bed he couldn't say he hadn't wanted a few moments alone with Claire after all he'd seen that day.

He felt the memories heaped up inside of him, like the day

had shaken them all loose and he hadn't yet had the chance to put them back. He walked through the house listening to the rain. On the kitchen table he looked at the old police radio he'd kept from his time as sheriff, the dials worn down to the metal, and the familiar etchings now carved loose of their paint. He put the kettle on, waiting for the water to begin rattling at the metal sides of the pot.

He didn't like what he'd done to himself. All that time behind him, all the decisions he'd made, all of it adding up little by little, knowing he had not made the sum greater than the parts. The judge on that last day of the hearing had taken him aside, asking Tom if he had anything to add. Anything that might make his situation any better.

"I can't tell it any other way."

"You're going to have to, Tom."

There was nothing to say. The past was the past, there was no changing that now. Tom wasn't the same anymore, he wasn't anything like the man he used to be. Headstrong to the point of being callous. Righteous. Those things just couldn't describe him anymore. His instinct for the day-to-day now tarnished. There was a lot to recover from and he was trying, even if it meant waking up the next day to work Deacon's cattle.

What he'd done to Angela Lopez hadn't been right. There was no getting around that, not now, not ever. It was the mistake that would define his life. He knew at the time he'd wanted Lopez to stand in for everything that was going wrong with Coronado: the loss of jobs, the empty storefronts, the death of Ray's family.

He'd learned to catalog this away inside him over the years. He was still pissed off over the thing but he knew he couldn't help that now. He'd lost that power. His one attempt to make things better already spent. Now, there was only the present, the rain outside slicking the wood siding of his house, the windows rocking in their frames. Tomorrow would be different, he hoped. Talking with Kelly had made him feel something about himself that he hadn't felt in a long time, that maybe there was still some use left in his life. Some hope for the future.

Out in the living room he heard the clacking of Jeanie's nails on the hardwood. She rounded the corner and came into the kitchen, running her nose beneath his hand, looking for attention. Tom's own glassy reflection there on the kitchen window. The whistle of steam as it broke out of the kettle. He didn't want to think about any of it anymore, and he sat with his mug of tea at the kitchen table while Jeanie nuzzled his hand. The drum of the rain out there in the night, pounding away inside him like his own thoughts.

Dario Campo stood on the wooden porch holding the Walther loosely in his hand. The clip still full, still weighted down with all its potential. He looked out at the gravel drive, at the dead brother there, the slightly darker pool of blood filling with rainwater. The cars gone now—Medina and the rest—all of them chasing through the desert after the Bronco.

Three of the men who'd been sent up from Mexico were now dead. Paid killers. Lalo, the biggest of them, lay on his back inside the house, his hands raised up toward his face and a pool of blood formed in the shape of a fan on the floor beneath his head. On the porch near where Dario stood—watching Medina's headlights cut long ribbons of darkness away from the rain—Hector, also killed, shot first in the upper thigh, then finished in a line upward that ended with a single shot in the side of his temple.

Dario knelt and took the HK submachine gun from the man and swung the strap over his shoulder, still watching the darkness of the desert, watching the swing and flourish of the headlights through the rain, reminding him of an ocean he'd once seen in a movie—the wash of a lighthouse over the water.

Entering the house with the HK on his shoulder and the Walther in his hand, he took a big step over the body in the doorway. He was careful about the blood. He didn't want to touch it. He felt a strange pleasure standing there in the darkened house with the smell of the plaster still strong through the room.

In the hallway upstairs he came to a small room. In what little light came in from the window, he stooped and found a waxed canvas coat, balled up on the floor, the indentation of a head still in the material. He picked it up and shook it out. A large coat, insulated with flannel padding. He put it to his nose and inhaled the smell of the desert. In one of the pockets he found a cash receipt from the Lucky Strike Diner outside of town. The date on the receipt one day before. In the other pocket he found a prescription drug bottle. He stood examining the label, trying to read the name.

Beneath the coat he found a set of boots and socks. He tucked the boots under his arm, and the socks into one of the jacket pockets. He folded the jacket and stuffed it under his arm with the boots. Leaving only the slight rattle of the prescription bottle in his hand.

Every room in the house empty and no sign of the heroin anywhere.

Dario came out onto the porch and stood waiting. He didn't know what to do next and he watched the headlights come back toward him over the flatness of the desert. The car high beams offering up just enough light to make out the name written on the side of the prescription bottle. Rain still falling everywhere in the desert, and a slight smile beginning to spread across his face. Three dead this night and at least one more to follow.

T HE BRONCO CAME ROLLING TO A STOP THIRTY minutes after they'd left the road. All three rear windows blown out. Rain fell heavy on the roof and slipped in through the window frames, collecting on the seats. Several minutes had passed since Ray had seen anything like a light, be it house or car.

"Looks like we're walking," Ray said.

"If it's all right," Sanchez said, "I'll just stay here." He was holding the side of his gut with a hand, and, as he finished speaking, he removed the hand, trying to push himself up on the seat. The palm of his right hand a beet-red color that even in the dark Ray knew was blood.

"Jesus," Ray said. "You should have said something." Ray reached up to flick on the overhead dome light. He was watching Sanchez. The hand back over the wound. A pale sweat showing on his face.

"It wouldn't have mattered."

"We could have tried for the town," Ray said.

"And if we didn't make it?"

"We could have tried." Stunned, Ray didn't know what else to say.

Sanchez removed his hand again and just sat looking at it in wonder as if something was written on his palm that he wanted to memorize. "It's the first time I've been shot. I can't even tell how bad it is," he said. "I don't even know what it looks like." His voice was strangely level, his young face heavy as clay in the bright overhead light.

Ray opened his own door, walked around the front of the Bronco in the rain, and pulled Sanchez's door open. He knelt there with the water falling on his back, his head just below Sanchez's shoulder. He pulled away the bloodied material to look at the wound. One hole bleeding a thin watery red. Blood all down Sanchez's pants and soaked into the seat. With his hands he supported Sanchez, leaning him forward so that Ray could check his back. No exit wound, the bullet somewhere inside.

"How does it look?" Sanchez asked. He hadn't moved at all while Ray examined him, only taking his hand from the wound, his muscles held tight, trying to avoid the pain.

"I think the worst is over."

"That's good," Sanchez said.

"Yes," Ray said.

There wasn't much of an option here. Ray took Sanchez's hand and put it back over the wound. With his teeth he ripped one of the sleeves from the shirt he was wearing, sliding it down off his arm. He balled it in his hand and tried as best he could to wring the rainwater from it. Ray made a bandage from the torn piece of cloth. He pressed it to the wound and had Sanchez hold it.

"I can't really feel it," Sanchez said. "Am I holding it tight enough?"

Ray looked at Sanchez's hand again. "You're doing fine."

Sanchez had rolled his head around on the seat and his eyes looked at Ray with something like glazed recognition, there and not there.

"Listen," Ray said, "we've got to do something about this. I need to try and get into town. There isn't much else we can do here."

Sanchez nodded, told him he understood.

Ray walked around to the other side of the truck again. Nothing but night all around them and the rain blowing in from the west in silver-blue sheets. "Jesus," Ray said under his breath, low enough that Sanchez couldn't hear him.

Ray closed his door. He went around the Bronco again and knelt in the mud beside Sanchez. "I'm going to go now," he said.

"Don't," Sanchez said. "Don't leave me out here."

"There's nothing I can do for you here."

"You'll come back?"

"Yes," Ray said. "I'll get you out of here and we'll head north for Las Cruces."

"You promise to come back?"

"I shouldn't be long."

"I know," Sanchez said.

Ray reached in over Sanchez to flick the dome light off.

"Could you leave it?" Sanchez asked. His eyes shifted upward toward the light, then back to Ray.

"If they see—"

"I'll be okay."

Ray didn't know what to say. Sanchez just sat there in the seat, his clothes soaking wet, the only skin visible his pale, sweat-stained face. Ray reached in and brought out the shotgun. There were no shells left. He looked to the backseat, where the hunting rifle was, but didn't move to get it. Finally, after just sitting there on his haunches, he pulled the Ruger from his waistband and laid it on Sanchez's lap. "You can use this if you need to. You're going to be fine," he said. "I'll be back as soon as I can."

Sanchez nodded.

Ray stood and Sanchez followed him with his eyes. Ray closed the door.

He walked out into the darkness, the rain becoming only a feeling on his skin, unseen and constant as the wind or the air. The ruts of the tires leading away toward the road, some five or six miles away, now filled with water and appearing in places like small overflowing canals.

Behind him he saw the pale dome light of the truck. He

felt the cold seeping through to his bones. Water dripped from his face, from his hands, from everywhere. Between bursts of wind he thought he heard a song playing. He didn't remember turning the radio on and he looked back toward the Bronco in a sort of stupid wonderment.

He turned to follow the little canals of water leading back to civilization. He began to run. He ran until his lungs burned and his heart ached. He ran till he couldn't feel his legs. Till his bare feet pulsed beneath him with every beat of his heart. The silver water falling, shaping the carved outlines of the Bronco's tires in the mud.

When he couldn't run anymore, he bent over panting with his hands held down on his thighs, gasping for air. He felt the blood in his head as he stood. The swell of it under the skin. Not a light anywhere in the desert. No road, no house, not one single thing.

Billy would be thirteen years old that spring. It was an odd thing to think about, standing there, his breath pulled down out of the air in rain-filled gasps. Broken capillaries somewhere inside his lungs. Mucus and the metallic taste of blood all down his throat. For all the trouble Sanchez had given him these last few days, he didn't deserve this. He didn't deserve to go like this, and Ray glanced back the way he'd come, trying to find his bearings.

Ray didn't know where he was. He rested his hands on his hips and looked out on the desert through the rain. He turned and looked to the north, tried to see through the night all the way to the gray-blue Hermanos Range he'd known as a youth. Nothing to see out there in the darkness except the darkness itself.

He turned on his heels. The last time he'd felt such desperation had been when Tom's deputy had come to his door over ten years before. That moment forever there in his memories, like it was now, ever present. All that came afterward simply a surge of emotion, carrying him forward toward those who were responsible.

Slowly, he began jogging back through the rain toward the Bronco. It took him ten minutes before he saw the dome light again. In another five minutes he heard the radio. Something up out of Mexico, the sound of an acoustic guitar followed by a woman's voice singing in Spanish.

Though he'd been willing life into the boy all through the night desert—following the trail they'd left back to the road, feeling the air enter his lungs, then pump back—he wasn't surprised to find Sanchez's eyes staring coldly at him from the interior of the Bronco. His hand dropped away from the wound and the torn piece of cloth held loosely between thumb and forefinger.

Ray reached in through the open door and closed Sanchez's eyes. The man half Ray's age, a boy any way Ray looked at him. Boasting about all the things he'd done in life, trying to live beyond his years. All that over now, all Sanchez would ever be now at its end, and Ray just there in the rain outside the Bronco looking in on him like a man looking in on something long since passed into the annals of time. Ray took back the Ruger from where it sat on the boy's lap. The rain falling. The radio playing. The boy long since dead.

DAY 3

DARIO HAD WAITED LONG ENOUGH. THE FIVE of them sitting in two cars, watching Gus Lamar's ranch a hundred meters away across the desert floor, lamplight in two of the windows and the staff houses off a ways, dark in every window. Five hours had passed while they'd waited, watching the house, waiting to see who would come. In all that time nothing had moved, the rain still falling but nothing to say Ray Lamar would come back to the ranch, or to say if this was even home to him anymore. Only the name on the prescription bottle and the image of the face Dario had seen to guide him here.

To the east the first light was beginning to show above the mountains, gray as it filtered through the clouds. And as they waited, they could see the clouds beginning to thin and the rain letting up until it became only drizzle on the car windshield.

He looked across at Medina, told him to pull the car forward. When they drew closer, he knew he would tell Ernesto to check the staff houses, while the rest of them went in after the old man who lived inside.

RAY WOKE IN THE TRUCK WITH SANCHEZ DEAD beside him. An early blue-toned light spreading across the sky to the east where the clouds had partially cleared in the night and a thin drizzle was now falling. Outside, the desert went on without mercy, gray and flat as a griddle pan, running along all the way to the mountains where the slope rose in waves of pinyon and juniper to the snow-topped peaks.

He'd promised Sanchez a trip north, a way out. But it wasn't going to happen, and Ray sat there trying to accept the life that he'd chosen. A life that had brought him here, connected him to Memo, and stolen from him anything he'd ever hoped for.

He didn't know what the day would hold. A slight glimmer of hope that he was still alive, and that there was light enough to walk by. The chance of a new beginning somewhere far out there, meager as it now seemed.

He felt his age. Every muscle aching as the new light spread over the mountains and the air shifted slightly, signaling the day to come. He knew that in an hour the sun would be up over those mountains, beating down on what remained of the window glass, and the metal body of the truck.

Ray sat for a long time in the driver's seat of the Bronco watching the mountains take shape out of the wet, grainy light. The radio long since dead. With a heavy hand, he eased the door open to feel the cold move in on him off the open land, parting fibers in the shirt he wore, bringing new life as it bristled against his skin.

With his bare feet on the ground, and the sun not yet up over the mountains, he felt cold and alone. The brittle pulse of the wind ran along the land in front of him, and the prick of the drizzle falling everywhere. All along the plain, the dotted shapes of creosote and chuparosa showing in a patch-work of dirt and gray-green vegetation. The receding track of their tire treads, once seen behind them, almost completely taken away by the rain.

All through the night the water had thumped down out of the sky, pouring in through the shattered windows and slick-ing the seats. The Bronco just sitting there in the open, and Ray knowing that whoever wanted to find him—wanted to find Sanchez—would find them soon enough.

Leaning into the back, he took up the hunting rifle, a thou-sand-meter scope on the thing and bullets almost two inches in length. Getting up out of the truck, he laid the rifle over the roof, then walked around to the passenger side. He went through Sanchez's pockets, taking his keys, taking his wallet, taking everything he found.

Ray bent again and took one shoe, then the other from Sanchez's feet, pulling them from beneath the boy's heels and then sliding them up over his toes. Now, with both shoes clutched in his hand, he leaned against the Bronco and one by one, measured the soles of the shoes with his own feet, estimating the difference. Both shoes too small. He took from his back pocket the knife he'd used on Burnham's Chevy seat and flipped it open. Holding each shoe in turn, he cut lines down through the heel material and then slipped them both on. They were a poor fit, but they'd do.

He was cold, hungry, and thirsty. One sleeve missing from his shirt and only his undershirt left to cover his right shoulder and bicep. Trying to move around as much as he could to create warmth, he gathered what he could from the Bronco and set out, taking his direction from the sun and the mountains. The rifle he carried in his hands, the Ruger pressed beneath his waistband to his stomach. He thought how, if he could, he'd come back for Sanchez, but looking out on the desert and the distance to walk, he doubted he ever would.

The drizzle now clearing a little as the sun came on, evaporating the clouds above. Sanchez behind him, sitting there with his pockets turned out and his arms folded across his chest while Ray walked due north, aiming to get as far as he could from the Bronco and all the history that lay within.

THE CALL CAME EARLY IN THE MORNING. TOM left Claire still asleep in his bed and drove out to the old Sullivan house. There had been nothing over the radio, just the familiar buzz of the static as he sat drinking his morning coffee.

He parked his truck off the road behind the county cruisers, cracked the window for Jeanie, and walked the rest of the way up the gravel drive to the house. The first body he saw lay uncovered just at the doorway to the house. Tom paused to look at the old pickup truck sitting on four slashed tires a few feet from the front porch. It was a truck he knew from his time as sheriff. A truck that had belonged to Jake Burnham, though he didn't know if it did anymore.

He stood there looking at the truck for a long while, thinking. Burnham had been somehow connected to Angela Lopez, and now here was his truck, the familiar dents along the left front panel, the dinged-up paint. Now at the edge of the fender was a silver pockmarking of fresh buckshot where metal had bitten into metal, shaving the paint away.

Whatever this was, whatever he'd stumbled across two days before on the highway and now out here at the old Sullivan house, it was beginning to look much too familiar to Tom. Where was Burnham in all this? Tom looked to where the dead body lay on the porch. Was it Burnham? With the face turned out of sight he couldn't tell.

Last night he'd gone to dinner at Kelly's and there'd been nothing left for them to follow, the two of them sitting out there on the swing set thinking it through. Already, in a way, discussing the death of the boy in the hospital like something in the past without an answer. Now they had Burnham's truck sitting on four slashed tires.

Tom stepped over the imprint of a tire tread and stood watching the scene. The blurred outlines of footfalls and tire tracks everywhere in the sand, not a single one of them clear enough to make a reliable cast from. About thirty feet out from the house, Tom watched where the young deputy knelt over the body of a man on the ground. Pierce took a photo, advanced the film, then stood and met Tom's eye.

"Got the call from Sheriff Kelly this morning," Tom offered.

"I saw you at the hospital yesterday," Pierce said, stepping back from the body to shake Tom's hand. "Edna said you might be around."

Tom knelt over the body. Mexican. Two bullet holes to the head. "Someone is a very good shot."

"There's another inside with a hole right between the eyes," Pierce said, something breathy and full of wonder in the way he said it. Like a young boy running to tell his parents something fabulous he'd seen.

"I've never seen anything like that," Tom said.

"Me neither," Pierce said.

"You got two bodies then?"

"Three. There's one up on the porch, looks like he was trying to get in through the door but he never made it."

"Any of them a skinny, old white man with a big, flat-brimmed Stetson?"

"Huh?"

"Just testing a theory," Tom said. He looked back at the four slashed tires on Burnham's pickup.

Tom said a quick good-bye to Pierce when he saw Kelly move out of the house, meeting her as she came off the porch. "What do you make of it?" Tom asked.

"It's hard to make anything of it," Kelly said. "I'm dead tired over this whole thing. I spent the night hanging out in the office, watching a snoring Andy Strope through the bars. My mind certainly wasn't ready for a morning like this."

"These morning calls are getting to be a regular thing between us, aren't they?"

"I hope not," Kelly said. "Have you ever seen anything like this? I sure haven't."

Both of them had turned and were looking at the man laid out on the porch. Nearby, Tom saw the top of the other man's head inside the doorway. There didn't seem to be any door at all on the frame.

"Three bodies," Kelly said. "Over a hundred holes in this house, and not one gun."

They walked up onto the porch and Tom knelt and examined the dead man, Mexican like the other. "What type of ballistics did you get back on Gil Suarez?"

"Hunting rounds, big ones, .308s."

"You find any .308s yet?"

"No. Not a single one," Kelly said. "As far as I can tell each of these men was shot with a nine-millimeter."

"A .308 would certainly have done more damage," Tom said. He looked from the body to the wood around the door. The wood siding looking like a billion termites might be living inside the house. "Shot this one right through the wall."

"I saw that," Kelly said.

"You see Burnham's truck out there?"

"I didn't like the look of it either."

"So where's Burnham? You know he works for Dario, and I doubt he was the one who shot all these men." Tom took a pen from his pocket and opened the dead man's jacket up so he could better see where the bullet had gone in. "Eli wants you to keep this thing quiet, but I just don't see how you can anymore," Tom said.

"I don't . . ." Kelly's voice drifted off, she was looking at Burnham's truck now and just shaking her head.

"These men aren't local," Tom said. "I'll tell you that now. What brought them here is what you're going to need to find out, and I think you know who you need to talk to." Tom let the man's jacket drop back down onto his chest. The shirt underneath still wet with blood and the pen now slightly red at its tip.

Kelly moved her eyes back to Tom. The slight click and advance of Pierce's camera buzzing in the background. "You mean Dario?"

"I don't know who else. Burnham makes the connection, it's not that hard to follow after that."

"We don't have anything solid on Dario," Kelly said. "Honestly, Tom, it's a horrible thing to say but after what happened with Angela Lopez it's a sensitive matter."

"The only person being sensitive about that is Eli."

"He's scared, Tom. Looking at these men here, shot up the way they are, I don't blame him."

"Whatever this is," Tom said, "it's nothing you can let slide anymore."

"I know that—I know that better than most, but I can't just go asking these types of questions without proper cause."

Tom smiled a bit. "I see a whole lot of cause around here, Edna. Too much. In fact, you might start thinking about calling in some help on this. DEA, Border Patrol, even the state cops." Tom looked down at the body again and then looked back at Kelly. "Strange how when a man moves to a small town and tries to keep his business quiet, it just becomes everyone else's business in the process. You know what Dario's been doing these last couple years, the whole town knows, but

I messed that up for us all and now everyone wants to look the other way."

Tom stood. He walked over for a better view of the man inside the doorway. A single shot right between the eyes. A shot Tom knew Burnham couldn't make even if he was standing five feet away.

He turned and looked back at Kelly. "You want to go through this with me?"

DARIO STOOD IN GUS LAMAR'S LIVING ROOM, looking over the pictures the old man had up on the mantel. Behind him, Medina waited in the living room doorway, a submachine gun hanging off his shoulder, while César and Carlos stood to either side of the big lounge chair, their hands held down on Gus's shoulders, fixing him in place.

"Help you?" Gus asked. He'd been asking the same thing for the better part of a half hour, wearing his sleeping clothes, his white hair mussed, and a coarse growth of silver all over his cheeks and neck. Dario hadn't spoken a word to him yet. He stood examining one of the pictures over the mantel, the face he saw there, angular like the old man's but darker.

"You're the father?" Dario said. "Ray's father." Drawing the name up out of memory, the name he'd read on the side of the prescription bottle.

Gus glanced from Dario to the set of pictures as Dario reached a hand out to take the picture down.

He was careful with the picture frame, using his sleeve, not wanting to leave any fingerprints. "I'm a friend of your son's," Dario said.

"I know who you are," Gus said. "You're not a friend of Ray's."

"No? Maybe not, but I know some about you, too, and I'm guessing you could tell me a little about Ray if you needed to."

Gus bucked a little in the seat and the men forced him down again. "You want to tell me why you thought you could just let yourself in?" Gus said, looking around the room at Dario, before moving his eyes across to Medina. "I haven't talked to my son in ten years, and anything you know about him at this point is more than I've heard in a long time."

Dario put the picture back on the mantel. He was careful about how he placed it, lining it up just as it had been. When he drew his hand back, he brought with him the heavy weight of the .45 he'd left sitting up over the mantel. The old man's eyes immediately fixed on the gun in Dario's hand. A slight smile flattened on Dario's lips as he saw the old man tighten up, and the reality sink into him. "If I tell these men to take their hands off you, you promise not to do anything stupid?" Dario said.

"I'm not making any promises," Gus said.

Dario's smile only grew bigger. He nodded to the two men holding Gus in place and they stepped back, taking their hands from his shoulders. "Let's start again," Dario said. He took a seat in the chair across from the old man, crossing one leg over the other and laying the gun across his thigh, his finger resting over the trigger guard. "You know me and I know you, and all I'm really after here—the reason we've come and we're all visiting you in your house this morning— is the answer to one simple question."

"I can't help you," Gus said.

Dario looked up at the pictures on the mantel again. He pulled back his sleeve and checked his watch. "You know your son is very good at what he does. He has a real talent. The only problem is that he's very stubborn."

"Stubborn?"

"He doesn't see that it's all over for him in this town," Dario said. Behind, the front door opened and Ernesto walked in. He paused for a moment, looking to where Gus sat in the chair, before Dario waved him over. He'd found four of the staff houses empty, but the fifth looked to have someone living in it. Dario turned back to Gus. "Someone is missing?"

Gus didn't say anything.

Dario raised the .45 off his leg and pointed it at Gus.

"Should we see who comes running?" He gave the trigger a pull and the gun bucked in his hand, releasing a sound loud as thunder and the cloud of gunpowder to go with it. In the wall over Gus's head, a hole the size of Dario's thumb could be seen in the plaster.

"Jesus!" Gus said. "I'm telling you I haven't seen Ray in ten years, I don't know where he is now. If he's in town, I don't know it, and he didn't stop by to say hi."

Dario could feel his patience running thin. He was tired and he'd given this man every chance he was going to get, but now it was all coming to a head. "Who is living out back?" Dario asked again.

"My brother-in-law."

"Who?" Dario snapped.

"Luis, he's a regular at your bar. He's probably sleeping it off somewhere, I don't know, I don't keep track of him."

Dario turned to look at Medina. "*Yo lo conozco*," Medina said, telling Dario he thought the man worked up the road, two miles away at the Deacon place, raising cattle. Dario turned back to look at Gus. "I'm trying to help you out here," Dario said. "I'm trying to help you but it doesn't seem like you want to be helped." Dario signaled for Ernesto, and when Ernesto came close, Dario told him to go outside and watch the front.

When Ernesto had gone, Dario said to Gus, "The man who just left lost his brother last night. I asked him to leave so that we could talk in confidence. Because of Ray his brother is dead. He's likely to kill you when he comes back in here, and I'm likely to let him if you don't have something for me pretty soon. Because the way this is going to work is not going to be pleasant, and it's not going to be short, and no one in this room will help you." Dario looked the old man over, trying to decide how he had taken it. The old man's face was thin and drawn. The cheekbones showing just below the eyes and a look of hate crossing his face for a moment, then going away again as Dario called for Ernesto to come back in.

Dario nodded toward Carlos and César, and the two men came forward again and put their hands down on Gus's shoulders. They were holding him still when Ernesto came forward and Dario told him to begin.

RAY WALKED NORTH THROUGH THE DESERT. HE carried with him his collection of guns. The clothes he'd worn the night before were caked in mud, the shoes he'd taken off Sanchez dusted in a chalky sediment.

He walked until his feet felt stiff as stone beneath him. The sun above risen into the sky. High billowy clouds floated for hours in the same position, while the first tendrils of heat began to play across the desert underbrush. He found large banks of land cut away from the desert by the rains, the dead-fall and underbrush of the mountains, miles away, brought down into the lowlands and strung out along the banks. He knew he and Sanchez would never have made it in the Bronco, that the land was too treacherous and pocked to go on by anything but foot or horse.

Miles in he came within sight of a road, but found no comfort in that gray slip of pavement along the valley floor. He watched the silver reflection of the sun work over the aluminum car bodies as they moved before him.

He turned away and followed the mountains to the east, not wanting to rejoin the world just yet, not ready to face the questions he knew would soon follow.

He was pretty sure the road he had seen would take him out of there. It would take him between the mountains to the north and those to the east. He walked on, feeling his shirt begin to stick to his back with sweat. He thought many times of losing the rifle, but he wouldn't give it up. Holding it like some talisman of the past.

There was little he could do but head north. He would have to call Memo at some point, to tell him about Sanchez and what had happened out at the old Sullivan house. There was no good way to tell it and he went on thinking his situation through and wondering how he was going to get to Las Cruces with no shelter, water, or food.

Several times he came to wire cattle fences. He passed

through private land and into public BLM land, then back again. He found depressions filled with rainwater. Much of the brown liquid already evaporated and the remaining water clouded in manure and buzzing with flies. He was dehydrated. Mad with thirst, but still he wouldn't drink from them.

He passed through land where cows stood and stared at him, working their sullen jaws before looking away again. He saw a coyote from a mile out and he raised the rifle and sighted it through the scope but didn't pull the trigger. The long bouncing step of the coyote, sticking close to the base of the mountains, then disappearing behind a hill. In the heat he surprised a bedded-down herd of antelope that went hopping over fences and soon were gone.

In the distance he saw the rusted scaffolding of forgotten wells standing up against the background of the Hermanos Range. The ocher-black skeletons he still recalled the names of. The Dean Garner, the Jack Freal, and the Oleg Stanovich now crested on the horizon. Landowners who had long since passed and for whom only a grave or well, rusted with time, existed to preserve their memory.

His own history now thrown in much the same as these men. His father's wells dry and all that it had meant for him and Marianne. And all that would result because of it. Ray out of work and their mortgage adding up, many months past due. Everyone around them scrambling for the jobs that were left. Marianne bouncing Billy on her hip, telling Ray every day that they would make it, that there would be more work. But he could see that there wouldn't and he had known already that he was as done with the oil business as it was with him.

A wish in his heart that he could go back in time and do it all again, but do it differently, starting again from the day they came out of the judge's quarters and stood on the court-house steps, newly married. The honeymoon they would take on the Sea of Cortez, eating fish tacos and walking the streets of the small towns still ahead of them.

Tired and wasted with the years that had come and gone, he crossed the road thirty minutes later, his clothes still caked with all they had seen and done the night before. Not one car in either direction. Columns of light shining down from above, where the sun had found cover behind a thin grouping of clouds.

He came to the ranch sooner than he'd expected and he knelt in the dirt at the edge of the property, catching his breath.

For thirty minutes he lay there looking the place over, fighting back thirst and hunger. As he watched, the wind came, carrying with it a low cloud of dust that ran along the ground toward the house, a small iron wind chime singing a solitary tune.

He rose and went cautiously on. It had been a long time

since he'd been here. It was a risk—the life he'd once lived here unrecognizable from the life he lived now.

Knowing he needed shelter, his clothes torn and stained with blood. He needed a place to hide away for just a day or so. There was little else he could do. He stumbled on, his feet scraping over rock and brush, his tired hands losing their grip on the rifle. He came to the stairs and pulled himself up along the railing.

Ray rapped twice on the wood frame of the screen door, waited, then rapped again. He went to the window and looked in, cupping his hands to the glass. He was just about to go around to the back when he heard the door latch give. When the door fell back on its hinges, Ray already had his hand around the screen door, pulling it open. The woman inside offered only the slightest of gasps as he put out his foot to catch the door before she could close it. "Hello, Claire," Ray said, looking past her now into the living room. "Is Tom around?"

"THERE'S ALL KINDS OF CASINGS OUT THERE," Kelly said to Eli. They sat in his office, one floor up from her own in the courthouse. "There's tire tracks to at least three different cars."

He stared at her for a moment then broke away, dropping his gaze to the desk.

"What's strange," Kelly continued, "is that there's virtually nothing inside the house. No casings, I mean. You hear me, Mayor?"

Eli gave her a solemn nod, then looked away again, moved his eyes to the window of his office. He'd been quiet for several minutes now. As if Kelly wasn't even there and wasn't telling him what was going on just outside his own town.

Kelly knew Eli didn't want to have anything to do with this. If it were up to him he'd probably just leave those bodies out there in the sun till their own gases bloated them big as beach balls. Elections were coming up. There were no jobs, no work—people leaving the town every week. And now there was this. There was a lot at stake. Kelly knew what he was thinking just by looking at the man. How he avoided her eyes, listening to what she had to say, but listening like he could just let it all roll past him without doing a thing about it or making any kind of choice.

"Whoever they were after was a good shot. A real professional—no mistakes." Kelly paused. "I think it's time we called in some help, Mayor."

Eli stirred in his seat, his eyes on her now, sizing her up. "That's all you have to go on?"

"It was a war zone. We won't really know till the ballistics report comes back from Las Cruces."

"How many gunmen are you talking about here?" His eyes fixed on her now, steady and waiting for her reply.

"I can't say for sure. We're thinking they meant to surprise someone out there. We're guessing it was this assassin from the hospital yesterday."

"Do we know yet who these men are?"

"None of them are in the system," Kelly said. "We're checking with the Mexican authorities now."

"And the truck you found?"

"The bench was slit open—down the middle—and the stuffing pulled out."

"You didn't find anything?"

"No."

"Who's it registered to?"

"Registered to a Jake Burnham."

"You know him?"

"He's one of the old boys we have here in town. No answer at his place when we went by, nothing really, just this truck."

"Fingerprints?"

"Still waiting."

"Can we keep this quiet?"

"I think we're past that, Mayor."

He was back to avoiding her now, his eyes turned away. A long pause and then he got up and walked to the window, where, she knew, down below in the street there were news vans waiting to talk with him. "I'm asking you now for a personal favor, Edna. Don't do this to me."

Out the window there was a high blue sky. The clouds from the night gone away and passed on into Texas.

Kelly watched him, and when he didn't turn back, kept looking out the window, she said, "Tom is saying there's too much missing. He thinks we'll find some bullet-riddled cars if we start looking."

Eli turned only slightly at the mention of the old sheriff's name. Kelly couldn't tell how he'd taken it.

"I told you I didn't want him involved with this."

"I had to."

"Is that why you've come in here? Is that why you're telling me this?" Eli turned away from the window and came back to the desk. He sat heavily in the chair, looking at her.

"I came here because it's my job to tell you."

"Tom Herrera isn't the law anymore. You get that? You understand what I'm saying to you?"

Kelly was considering it. She'd been thinking about Tom for a while now and she knew if Eli had had his way ten years ago, Tom would be locked up right now. Only he wasn't, and Kelly had had a lot to do with that. Maybe too much, but it was something she'd taken on her shoulders a long time ago. Most of all, she knew Eli wasn't going to help her now, and she needed help.

"You find any drugs?" Eli asked.

"No."

"Money?"

"No."

"There's no reason for anyone else to get involved in this thing then, is there?"

Kelly waited for him to say more and when he didn't, she said, "This could just be the start of a real problem."

"You don't think it's finished then?"

"I think it's time we called someone. We can't keep this to ourselves. Four bodies in two days is a lot to account for."

"We can handle it."

"No," Kelly said. "We can't."

Eli looked as if he wanted to say something, but then didn't.

"We need to get a plane or a helicopter, and we need to get it in here soon," Kelly said. "There's three other cars out there somewhere and a whole lot of desert to cover."

"Who are you going to call?"

"DEA or Border Patrol, whoever can get something in the air."

"They're going to be all over this," Eli said, his voice giving it all away.

"It can't be helped," Kelly said. "None of us can, not anymore."

OUTSIDE, THE SUN FELT WARM AND THICK ON Dario's skin as he stepped down off the porch to stand in the light. He carried with him a dish towel and as he stood, surveying the surroundings, he toweled his hands down and watched as the blood came off onto the material.

Up the valley he could make out the aged oaks, barren of leaves, the branches pointing upward into the air like skeletal hands. In the end there was nothing he could have done for Gus. And he didn't really think the man had feared death until it had been upon him, those last painful breaths of air before his lungs stopped moving and the hiss of wind went out of his lips.

Now, Dario would wait. He would hold his ground, go back to the bar and wait for what he knew would eventually come. The anxiety he looked forward to, growing in his heart with each hour, wondering when Gus would be found. And then what would become of the anger that would follow.

Behind him the men were coming out of the house just as he had a minute before. The sun strong on their faces and their eyes sliding, almost reptilian, as they came off the porch, looking from side to side down the valley.

When they'd gone past him and moved on to the cars, Dario took from his pocket the small prescription bottle and placed it on the last step of the porch. Raymond Lamar's name faced out toward whoever might find it first.

With the day's work ahead of him he turned and met Medina by their car. Dario knew he would be moving on soon enough, but for now he would wait. He would finish what needed doing—he would try to make the most of it—before he was shipped off to the next town, where life would go on for him the same as it always had.

W ITHIN FIVE MINUTES OF LEAVING ELI'S office, Kelly was on the phone with the Border Patrol. Through her open office door she saw Pierce listening to her as she explained the situation. When she was done she depressed the switch hook and waited for the tone.

Not a damn thing to do but wait. She called over to Tom's place, but got no answer. In the morning, looking over the house, they'd paced out the gunfight, Tom asking about any .308s she might have found, and Kelly had nothing to tell him.

She put her gun belt on and then her hat. "Fuck it," she said. Moving around the desk toward the office door.

"Fuck what?" Pierce said.

"It." Kelly passed Pierce where he sat. She didn't know quite what she was going to do yet, but she was done depending on Eli, on Tom, on everybody who might know something and said nothing. "Radio me if anything happens," she told Pierce.

Outside, the rainstorm had gone by hours before in the night, and the sky hung motionless above, clear and blue. Weather reports saying it was only the first band of rain expected for the region. All of it coming in from the West Coast. California soaked with it. Storm drains overflowing and all of it running right back down into the Pacific.

She walked to her cruiser, watching the glint of the sun on the metal and the dust all over the body. Nothing seemed clear to her in the way it had once been. The town seeming to tip away from Kelly as the sun rolled away above in the sky. Last night's rain coming like a flood, leaving disaster in its wake—all of it crowded in upon her and the thought in her head that it would be nice if that was all she had to deal with.

TOM SCOOPED THE LAST OF THE EGGS OFF HIS plate, paid the bill, and then walked outside to where his truck sat in the parking lot of the Lucky Strike Diner. He'd left the Sullivan house feeling wound up, unsure of what to do next. He knew his father and Deacon would be expecting him by now, waiting on him to come up the long road and start the day's work. But he wasn't ready just yet, with the frozen images of those men laid out in front of the Sullivan house. All the blood washed away in the rain from that body thirty feet from the porch, like the man had just been dropped from the sky.

He glanced at his watch, a quarter past eleven. Three hours late for work already. With his finger he depressed the hook on the pay phone, listened for the tone, and then dialed the number. When he got Deacon's wife on the phone, she said Deacon was outside with the cattle, and Tom told her he'd overslept, and would be by as soon as he could.

Claire's Volkswagen was still in front of his house when he pulled up. The little Beetle just sitting there like it had the day before. He needed to grab his gear for the day and get going. No time for this, he thought, as he opened his own truck door, waiting as Jeanie found a foothold. No clouds left in the sky and a painting of mud on the body of the Volkswagen behind the wheels. The sound of the pigs in their pen, heard through the wire fence, and the smell of their manure in the midday air.

He closed his truck door and went up the porch stairs. By the time he had the front door open, he knew something wasn't right. Jeanie making a low grumbling sound in the back of her throat as Tom let the door swing open on its own weight. Claire there on the far cushion of his couch and his cousin, Ray, sitting in the old lounge chair.

On the coffee table, peeking from beneath the magazine in

front of Ray, the long barrel of a hunting rifle, and close by what looked to be a Ruger handgun. Claire gave Tom a desperate look but didn't say anything. Tom's attention not completely on her, but on what Ray was going to do and why he was here in Tom's house after all these years. Though Tom could guess.

"That rifle take a .308 cartridge, Ray?"

Ray leaned forward and pushed the magazine away so that the wooden stock of the gun could be seen. "I believe it does," he said. "Go on and close that door, Tom. Leave the dog outside for a bit, would you?"

Tom pushed Jeanie out and closed the door, he could still hear the dog making that low growling sound outside, followed close by a series of barks. Turning to face Ray again, he said, "You're not in the best shape, Ray. You're looking like maybe you had a hell of a night and maybe not that good a morning."

The clothes Ray wore were dried a reddish-brown tint from the desert. One sleeve missing from his shirt, and a set of ill-fitting shoes pushed up on his feet. "You all right, Claire?" Tom asked, turning now to face Claire where she was watching him from her side of the couch. Tom with no idea how long the two of them had been here like this, but willing to guess it had been a while and that the mayor and the rest of the staff would be wondering where Claire was at this point, just as Deacon was wondering about him.

"I'm fine," Claire said. "Your phone's been ringing though. There's a good number of messages from Deacon."

"Take a seat, Tom," Ray said, pulling himself up in his chair and gesturing to a spot next to Claire. "There's been some changes around here, I see. I never expected you to end up working for Deacon."

Tom sat, looking to Ray. The guns on the table between them, just as close to Ray as they were to Tom. The only difference, the barrel of that hunting rifle lay faced toward Tom. "You know you've always been welcome here, Ray, but not like this."

Ray looked to the coffee table and then moved a hand out and set the guns out of sight on the floor. The feel of the couch shifting as Claire tensed at his movements. When Ray looked back up at Tom, he said, "I'm in trouble."

"I know," Tom said, watching his cousin now, trying to understand what he would do next. "There's people that are looking for you and not just the law. The DEA is going to get the call at some point today, if they haven't already. You made a pretty good mess out of things."

"I shouldn't even be here," Ray said. "I came back because I wanted to start again. I thought I'd give it a chance. But it didn't work out that way for me and I should have been gone from here two days ago. All of it's fucked now, you understand?" Ray pushed a hand up his face, scrubbing hard at his cheek with his palm.

"I don't understand," Tom said. "I told you you're welcome here and I mean it but you need to help me with this if I'm going to help you." He looked from his cousin to Claire. "You mind if Claire just calls in to her office, just lets them know she's sick or something? With all that's been going on around here there'll be people looking for her soon enough, if they aren't already."

Ray took his face back from his palm and ran his eyes across to the phone where it sat on a side table by the door. Ray nodded toward the phone and Claire hesitated, then rose, watching Ray the whole time.

When Claire began speaking into the phone, Tom said, "Burnham's dead, isn't he?"

Ray nodded. He was watching Claire where she stood at the phone.

"All of this over some drugs?" Tom said.

"A lot of drugs," Ray said, turning back to look at Tom. "Though I'm starting to think it's about more than that."

"The cartel?"

"I don't know," Ray said. "I'd have thought maybe so, but I'm just working here, I'm not the one in charge. You should know that about me."

"You've been gone a long time, Ray."

"Whatever's been done," Ray said, "the actions I've taken—I didn't mean any of it. I was just doing my job. You should know that, shouldn't you?"

Tom sat looking out on the sunlight that drifted in through the living room windows and lay flat along the floor in a yellow rectangle. "I'm not the sheriff anymore, Ray. I don't have that sense of duty. There's no right way anymore." Across the room he saw where Claire was standing watching them both, her hand held down on the phone as it sat in its cradle. "I don't need to do what's expected of me," Tom said.

Ray worked his jaw, the muscles showing on the side of his face. He wouldn't raise his eyes from where he'd dropped them. "I'm sorry about all of this," Ray said. "About you losing your job and about this now."

Tom glanced to Claire again, he didn't know why, but he needed her approval, he needed to know if what he was about to say would matter to her and in what way. "I'm telling you I can help you if you care to be helped," Tom said to Ray. "There's people here who want to help you."

Ray still wouldn't look up. Claire shifted a little where she stood, looking unsure of whether she should return to the couch. There's no right way, Tom thought again. There was no clear path, not anymore. The road he'd followed had taken him here and he'd thought for the longest time that it had been the right road, but now he thought maybe it hadn't been and there were greater things at play in this world than doing what everyone expected of you. "I can help you," he said to Ray again. "I want to help you."

THE BORDER PATROL PLANE HAD PASSED KELLY fifteen minutes before, the drone of the engine working over the landscape long after the body of the plane was lost from sight. She didn't know what they would find, or if they would find anything. She sat with her feet pulled up on the bumper watching the plain of the desert fall away before her toward Mexico, only ten miles away to the south.

She didn't have much hope in any of it anymore, the law, this town, the mayor, or even herself. All that she'd learned over the years seeming to have abandoned her. A feeling inside her of pure loneliness, and a certainty that whoever had shot up the Sullivan house last night, leaving those men dead in the dirt, was gone now. The Border Patrol plane was simply wasting its time as it came back north, wasting her time, too.

She couldn't help but think that if she'd just been a little faster to bring her concerns to Eli, to stand up for herself, maybe she wouldn't be sitting here on the bumper of her cruiser listening to the useless drone of the plane. Maybe she never should have taken the job, maybe it had all ended for her the moment it had ended for Tom. The last few days had made her feel hopelessly beyond herself, cut loose and helpless to stop anything in this town.

From inside the cruiser the radio crackled on and she

jumped at the sound, her nerves quickening. She was off the hood and inside the car by the time Pierce began relaying the information about the Bronco the pilots had found just north of town.

"What did they see?" Kelly asked. She had the radio pulled out on its cord and held close to her lips as she watched the sky to the north, trying to get a position on the plane.

"They said there's something in the passenger seat," Pierce answered, the static shift of the radio bouncing up out of the speaker, and in the background the relay of the pilot's voice through the intercom at the office.

Already she had the door pulled closed behind her and she was turning the key in the ignition. The town just up the road and then the desert highway leading north. Somewhere up there the plane was circling and she felt ready for whatever it might bring.

A LL THE MEN WHO REMAINED — ERNESTO, Carlos, César, and Medina — stood out at the bar, drinking and talking. Dario in his office with the door closed. The phone held to the side of his face.

"*Félix está muerto*," Dario said.

"*Lalo está muerto*," he went on.

"Hector está muerto."

There was a bitterness in his mouth as he said their names. All the men he'd known, doing this work, carrying on like this through life like death would never find them. But it would, and Dario knew his time would come, when he'd have his chance to test himself against the inevitable. Trying as best he could to draw blood.

It wouldn't be long now and he listened to the men out there at the bar, all of them knowing it was only a matter of time. Gus Lamar's body up there, sitting in his own house, waiting for whoever might find him first.

On the other side of the line he heard the voice, scrappy with distance, bouncing up out of the receiver as if pulled up through the desert itself. "No," Dario answered as he thought about the night before and the skill of the gunmen and what might happen if they came through that door after Dario and the men inside. He needed more time. He needed more of everything. The only real fun he'd had in the town since he arrived, he'd had the night before in the rain and then again that morning in Gus Lamar's living room. He wanted to test himself, needed it like the fix to a sickening addiction. "No," he repeated, *"no tengo las drogas."*

The only response Dario could hope for now was that Juarez would send more men.

TOGETHER THEY LISTENED TO THE MESSAGES on the machine. Deacon's voice growing tighter as the time ticked by and the messages came to their end. The scent of his clothes burning in the barbecue out back coming to Ray through the screen, acrid as burning tires—Sanchez's shoes and wallet thrown in on top of it all. He hadn't known he'd ask for help until he'd done it. And now he wore a set of Tom's jeans and a dark woolen button-up, to replace his own. He still didn't know what he was going to do but they'd laid out enough for Ray to know they were heading to his father's place, where Tom said Ray would still be welcome.

The pager on his hip had vibrated several times already and Ray had looked at the number and put it away again. No time now to call Memo back. No idea what he would say to the man, or how he would tell him about his nephew. A doubt in Ray's mind that it would change anything. Memo would want the drugs regardless. What happened to Sanchez wasn't on Ray, though he feared somehow Memo would find a way to blame Ray for the boy's death.

From the start, when Claire had opened the door, Ray didn't really know how it would go. He'd forced himself inside, worried that someone might see him. The fear built up in a way he hadn't felt in years. The feeling that he was at an end, his end, or possibly even Tom's—not knowing what he might do if Tom had been there and pushed him back out into the wilds.

All through the desert he'd worried about being caught, and even as he'd come to the porch, the sound of the highway behind him, fourteen-wheelers and tankers moving past on their way from one job to another. His fear lessened now that he was around people who knew him again, who'd grown up with him, known him before his life had gone the way it had. An uneasy certainty going through him the whole time, since coming down the road toward Coronado three days before, that he would be found, and all that he had done in the time since he'd left, in order to escape his past in this town, would be stacked against him.

The tape spun to a stop and he heard the machine click and rewind. Deacon's voice still fresh in Ray's memory and Claire waiting there behind them on the couch as Tom looked up at Ray and asked why there would be a message on the phone from Deacon, asking where his father, Luis, was. Why he wasn't at work, when so many days in a row he'd never been late, never missed a day. Tom's eyes searching Ray's, looking for some answer, and Ray with no answer to give but to shake his head, looking from his cousin to the answering machine there on the table by the phone. Dropping his eyes away, if only for something to do, to break off his cousin's stare, because Ray knew now why Luis hadn't shown up to work that day, and had known since this morning when he'd changed out of his clothes, looking for his prescription bottle of pills.

T HE BRONCO SAT IN THE FLATLANDS ABOUT three or four miles off from the big mountains farther on to the east. Accessible only by an offshoot of the gravel road that quickly turned loose and empty, crumbling away at the edges, and cut through by large open areas of wash.

Kelly got up out of the cruiser, taking in the landscape, the dull brown of the creosote and burro bushes running all the way out across the flatlands. The smell of the rainstorm hanging fresh in the air as the sun dried the land. Overhead the wide circle of the Border Patrol plane was audible as it looped across the sky above, its wing tip pointed down at them like a finger. From where she stood it was clear the Bronco's rear windows had been blown out. The metal pockmarked by the same automatic fire they'd seen that morning at the Sullivan house.

Through her open cruiser window, she heard the pilots come on the radio and as soon as Pierce gave them the go-ahead they cut for El Paso.

"You smell that?" Kelly said, her nostrils picking up the scent leaking from within the Bronco.

"Worse than this morning."

"Much worse," Kelly added. She walked over to the Bronco, careful with the placement of her feet. The rainstorm had erased much of what she could see on the dusty surface of the desert, where the grasslike sedge grew up through the cracks, and the brush cast a thin veneer of color to the land.

She came around to the passenger side and pulled the door open. The man inside had been shot in the side of the abdomen. For a long while Kelly stood there staring at him.

Except for the blood, he looked as if he had just sat down for a nap and not woken. Barefoot with his chin resting forward on his chest, he seemed oddly comfortable.

"What do you think?" Pierce asked.

"I think it's strange he would be sitting in the passenger seat like this."

"All this," Pierce said, moving his arms to encompass the bullet-riddled sides and shattered windows of the truck. "And that's what you think is odd."

"Where are his shoes? Why would he be sitting here in the passenger seat like this?" Kelly said again, running each thought down to its source.

Pierce put a hand up over his nose and leaned in close to look at the body. "There's somebody missing, isn't there?" Pierce asked.

"There's a whole lot missing," Kelly said.

TOM HAD SEEN THE WAY THE MESSAGES FROM Deacon changed Ray. The downturn of his lips and the constant shift of his eyes to Tom's front windows and the land beyond, looking as if he wanted to be anywhere but where he was. "Should I be worried?" Tom asked.

"Is Luis usually late for work?"

"No," Tom said. "Not usually, but sometimes he goes on benders and he'll miss a day. Judging from when I saw him last, just a couple nights ago, there's a good chance he's home in bed, sleeping it off."

Ray was looking out the window again and Tom knew it was time to leave. Every minute they spent here at his place was another minute Kelly or someone else might stop by for a visit and find Ray there.

"Have you thought about what you're going to say to Billy?" Tom asked.

"I've been thinking about it for ten years," Ray said. "I still don't have the answer."

"You're going to be fine," Tom said. "He's a good kid. He's more of an adult at the age of twelve than maybe even my father is."

Ray smiled a little. He was still looking out the window toward the highway. "I've thought a lot about coming back here," Ray said. "I've wanted it for a long time and before all this I thought maybe I'd make a go of it, but I just don't know if that's possible anymore."

"Give it some time," Tom said. He didn't know what else to say and he could see his cousin had been living with the guilt of what he'd done, leaving Billy the way he had, leaving them all. "Are you ready?"

"Yes."

They went out to the Volkswagen and got in. The hope in Tom's mind that all would be okay, and they would drive over to Gus's without anything going wrong and then somehow they would drive Ray north. Tom with no idea what they would find. The message from Deacon and the memory of driving Luis home only two nights before still fresh in his mind. A hope in Tom's gut that his father would be there, passed out and smelling of alcohol.

Tom drove the Volkswagen and Claire sat in the front with the dog held between her knees so that the mutt wouldn't growl at Ray in the back. In Tom's hands, the Beetle felt like it skimmed over the road's surface like a boat over water, a wake of dust rising up behind them as they came off the valley highway. In the distance the Hermanos Range sat like teeth around the valley floor, bowed out toward the north where the highway went through. Each peak covered in a gloss of snow where the storm had come the night before and shaved it clean.

When they came out into the flatlands that had held the Lamar oilfields twenty years before, Tom could see Gus's house sitting there as it had all through his childhood, the stables off to the left and the staff houses behind. He pulled the Beetle in, his eyes searching back toward his father's place, where he saw his father's truck was missing.

From the backseat Ray leaned forward. "How long has it been since you've been here?"

"I was here a couple days ago," Tom said, looking to the porch where the screen door sat against the frame. "Strange as it now seems, we talked about you."

"You see anything—" Ray paused. "You see anything that doesn't look right?"

Again Tom leaned forward, scanning the landscape with his vision. A swirl of dust kicked up far down the valley and then blew itself out, pushing a dry weed before it. He elbowed the car door open and stood. "You have a reason you're asking?"

"No reason," Ray said, sliding the driver's seat forward so that he could get out of the small car to stand next to Tom. "I've just gotten cautious, that's all. The last few days haven't gone as well as I'd hoped."

Tom gave Ray a sideways glance but didn't say anything to him. Gus should have been there by now, standing at the doorway to invite them in, spit at Ray or hug him, he should have been there to say something. Their relationship never a good one but Gus's words to Tom only a few days before suggested Ray would be welcome. Gus saying how he still cared for his son even if he knew Ray had chosen badly in life.

The sun felt hot on his skin. A bright yellow orb above

DEAD IF I DON'T

them, passed over its half point. The shadow of the porch roof, slightly canted away from them, hit the ground at an angle. Looking back at Claire, he told her to wait there. "Let the dog out and watch her to make sure she doesn't get too far. Ray and I are going to go in for a moment and talk with Gus."

Ray paused as they came to the porch, an orange prescription bottle there on the first step. Bending, Ray took it up and looked at it, the dosage written in clear print along the side but the name concealed beneath Ray's fingers.

Tom heard his cousin curse under his breath and then watched as Ray slipped the bottle into his pants pocket.

"You not telling me something?" Tom asked, his voice low.

With his right hand, Ray had brought up the Ruger from his belt and he was looking to the house. "You know when the curtain comes down at the end of the show, and you get that sick feeling that life—real life—is waiting for you outside?" Ray said. "I have that feeling now and there's nothing I can do to stop it from crawling all over me."

Tom didn't like the feel of it at all and he went up the stairs with Ray next to him on the steps, the rifle strapped over Ray's back and the Ruger held close at his side. That bottle on the porch had meant something to Ray, but Tom couldn't say what. Ray moving up the stairs now like he was expecting trouble inside.

"Wait here," Ray said. With the gun raised toward the door he gestured for Tom to get the screen.

Tom reached a hand out and pulled the door open, the wide desert behind them and Jeanie now out in the dust at the bottom of the porch, standing stiff-legged looking up at him.

A passage of time working over Tom that he couldn't identify. Jeanie and Claire waiting for him on the stairs while Ray went inside. Nothing for Tom to do but stand there hoping for some signal from Ray. Nothing about it feeling right, and a loud keening soon heard from within, abrupt in the silence.

When Tom found Ray, his cousin stood across the room, a rough splatter of blood on the wall and Gus slumped forward in one of his living room chairs. The face a mash of blood and bone, skin cracked like a spiderweb across the old man's face, where the nose had been smashed in at its center. The only thing to tell Tom he was looking at Gus the wedding ring that he still wore on his finger.

Deputy Hastings stood three feet away from the open door of the Bronco, looking in on the dead man in the seat. "No footprints leading away?" he asked.

"You heard that rain last night," Kelly said. "Pierce and I drove out here and didn't even see a tire track till we were a hundred feet out."

"And this one?" Hastings said, still looking at the gut-shot man in the passenger seat.

"No ID, no wallet, nothing," Kelly said. "We won't know who he is till we can get him into the morgue and run his prints."

"It doesn't make much sense, does it, Sheriff?"

"A man sitting gut-shot in the middle of the desert with his shoes missing, no it doesn't."

"None of this scares you?" Hastings asked.

"Scares the shit out of me," Kelly said, turning to look back at her cruiser, where Pierce sat inside on the radio, guiding the ambulance that would take the body back to the morgue. "We don't have the resources for this."

"You talked to the mayor though, didn't you? Didn't he tell you to go ahead with whatever you needed to do?"

"Not in those words exactly."

"At times I wish I didn't have this job," Hastings said.

"Let me guess," Kelly said. "This is one of those times." From a little ways out she caught the sound of tires running up over the desert and the creak of springs. Turning, she saw the ambulance come into view. "You still have Agent Tollville's number over at the DEA?" she asked.

"Tollville? We haven't talked to him in a while now. Not since the mayor brought him down to look at what happened to Angela Lopez."

"He used to be a friend of Tom's. I doubt they are anymore,

but they used to be friends. He might be willing to help us out."

The ambulance pulled up and the medics jumped out, both Hastings and Kelly watching them as they gathered their gear. "What about the drugs?"

Kelly smiled. "You mean the fact that there aren't any?"

"Something like that."

"If it gets the DEA down here I'll fill bags with baking soda if I have to," Kelly said, grinning now and waiting for the medics.

IT CAME ON TOM STRONGLY, ALL IN ONE SWEEP-ing movement, his legs carrying him out the door onto the porch, where he gagged and coughed, feeling his own bile bitter at the back of his throat. Gus dead and Billy missing.

He ran a hand beneath his lips, wiping at the saliva on his chin, his knees bent down onto the wood of the porch and Ray still inside with Gus. No sign of Billy anywhere Tom had looked and a desire now to find both his father and the boy. The world had slid away from Tom in that moment, all of it teetering toward the edge and then going over. No feel for it anymore.

Getting to his feet, he stumbled down the stairs, Jeanie

now beside him and Claire up out of the car. Without saying anything he rounded the house looking for his father. Three times he called his father's name, waiting each time for a response that never came.

When he reached the little apartment where he'd grown up, and his father still lived, he could see where the window nearest the door had been broken out. The door stood slightly open and there was a darkness within that Tom didn't know what to do with.

He called his father's name twice more, letting his voice move ahead through the rooms before he, too, came to them, opening closets and checking behind doors. Tom only loosely aware of Claire as he searched, her voice coming to him out of the midday light from outside, her silhouette there in the doorway as he stumbled back toward her.

An intensity to the look she gave him reached down inside and scraped against the muscles of his chest. Tom with no words yet to answer her as she asked him again and again what was wrong, what he'd seen inside Gus's place, and where Luis was. He put his hands to his knees and dry-heaved several more times, the sun felt on his back as it hit his shirt and he fought to get air into his lungs.

It was a while before he was able to form the words, and he watched her face turn pale with the news.

"What about Billy?" she wanted to know.

He didn't have an answer and he ran his hands up through

his hair, pulling against the skin of his temples before letting his hands drop again. There had been a lot of blood inside Gus's living room. More than Tom had thought possible for one man.

R AY WAS ONLY MODERATELY AWARE OF THE hacking of his cousin outside, choking at the air. Ray felt a pulse of blood in his veins that spread like a stain through his chest and swelled at his throat. It had been a long time since he'd allowed himself to feel this way and he was aware now of the anger surging inside him, threatening to break through.

His father there in the chair, the blood on the floor where it had run from his body and collected in a pool.

So much blood already. Everywhere.

Ray took a step back. He hadn't yet allowed himself to move, but he did now, feeling the muscles in his legs come unlocked. A pain all down his chest, all the way to his feet as he moved away, his eyes still on his father. Not since his wife had been taken from him had he felt this way. Like an axe had been hefted into the heartwood of his life and the tender golden flesh beneath exposed.

He turned and ran his eyes around the room. The place just

as he'd remembered it. Nothing changed from when he was a child here to the days he'd had with his own son crawling around on the living room floor. Gus and him sitting back as they watched the boy move in erratic lines across the carpet. So much gone and a pain held deep in his chest.

When his breath came back to him, it came in a surge—all at once—like someone surfacing from the depths into air. His lungs hungry for the world above and his pupils dilated black and wide, as if coming into light from a great darkness. He fell back with a hand held out for support on the fireplace behind. The flash of memory shifting across his vision like a slide reel, image after image from a life now completely lost to him. His wife standing on the courthouse steps, the birth of their child, their first night in the new house outside of Coronado, the call of sirens before the knock came on his door, the wreckage of his wife's car and the black scrape of tires across asphalt that would never make sense to him.

Where was Billy? A desperate need to know now rose all the way through him. Where was his son?

He slumped to the floor. Every bad thing that had ever happened in this town to anyone he loved—his father, his wife, his child, even Tom—was his fault alone.

K ELLY KEPT STARING AT HER HAT WHERE IT
lay on the office desk. Hastings sitting on the other
side, waiting to hear what she had to say, and Pierce gone
along to the morgue with the medics. In her hand she held the
report that had come in via fax from the authorities down
south. Every one of the men they'd found out at the Sullivan
house that morning had some sort of record down in Mexico.
Violent crimes. Two of them recently released from a jail in
the Mexican state of Sinaloa. At the top of the sheet, Hastings
had scrawled the number for the DEA office up in Albuquerque.

She'd put her hat there on the desk when she'd come into
the office and now she couldn't stop looking at it. Flat brimmed and wide. Her own sweat stained into the material. The
hat not that different from Hastings's, only the tassels around
the brim enough to distinguish it as the sheriff's hat and not
one of her deputies'. She felt worn down—frustrated by all
that had happened and all that she'd been unable to prevent.

"No time like the present," Hastings said, looking at the
phone on her desk.

"No, I suppose not." Kelly picked up the phone. She was
still waiting to hear back from Pierce at the morgue, waiting
to hear who the man was they'd found in the Bronco, and
while she waited, she thought she might as well get on with
it.

When the secretary at the DEA picked up, Kelly identified herself and said, "I'm not sure how much Agent Tollville may have already heard about us down here in Coronado, but I'm calling because I'd like his help regarding what we've found so far."

Kelly waited while the secretary put her on hold. With the mouthpiece covered, she asked Hastings to give her some time alone.

After he'd gone she looked at her hat still sitting there in front of her. With the back of her hand she swiped at it and watched as it fell to the floor out of sight. When Agent Tollville came on the line, she began to explain the situation.

I T WAS JEANIE WHO FOUND LUIS AND BILLY twenty minutes later, their clothes soaked in the same mud that Tom had seen coated all over Ray that morning. The desert grime dried into the material. Luis with his arm around the boy, holding him close to his chest, and the boy shivering slightly even with the sun directly over them. Luis's eyes, dust-swollen in their sockets, looked back at Tom with an erratic twitch that seemed to skitter from Tom to Claire and then back toward the house.

"I saw them," Luis said. "We were inside when they came,

Billy in his room and me sleeping on the couch. Gus woke us and told us to go out through the kitchen as fast as we could. We've been here ever since." He was leaning now with his back to the rock, the last bit of shade on his face, while his legs lay splayed out before him in the roasting sun.

"Come on, Dad," Tom said, reaching a hand down first to pick Billy up off the ground. "Come with us, it's going to be all right now, it's just us."

Luis shrugged his son off and pushed himself closer into the rock, bringing his legs up with him. Eighty-one years old, he looked frail and small, with his eyes darting all over the desert.

"Who did you see?" Claire asked. She dropped down to Luis's level, resting on her haunches as she spoke.

"I thought you were them," Luis said. "When I saw you come down that road, I thought you were them again, come back for us."

With his hands, Billy told them about the light from the house and how Luis had kept them hidden all through the night and into the morning.

"Come on, Dad," Tom said again. He signed to Billy, "Can you help me with him?" Then to his father, "It's safe now, it's us. There's no reason to be scared, not anymore."

Luis fixed Tom with his gaze, looking up at him as if for the first time. "I heard the shot, I never even went back," Luis said. "You saw what they did to Gus?"

Tom didn't want to say it in front of Billy and he turned away so that the boy wouldn't read his lips. "He's dead, Dad."

"I can't go back there," Luis said. He began to repeat the words like a mantra, speaking not to them but past them to the world.

Tom looked to Claire. "Take Billy," he said. "I'll get my father up."

Tom waited while Claire led Billy away, and then he reached down and dragged his father to his feet. Tom was surprised at how thin his father's arms had become, the muscle tight beneath the skin, the skin itself, felt through the shirt he wore, loose on his bones.

With his hand behind Luis, they walked back toward the outbuildings, Claire ahead of them with Billy. Outside, beyond Gus's house, Ray was waiting for them. The gun now tucked away in his belt again and the rifle strapped across his back. Up ahead he saw the boy flinch as he saw his father, no idea if Billy recognized him at all. A lot of time had passed and the pictures on the mantel were the only real connection between them anymore.

Claire led Billy into Luis's place. Luis didn't even seem to register Ray as they approached, and Tom brought Luis into his apartment and laid him down on the bed, waiting over his father till the old man turned away to the wall and stayed that way long enough for Tom to know he wouldn't turn back any time soon.

"He saw them?" Ray asked. He was standing in the door-way looking in on Tom where he sat at the edge of his father's bed. Claire stood a few feet behind, a blanket thrown over Billy's shoulders and Claire's hands rubbing warmth onto the boy's back.

"He saw them," Tom said. "But he's not going to talk about it, at least not now." Tom looked from Ray to Billy, trying to see if the boy understood.

"And the boy?" Ray asked.

"You know he couldn't have heard anything. Luis was protecting him through the night. He didn't hear a thing, and he doesn't know anything more than what we can see for ourselves."

Tom watched to see how his cousin had taken it. Ray's father was dead inside the house, and there was nothing Tom could say to change that. There was only dealing with where they were now and what they would do. He watched Ray for a moment more, long enough for Ray to lean his weight into the door frame, slump-backed, with his head searching the ceiling above.

"Luis is in shock, Ray," Claire said. "He probably has pneumonia being out all night in the rain." She stopped and worked her hands together, the dirt rolling from her palms as she pressed them together. "I'm sorry about what happened to your father," she said, almost as an afterthought, though Tom knew her well enough to know it wasn't. "I didn't know him well but I understand from Tom that he was good to both of you."

Ray nodded. He was looking now toward Billy, and then when he saw Tom's eyes on him, he turned back to Luis. "How is he?"

"He'll get better," Tom said. "They both will. They need some time and they need some rest, but they'll get better."

"I never thought it would go this far," Ray said.

"I know," Tom replied.

Tom had never thought life could ever be like this. But it was, and they stood apart from each other for a long while in the silence that followed until Ray shifted, turning back toward the house, and said, "You'll help me bury him, won't you?"

"YOU KNOW ANY OF THOSE BOYS?" KELLY asked. She was sitting in the passenger seat of Hastings's patrol car, watching as an old Buick with Mexican plates went past and parked around the corner behind Dario's bar.

Kelly watched the men begin to appear from the side street, filing out onto Main.

"New recruits for one of the wells?" Hastings guessed.

"No," Kelly said, "I really don't think that's the way this town is headed." She looked around toward the courthouse up the street and their office in the basement. "How long since we called Tollville?" Kelly asked.

"Can't be more than half an hour," Hastings said.

They sat in the patrol car, Hastings behind the wheel and Kelly in the passenger seat, watching as the men went in through the front door. The last of them paused outside to light a cigarette, shading his face for a moment with his cupped hands.

"They don't look like any locals I've seen," Hastings said.

"Reinforcements," Kelly said.

"I'll be glad when Tollville shows."

"Why?"

"He might at least be able to tell us something we don't already know."

They were parked a hundred feet up the street from the bar, and when the man pulled his hands back from his face, they could see he was looking directly at them. Kelly raised a hand, waving at the man, letting him know they were there looking right back at him. He went on smoking, and after about twenty seconds of just offering up a dead stare, he threw the cigarette down and went inside.

"I believe that was littering," Hastings said.

"You want to be the one to go get him?"

"I'll let him slide if you will."

"No," Kelly said, "I don't think I can on this one." She was up out of the cruiser with the door shut behind her before Hastings had a chance to talk her away from the place. No telling how long it would take Tollville to get down to Coronado and Kelly with no more patience for waiting.

Too much on her plate now to look any other way, no idea what had happened to Burnham, but a dead certainty about the boy in the hospital, the three out at the house, and the gut-shot man in the Bronco. It was a veritable killing spree, and she was looking at the bar door as if it held all the answers she needed.

DARIO STEPPED AWAY FROM THE MEN WHEN Kelly came in. He'd been sitting with his back to the bar, speaking with the new men, just up out of Juarez, telling them all what they'd need to know and what to expect. None of them rousing even a mutter as they'd listened to him. Medina, behind the bar, was the first to raise his eyes as the door slid open and then, almost with the same movement, gave Dario a slight nod of the head, pointing with his chin toward the front of the bar.

Dario had known it would happen like this. Expected it from the start—waiting as he had been all this time in the bar. He hadn't expected the woman to come alone like this. Gus Lamar out there in the house, dead in his living room chair, and the bottle of prescription drugs waiting on the front steps. Now the reality of the woman there in his own bar, standing there alone, as if he'd simply invited her in for a drink. A strange admiration he now felt at the sight of her there alone, letting her eyes adjust to the gloom.

As Dario stood from the stool he was aware of the quiet in the room. Kelly taking her first few steps toward them and the stillness he felt behind him like the electric tension in the air before the lightning breaks far overhead. A smile on his lips he could not control. The squeal of a stool as one of the men stood, not knowing yet what the play was and how close they were supposed to let Kelly get before something was done. With his hand still on the bar, Dario raised his fingers in a small show of supplication. Kelly walking toward them to take a seat a little ways down the bar, away from the group of men, her hat now thrown out on the bar and her fingers drumming on the wood.

"Sheriff," Dario said, the smile still on his lips as he took the seat next to her. A tinge of excitement rumbling through him. The thought in his head that every day after this one would be different from any that had come before.

"¿*Cerveza?*" Medina asked, not bothering to move off the back bar, where he'd been leaning since the men had entered.

Kelly ran her eyes down the bar, appearing to take it in, no one except her and the men in the place. "A drink, Sheriff?" Dario asked, his hands on his lap as he swiveled on the stool to speak with her.

"Soda water and lime."

When Medina turned to him, Dario ordered a coffee. He watched Medina take a glass from the back bar and fill it with ice. In the mirror over the bar he could see Kelly's shoulders and the top of her uniform. Down the bar on one side the men were beginning to take their seats again, and he heard Medina say something to them and then the mutter of a reply.

When the soda water came, Kelly folded out a couple dollars from her pocket and put them on the bar. Dario watching as Medina slipped them off the bar in the same movement he used to set Dario's coffee before him. Still no one's voice had risen above a whisper. Beside her, Dario sipped from his cup, waiting for what he knew would come, the inevitable reason she was here and the answers he was not prepared yet to give, but that he knew he would. His time in this town drawing to a close, and the feeling all around him in the air that the world had quickened and begun to spin all that much faster.

"Dario," Kelly said, turning on the stool and holding her hand out toward him, "I think it's time we met formally."

R AY STOOD IN THE STABLES, EXAMINING THE picks and spades, the blades rusted and unused and the wood almost petrified with age. His father's body already carried to the cluster of oaks up the valley where his mother had been buried twenty years before, and which held Marianne.

Ray brought a shovel up and then, running a finger down the handle for splinters, he put it back, bringing his hand up and looking it over where the dull vermilion of dry blood showed between the whorls of his fingertips. He had been standing for a long time looking at his hand when Tom came in and ran an open palm up the nose of one of the horses where it stood in its stall.

"You should talk to him," Tom said. "He'll understand you. He reads lips like me or you read the newspaper."

"I don't imagine he'd want anything to do with me."

"It's been a long time, Ray."

"Don't you think I know that?" Ray said, the volume growing in his voice, uncontrollable. "It's been too long. Looking at him now I can tell you I don't know him and he doesn't know me. Can't we leave it at that?"

"It's whatever you want to do, Ray. But you should know you and Billy both lost a father today and there's something you owe that boy that you can't just ignore anymore."

Ray looked away, everything changed and none of it how

he'd thought it would be. He looked back to the spades and picks leaning against the side of the stable. "Is that why you came in here?"

"I'm going to need to make some calls," Tom said. "I'm going to need to explain to Deacon where I am."

Ray put his hand down and let it hang by his side. "I don't think that's a good idea," Ray said. He looked up at his cousin, waiting to see what would be said.

"I can still help you," Tom said. "But you need to understand things have changed. This isn't about some cartel men you shot out in the desert, this is Gus we're talking about now and I don't want this to go any further. I have Billy and my father to worry about, and Claire."

"And yourself," Ray said.

"I didn't say that," Tom said. He stepped away from where the horses waited with their heads and necks pushed out over the stall doors. "Look, I can tell Deacon my father got sick— that he drank himself sick. It will buy you some time to get out of here, but after that I am going to the sheriff and I don't plan to lie to her."

"You'll buy me time?" Ray said, his voice slow and deliberate in the stillness of the stables.

Tom shook his head, looking away out of the stable doors. "Do what you like here," Tom said. "Bury Gus. I can't be part of this any more than I already am. I'll take Claire and we'll head into town, and we won't say anything about what we saw out here till you have time enough to get away. It's all I can promise."

Ray looked at his hand again. He ran it down his pants, pressing his fingers to the material. "What about Luis?"

"Claire's with him now, she's got him up and he's drinking water and talking again. I've got his truck keys and when this is all done, I'll pick up his truck in town, then drive back here and be with him."

"He say who did this?"

"The man Burnham worked for, the same you probably already have an idea about," Tom said. "I don't want to say any more. I don't want to be involved in this."

"Your hands are clean then?" Ray said, a grin on his face as he said it and a pain in his chest as his voice broke a little and he quickly regained himself. "I'm not judging you now, I'm just telling you the facts. I thought better of you than this. I don't know if I can let you go."

"What are you saying?"

"We had a deal, didn't we?"

"Nothing is the same as it was only an hour ago," Tom said. He walked closer to Ray. "Luis said he wants to help you bury Gus. He said you can take Gus's truck if you want to run. I can't stay here any longer though. I thought I could help you but I see now that I can't."

"What about Luis?"

"If I'm not back in time with his truck, he can take Billy

and ride one of the horses up to Deacon's like he did yesterday for work. I expect that will be what he'll do once you have Gus in the ground."

Ray turned and looked at the tools again, feeling something inside of him pushing against his skin. "How much time do I have?" he asked, his eyes still on the spades.

"Two hours at the most. I don't think I could explain for any more than that."

"Okay," Ray said, his mind working, adding mileage and time all into one. "Okay," he said again.

KELLY TOOK ANOTHER DRINK, THEN PUT THE glass down on the bar. She was aware that no one had said anything for a minute or more. She rolled the glass around, making small watery circles on the wood. It had been going on like this for a long time now and it was going nowhere. "You're saying you have no idea about the old Sullivan house outside of town?" she said.

"None," Dario responded.

"None at all?"

"No sane person would have been out in that weather."

"That's probably right," Kelly said. "No sane person

would have." Kelly watched Dario take a drink from his coffee.

"Did something happen out there?" he said.

"Something did."

"Well," Dario said, laughing a little as he said it, "don't lead me on and then not finish. I swear I can take it." There was the slightest of accents to his voice. Not a bad-looking guy. Midthirties. No scars. No tattoos. He could have been just a guy at a bar drinking a coffee.

Kelly lifted her glass and felt the cool soda as it passed her lips. She thought over her position. It really didn't matter whether she told him or not, but she was interested to know how he would respond. "We found three dead bodies," Kelly said.

"That's horrible." Flat toned, his voice giving nothing away.

"Yes."

"And now you're going around asking questions?"

"That's how it works."

"How many before me?"

"How many what?"

"How many people did you go to before me?"

"You're it," Kelly said.

TOM DROVE SOUTH ON THE HIGHWAY WITH Claire. At the big courthouse he pulled around back and brought the Volkswagen to the curb. "You go on ahead of me," Tom said. "There's no point in both of us getting in trouble for this."

Claire looked at him where he sat in the driver's seat. Jeanie behind him. "What do you expect me to say?"

"I don't expect you to say anything. I'm sorry about this. I'm sorry I brought you along with us when I should have known there was trouble."

"You had no way of knowing," Claire said. She put a hand back over the seat and nuzzled Jeanie where she sat. "I've known Ray almost as long as I've known you, and I knew how it would go when he showed up, and I knew how you would react."

Tom smiled for a moment, both of his arms pushed out on the steering wheel, waiting on her to get out so that he could go around the front and make whatever he was going to say official. "You know a lot about me," he said.

Claire laughed and leaned into him, putting a hand up over one of his arms and pulling it down. "Maybe that's why it never works out for us."

"Maybe," Tom said. He gave her a weak smile and looked away down the street.

"You don't need to tell Kelly anything," Claire said. "I

wouldn't blame you for it if you just turned this car around and took us both back to your place."

"That's a lot you're saying there," Tom said. "I can't tell you I haven't been thinking the same thing on the way down here, but Gus is gone now and I can't simply forget that."

"You think by saying something you'll be doing any better?"

"Luis saw who did this," Tom said.

"Dario?" Claire said. "How long do you think Luis or even you will last if Dario finds out there's someone going to stand up to him?"

"My dad will be all right. I told him what I was planning to do and he didn't try to stop me," Tom said. "I'm trying to do what's right."

Claire still had his arm wrapped with hers and he could see her eyes were wet along the edges. "Sometimes what you think is right, isn't right for everyone," she said. "You're not the sheriff anymore, you never seem to understand that. What you're going to do may end up hurting more people than you think."

"Who?" he said. "I told you already I talked to my father, he knows what could happen and so do I."

"No," she said.

"Then who?"

"Me," she said, rushing the word before he was ready for it. "You're doing a fine job of thinking about yourself."

"I'm going to leave your name out of it."

"You just don't get it," Claire said. She took her arms away from him and moved toward the door. "What happens to me after all this? What happens to us? I don't want to see you get hurt again. They'll take away more than your badge this time."

Down the street a car came around the corner and headed their way. Tom watched it till it went past, the woman in the driver's seat not even bothering to look their way. "I can't talk about this anymore," Tom said. "I told you how I feel, and I can't sit here like this anymore. If someone sees us sitting here together, everything I say later will come into question."

"Just drive us back to your place," Claire said. "That's all I'm asking."

"You know I won't do that," Tom said. He was looking up at the back door of the courthouse, aware that anyone could come out of the building at any time. "Get out," he said.

She stared at him coldly, the sparkle of tears in her eyes. He told her he would park the car up the street and where she could get her keys and then he reached over and pushed her car door open.

When she was gone he drove the Volkswagen up a block and parked it. Leaving the keys up under the back right tire, he came down the street with Jeanie trailing him on her leash, and crossed toward Main and the front entrance of the courthouse.

It wasn't till he passed the courthouse parking lot that he slowed, looking at the one cruiser outside. No idea if it was Kelly's car or if it was one of her deputies'. Only two cars left in the department after the one at the hospital had burned. He checked his watch. Still plenty of time before something needed to be said and he would drive his father's truck back north, he owed Ray that at least.

"Claire told me you were a pig farmer now."

Tom turned to find Eli at the top of the courthouse steps. The mayor taking the stairs quickly, stopping only when he was a few feet away from Tom. Ten years since they'd said more than a greeting to each other.

"I also heard you've been assisting Edna with the killing of that boy."

"I've been trying to help out," Tom said.

"Pigs," Eli said again. "I guess I should have seen it on you from the start."

"I'm not in that business anymore," Tom said. The anger growing inside him as he stood there and the thin smile on Eli's lips that Tom had always hated. "I left it a while ago to get into cattle. I thought maybe you'd heard that from Claire, but maybe not."

"I didn't know you two were still together."

"We're not," Tom said. At his leg he felt Jeanie yawn and lean into him. Her canines showing as the air whistled up out of her throat.

"I see you still have that mutt."

Tom didn't say anything. He knew exactly where this was going, and he didn't have any desire to help it along.

"It's a poor replacement for a woman," Eli kept on. "But I guess there's not too many that will still have you."

Tom smiled, forcing the muscles in his face. Eli and him on the sidewalk and Tom knowing that if they kept on this way he was going to hit the man. "Have you seen Edna?" Tom asked.

"I don't know where she is," Eli said. "I told Edna to fire that young deputy two days ago but he's still around, waiting in the department office with the DEA agent that came down from Albuquerque today."

"Who's that?"

"You know him," Eli said. "Tollhouse or something? The same one who came down for your hearing."

Tom shifted his weight from one foot to the other, his palms grown sweaty where he clenched them at his sides. "I think I better be going," Tom said. He nodded a good-bye to Eli, taking the first couple steps toward the department doors around the side of the building.

"You know Edna's not going to need you anymore," Eli said, still standing there on the sidewalk, watching Tom until Tom tugged at Jeanie's leash a little, urging her on. "This is out of your hands now. The sooner you and Edna understand that, the better off this town will be. You know that, right?"

"I'm not much more than a farmer these days," Tom said,

walking now, not looking back as he made his way toward the
basement offices and whatever he'd find there.

R AY LEANED HIS WEIGHT ONTO THE SHOVEL
and looked in the hole. It was about six feet in length
and three feet in depth. Sweat collected on his brow and then
ran the length of his face, dripping from his chin and speckling the ground. Across the grave from him, Luis sat with his
back to the big oak tree, drinking from a canteen of water.
The wrapped body of Ray's father lay next to him on the
ground. Farther on, he saw Billy where he sat fifty feet off,
resting against a far oak watching Ray.

"You could have gone with them," Ray said, looking across
at Luis. "You probably should have."

"Here," Luis said, tossing the canteen to Ray. "Rest a little
and let me work." He lifted himself from the ground and
brought with him a pick that was leaning against the trunk
of the oak.

Ray unscrewed the top of the canteen and stood staring
into the darkness within. The feel of water inside the thin
metal body, cold against the sides. For a while now he'd felt
life sliding away from him. His daily routines gone. The guilt
risen inside him over what had happened to Marianne, about

what he'd done all those years before, working for Memo and putting his wife in that position. The pills his only defense against much of it, the dried look of his wife's eyes as he'd looked into them for the last time, always open in his memories of her. Like some part of him that was forever awake, but would never rise. She was many things to him, but the most she would now ever be—Ray knew—was a body in a grave only fifty feet away.

In the hole, Luis raised the pick and began to chip away at the earth, loosening the clay soil. "You didn't have to stay," Ray said.

"I stayed because it's my place to stay," Luis said, pausing in his work. "I saw who did this to him, and I didn't do a thing about it. I was scared, and I wanted to do something but I couldn't."

"You did nothing wrong, Luis."

"I did everything wrong," Luis said. He was looking up at Ray, and already there was a fresh sheen of sweat on his forehead.

"The ones who did this," Ray said, "you know them? You'll testify against them if it comes to that?"

"I've done my part to hurt this town. I've drunk their liquor and paid their way through this town and it's all led to this."

"Dario?" Ray said. "The bar in town?"

"You know the one, same place it's always been. Everything

has changed through the years, and I've been too much of a fool to see it." Luis raised the pick and brought it down into the earth. He raised it again and brought it down again, the huff of his breath now heard. "I've been drunk for too many years," he said. "I should have seen what I was doing. Going through life with blinders on. Your father saw it. This last year, spending time with the unions trying to build the town, while I spent my time investing in its fall. Now the workers are leaving, the wells drying up, while Dario keeps digging farther in.

"Two nights ago I was sitting in that bar," Luis went on. "The place seemed ready to self-destruct—the whole town, like a black hole opening up to swallow down every street and building. Everyone talking about how they were going to burn the Tate Bulger wells out. All of it seems so stupid now, your father dead, and all he's done to protect this town at an end."

Ray watched him where he worked in the grave, under the oak, his father's body wrapped in a patterned floral tablecloth of forget-me-nots. The blue coloring of the sheet stained red in places where the blood came through. "What's going to happen to Billy?" Ray asked.

"He's my responsibility now," Luis said. "You don't have to worry about that. I'll watch over him most of the time, and Tom will take him sometimes. It will be just like it's been."

"I'm sorry about all this," Ray said. He didn't know what

else to say. He knew he couldn't stay. At one time, only days before, he'd thought something different, but he knew he'd given that right up and it wasn't his place anymore, not at all. "Gus was his real father," Ray said.

He tried to remember his father the way he used to be, the way things used to be, before Ray had taken up with Memo. Before the wells on his father's property had gone dry and Ray had been forced to leave the land he worked every day with Luis and his father. "You've done nothing wrong, Luis," Ray said. "You're not like me. You've got nothing to blame yourself over."

Looking up at the sun now slowly beginning to set beyond the western hills, Ray estimated the time. His father's body on the ground next to the grave. Never enough time. Everything running out on him and a world he'd long since pushed away now collapsing all around him. He tried to remember how he'd felt all those years before, when life had seemed so figured out and solid. What had he thought? Who had he been? The image of himself all those years ago nothing but a paper cutout of a man that seemed to bend now with the wind.

"Luis," he said, waiting for his uncle to look up at him. "I can't stay around here anymore. I know I should, but there just isn't time."

"I know," Luis said. He had turned to face Ray, putting the pick aside and climbing from the hole. "You be careful out there. Gus would have said the same." Luis reached a hand out to Ray and waited. "You're going to be okay, you know that, right?"

Ray took Luis's hand. "One way or another I know that," Ray said. "I wish I could stay and see this finished." He let go of his uncle's hand and nodded a good-bye, pausing to look to his father there on the ground, before turning and walking toward the house, the boy watching him still.

"Tom told me you read lips," Ray said, stopping for a moment and waiting for the boy to nod his head. "I'm sorry about Gus. None of this should have happened and I don't know if you'll ever understand quite what I mean. I don't expect you to and in some ways I don't want you to either." He stepped a little closer, scrubbing at his face with a single hand. "I've never been a good person. I'm not made for this world, not anymore. You'll figure that out someday, like I figured it for myself." He paused, taking time, but not really knowing what else to say. Ten years had passed and he'd abandoned the boy without even a postcard sent in all that.

He took another step and now he was close to the boy, his son, and he knelt within arm's reach of the boy and put a hand out to Billy's cheek, trying as best he could to make the connection. "I'm sorry," Ray said. "I can't say anything more than that."

Billy turned and looked away. The brief warm touch still there on Ray's hand where his fingers had grazed his son's cheek.

He was aware that behind him Luis had stopped working and was listening to everything Ray said. The boy, his son, just sitting there, looking away from Ray. "I deserve that," Ray said, "I deserve far worse and someday I hope it will be better between us." He had no idea if the boy understood him. His face turned away as Ray stood, waiting only a moment before walking away. His feet carrying him toward his father's house, where he knew everything inside was just as it had always been.

"THESE BODIES," DARIO SAID. "YOU THOUGHT I'd know something about them?"

Kelly looked across the bar at the men sitting opposite. "They seemed like the type of customer that might be in here."

This made him smile even bigger. "What," he said, "Mexicans?"

"Out-of-towners."

Dario smirked and looked across the bar at the men on the other side. Medina down the far side of the bar, polishing the same glasses over and over again.

"You always this busy during the day?" Kelly asked.

"Sure," he said. "Around lunch we get a lot of these guys coming in here."

"I don't see much food."

"We don't have a lot of customers come in here looking for food," Dario said.

"I bet." She made a quick pass of the room with her eyes. "What type of customers would you say you get in here?"

"The hardworking American type," he said.

"I can see that," she said. "There's not much to it. Just you and Medina?"

"It's usually about all we need."

"And if you need more?"

"We make do."

"These men oil workers? They hardworking American types?"

"After the layoffs they've been coming in less and less, saving their money or heading north for work."

"Worry you?" Kelly said. "Your business drying up."

"There's always other ways to make a little extra."

"Blue-plate specials?"

"There's always something," Dario said again.

Kelly finished her soda water. She thought over what had just been said.

"Would you like another?" Dario asked, motioning to the empty glass on the bar.

"No," Kelly said.

Dario held her gaze for a moment. She could tell he wanted her to say more, to keep talking, but there was nothing left to say. She got up to go. She could feel the weight of the gun belt

DEAD IF I DON'T

around her hips, the cuffs, the flashlight, the radio. All the various things that made her what she was. Sheriff, law, protector—though she was starting to think there wasn't much point in it. She was standing with a hand on the bar, aware that everyone's eyes were on her, almost willing her to leave. "Do you mind if I ask you one more thing?"

"Go ahead."

"You heard about the boy in the hospital?"

"I heard about him."

"Does that seem strange to you? Nothing for years and then in the same day this boy is murdered, followed that night by three more?"

"It's a horrible thing."

"Yes," she said. She looked at the empty glass on the bar, just for something to look at, a distraction from what she really wanted to ask. "There's a rumor going around that the boy was related to the cartel in some way."

"Is that what you think?"

"The same rumor has been going around about you," Kelly said.

Dario smiled. "Cartel." He blew off the word with a little passing movement of his hand. "That type of thing is back home in Mexico. Not here."

"Back home?"

"Juarez."

"What did you do before you moved to the States?"

"I was a police officer."

Kelly looked at him, trying to decide if he was being serious.

"Hard to believe?"

"Honestly, yes."

"It's the truth," Dario said. "You can look it up."

"Rough town," Kelly said.

"Very rough. There was a lot of violence. A lot of murders."

"Is that why you left?"

"Yes," he said. "It is very peaceful here."

"It *was* very peaceful here," Kelly corrected.

"Yes," he said. "You are right. It was."

She looked at the empty glass again. The men talking in low, controlled voices, occasionally glancing over at them. Kelly knew just by standing there she was making them uncomfortable and in the same moment she wondered if she had pressed her luck coming here.

"Would you like something else?" Dario said.

"No, I'm fine."

Dario reached out a hand and took the empty glass off the bar.

Kelly considered him where he sat. Whether he was telling her the truth she didn't know. Perhaps he'd said that thing about being a cop just to try to get sympathy from her, perhaps it was true. She dropped her eyes to the floor, nothing outside for her. No place for her to go. "I want your advice on something," she said, speaking not to Dario, but to the coffee cup in front of him, like she was talking to herself, sounding out the question as she asked it. "What would it take for this to go away? For this town to go back to the way it used to be, to the peace you say it's known for?"

Dario breathed out and for the first time she realized he'd been holding back, letting her speak, waiting even, for what she might say to him. "There is no going back," he said.

"I didn't tell you everything," Kelly said. She raised her eyes to his and waited. When no response came she told him about the Bronco outside of town, about the DEA and the Border Patrol. She said it was over. "Whatever game we've been playing here in this town, it's over, it's done, there is nothing more for any of us," she said.

Dario lifted the coffee cup and then put it back down, he wet his lips with his tongue. "There's always something to look forward to," he said.

"You miss being a cop?"

"No," he said, "but I think I understand something about it, something about that life and why you came in here looking to talk with me."

"Why's that?"

"You want something more from this life," Dario said. "The things that go on here, that wear away at you every day, that just keep coming. They're all the same to you and me, to people like us. Shouldn't we want more, a little break from the monotony?"

She didn't have an answer for him and pausing to consider what this meant, she asked, "What if the rumors are true?"

"What rumors?" Dario asked.

"That you're working for the cartel."

"What if they are?" he said.

"You know if I find something and it leads me here, I won't be back just to talk."

"I know," Dario said.

"You've run a good business. Really quite impressive."

"Thank you."

"But it's slipping away from you," Kelly said. "Don't you see that? Don't you see how it's going to end for you in this town?"

"I'm just a barkeeper," Dario said. "That's all. I don't intend to give that up now."

WHEN TOM LED JEANIE INTO THE DEPARTMENT Pierce sent them straight through to the sheriff's office in the back, where Tollville was waiting. He and Tollville had been friends once, or as close to it as the distance would allow, and Tom stood looking at the back of Tollville's head for a long time before he finally went in and shook the man's hand.

"It's been a while," Tollville said. He was sitting in the

chair reserved for guests and he had turned slightly to look up at Tom where he stood by the filing cabinets and papers in the corner of the small office.

"I didn't think they'd send you," was all Tom could think to say.

"Edna called me directly. I was wondering when she might, and to tell you the truth I'd been expecting the call a day ago."

Tom looked around the room for a place to sit. The desk in the center of the room with Kelly's chair on one side and Tollville sitting in the other. "I doubt she'd mind," Tollville said, raising his hand off his lap toward the chair opposite.

Looking around the office for a second, searching for something to do with Jeanie, Tom lifted the desk a little, toed the grip of Jeanie's leash beneath the leg, and then let the desk down. When he was satisfied the desk would hold her, he sat.

Sitting across from him, Tom thought that Tollville looked much the same. Skinny with close-cropped hair and the hollow cheeks suggesting he didn't have the time for a good meal or didn't much care. As he used to, he wore a suit even in the heat of the late-afternoon sun coming through the windows, the motes of dust strangely milky as the sun set away in the west. The jacket he wore rumpled beneath the pits. The only change Tom could identify about him was the whiteness in the man's hair.

"You look the same," Tom said.

Tollville offered a weak smile. He had his hand out on a manila folder that lay flat on the desk, and he worked his fingers over it a couple times. "Edna told me you've been helping her out," he said.

"That's right," Tom said, watching the man's fingers dance over the folder on the desk.

"Well, even if you weren't, I'd still want to talk with you."

Tom looked out of the office to where Pierce sat, going through a stack of paperwork. The young deputy the only one in the department and a collection of empty desks and chairs all around him.

"Edna faxed up a copy of some prints she took off a dead man they found a few miles outside of town, sitting in a stolen Bronco." Tollville slid the manila folder across the desk and waited for Tom to take it. "I took a helicopter down just because I thought I needed to be here." Tollville watched Tom where he sat, his eyes jumping from the folder on the desk to Tom's eyes. "Recognize him?"

Tom opened the folder and pulled out a mug shot of a young Mexican man. "I don't know him," Tom said.

"The prints Edna faxed up got me pretty interested to see what was going on down here."

"You know this man?" Tom said, turning the mug shot over to look at the report that followed.

"I know his family."

Tom smiled. "Is he in the mob or something?"

"Closest we have to it here in New Mexico."

"You have to be joking, right?"

"No joking," Tollville said. The chair he sat in creaked a little with his weight. Sitting, he didn't look nearly as tall as he was.

Tom put the folder flat on Kelly's desk, the two sides open and the picture facing up. The man's name didn't ring any bells.

Tollville leaned forward and jabbed a finger at the picture. "This guy here is pretty small-time. A few years back he tried to boost one of those big fourteen-wheelers. But when he gets behind the wheel he can't quite figure out how to drive the thing." Tollville was smiling again, enjoying himself. "He ends up making it about two blocks, burning the clutch all the way, and then just loses it and dead-ends the truck in some poor guy's pet shop."

"That's like something out of the world's stupidest criminal tricks," Tom said.

"Probably would have made the cut, only when the truck went through the wall of the pet shop it killed about six cats, two Labrador retrievers, and a fifty-year-old cockatoo. Animal cruelty and all that," Tollville said, obviously enjoying the story. "The police found this guy trapped in the cab, pissing himself. The doors all jammed up from going through the front of the place."

"So what about this file gets you on a helicopter and gets you down here?"

"His uncle, Memo, is the biggest drug supplier we have in the state."

"Did Kelly say if there were any drugs in the Bronco?"

"There's always drugs when Memo's involved."

"You think he is? What if this Sanchez kid was just up to the same old tricks?"

"What gets me down here is the body count," Tollville said. He was leaning forward in the chair, speaking quietly across the desk. "Memo's nephew couldn't have done any of this even if he'd started training for it the day he got out of prison."

Again Tom looked out toward the young deputy, Pierce's back to the two of them where he sat at his desk. "It's a good story," Tom said. "But I don't understand why you'd want to talk to me about it."

"Twelve years ago things started to go real bad between Memo's family and the Mexican cartels," Tollville continued. "Memo had been their guy over here, and then ten years ago, after the trouble you all had down here, U.S. members of the cartel just start turning up dead. They walk into a room, the door closes, and then boom, they're gone. It happened all up and down the border. It was a real piece of work. Fifty percent of the people we were keeping tabs on either disappeared or ended in very bloody ways." Tollville paused. "I can't prove a thing. I mean, we all knew Memo was killing people before all this happened, but this was bad. It was all-out war, no-sur-vivors time. And then it just stops. No killings, no dead bodies, nothing. And that just doesn't happen. It drags on for years, then peters out, but it doesn't just stop."

"You're thinking it's starting up again?"

"This is the interesting part," Tollville said. "Ten years ago I get called down here to check into this thing with you. It's the first real lead we'd had in a while. Off the record, we all knew Angela Lopez was dirty, which is about the only reason you didn't end up in jail. But what's exciting is that it was the first time we got to officially look into the life of one of these cartel figures."

"I'm glad you enjoyed yourself," Tom interrupted. "I lost my job over that."

"You're lucky you didn't end up in jail," Tollville said. "Going after her the way you did. Without any evidence, and only a tip—which I suspect came directly from your cousin—to rely on."

"I was just doing my job," Tom said.

Tollville held up his hands. "Look, I'm not saying Lopez didn't have it coming. She qualifies as a bad person in the DEA's handbook, bringing in all that dope. But she didn't have anything but some money and a baby daughter in that house when you came to her door. What happened to you had to happen to you, Tom. There was no other way around it. And that's the thing that gets me down here. Two events like that in one small town, it's too much of a coincidence."

"That and the bodies."

"Yes," Tollville agreed. "That and the bodies." He waved a hand at the file. "A guy like Sanchez doesn't do damage like this. He doesn't do much damage at all, at least on purpose." Tollville put a hand out and picked up the picture there on the desk. "I didn't put it together back then. But I dug around a little this time and I did some checking. Your cousin Ray's files are sealed. You remember me looking into him all those years ago? We got some good information then, didn't we? Now his files are sealed again. Do you know what that means?"

Tom shook his head. He knew exactly what it meant. He'd forgotten Tollville's smugness, how his clearance made him think he was smarter than he was.

"Someone powerful had those files closed. Someone with connections."

"I don't know anything about this," Tom said.

"Your cousin worked for your uncle, correct? They were in oil together?"

"Along with my father," Tom said.

"But before that Ray was in the army, wasn't he?"

Tom nodded.

"The way I'm looking at this is that Memo has his nephew, the one Edna found out in the Bronco this afternoon, tag along with a fellow like your cousin. Figuring that the kid can't do any damage, can't screw up too bad. I mean he's in the family, Memo has to watch out for him. But then something goes wrong, Gil Suarez gets away, makes a run for it. And all that tension that's been building between the cartel and Memo starts to boil over."

On Kelly's desk the phone began to ring. Jeanie raised her ears but didn't move from her spot beneath the desk. Out in the office Pierce turned, then rose from his desk and started toward them. After only half a step, every phone in the office was ringing.

Tom looked down at the phone and then he looked up at Tollville.

"Your cousin isn't in oil anymore, is he?"

Tom watched Pierce where he stood, the phone cord dangling from the receiver he held in his hand.

"I haven't seen Ray in a long time," Tom said. Behind Tollville, Tom saw Pierce raise his radio to his lips and depress the button.

Tollville turned and looked to where Tom's gaze had fallen.

"What now?" Tom asked.

"We wait," Tollville said. "If this is anything like ten years ago I expect there will be some cartel figures going down in very bloody ways."

On the radio, Pierce kept repeating the same few words over and over again. "Tate Bulger." "Smoke." "Fire."

ARIO SAT IN HIS OFFICE. THE AMMONIA SMELL
of piss and bleach leaking in from the nearby bathrooms, and the low sound of the men out in the bar. The
sheriff gone and Dario feeling a strange loneliness as he listened to the men outside and knew he wanted nothing to do
with any of them. He had been honest with Kelly in a way he
thought he hadn't been honest in a long time.

Still, he was disappointed to hear about the body she'd found
out in the Bronco. All that he had hoped would come—his own
gamble, his test for the inevitable—now nothing but a disappointment. Kelly had not come to talk to him about the old
man they'd left beaten bloody at his house. Dario's knuckles
still tender where he'd crushed them into the man's face, split-
ting the swollen skin and watching the blood bloom. Kelly
had come because everything in Coronado was now moving
toward its end, and perhaps Dario knew that just as she did.

He dug out the small knife from his desk, and listening to
the men outside he threw it time and time again toward the
floor, watching the blade stick and quiver. No idea if the body
out there in the Bronco was Ray Lamar's. No hope anymore
for anything. Dario's life just the same as it had been days and
weeks before.

He heard the voices of the men rise for a moment, and then
the dissonant sound of laughter. He didn't understand anything about this life. Just a day before they'd been in a gun

battle, and now they were laughing about it. All he understood was that one day it would be his turn and he doubted anyone would care.

R AY SAW THE RED GLOW OF THE OIL FIRE WHERE it lay flat and orange as an eclipse along the horizon, all of it dark in the night and the thin band of light where the well burned. Ray drove his father's truck, the harsh smell of oil all over his hands and the deep carbon scent of fire floating around in the cab.

He slowed as one of the county cruisers flew by, heading south, the bubble lights going around and the silent pull of the wind as the car went by in a wash of air. Ahead the dim aura of light showed above Coronado.

Any hope for his future now gone with the death of his father and the rejection he'd felt from Billy. Ray didn't know the boy like he'd thought he would after all these years. What had he expected? What had he thought the boy would do? Had he thought Billy would just run into his arms like some happy movie? Well, that just wasn't how it was, or ever would be. Not for Ray.

On the seat next to him was a double-barreled shotgun he'd taken from his father's house, the metal gleaming from the years Gus had spent caring for the thing, disassembling it and wiping at it with a rag he kept especially for that purpose. Ray had found the shotgun in the hallway closet, where it had always been.

Farther back he found the thin, aged cardboard boxes. Three of them there, each one containing a different shell, number-eight shot for quail, number-six for duck, and number-two for mule deer or antelope. He pulled a selection of shells from each of the boxes, feeding them down into his pockets as he went.

"Are you about to do something stupid?" he said. Speaking to himself as he went on down the road, remembering a night years ago when Marianne had asked him the same question. The oil gone from the land and Memo still new to their lives. Ray just kneeling there at the closet with his hands held down on the Ruger and the clip slid out far enough that he could see how many bullets were inside.

A month later she'd be dead and he'd go on to do a hundred other things he couldn't take back and that he'd always regret. His father was one of them now and he looked over at the shotgun and thought how his life had gone wrong all those years before and there was no stopping it now.

On his hip he felt the pager giving off a steady vibration. He pulled it up and looked at the number again. He was sure Memo must have heard by now about the Sullivan house, and maybe even about Sanchez, either on the news or listening in over the police scanner. Ray didn't care. Memo's business wasn't

Ray's anymore, not in the way it used to be, and those drugs could just rot under the desert soil for all it mattered to Ray.

In his rearview he saw the glimmer of red and blue as the cruiser disappeared into the night behind him. He put down the window and threw the pager out. He didn't want anything to do with it now and he could feel a storm brewing inside him he could do little to quiet. No plan at all for his future except for the road ahead and where it led.

K ELLY FELT THE WIND SHIFT. THE HEAT moving over onto them till the air boiled against their skin, and Hastings raised a hand and started to back slow toward the cruiser. The black smoke overhead disappeared into the night, and the rush of the fire coming off the wells spilled up into the sky as if out of a jet engine.

"Christ," Hastings said, his hand held up toward the flames, shielding his face from the heat.

Kelly backed away, watching how the fire billowed up. Flames rising thirty feet into the air and snapping at the black clouds of oil being burned, the skeleton of the well now only a thin cage of metal around it all, pulsing red with heat where it came exposed and naked from the fire.

None of it felt right to her and she backed away toward the

cruiser with the rush of the flames heard in her ears like a high wind cutting across a mountain ridge. Where were the protesters, the oil workers with their signs and picket lines? The whole landscape completely empty and only her and Hastings backing away as the heat rolled over on top of them. The volunteer firefighters not there as she'd hoped they would be. Probably still pulling their boots on.

Pierce had gotten her on the radio as soon as she'd come out of the bar, his voice breathless as he told her about the calls coming in from all over the valley. The tower of black smoke climbing dark into the last pale strands of sun over the Tate Bulger well to the southeast.

The heat on them and Kelly making it back to the cruiser first, her fist jamming the transmission into reverse as Hastings took his seat. They spun back along the access road, the well spitting flame before them and the sand beneath their tires kicked up through their headlights as Kelly tried to keep them out of the heat.

Nothing was right about any of it and when she got Pierce on the radio, she asked for his position.

"Just where you told me to be," came the response.

"You're not too close?"

"I'm a block up from the bar, I can see the front door and I can see if anyone leaves."

"Good," Kelly said. "Stay there, we'll be back as soon as we can."

Tollville and Tom Herrera waiting for her in her office, listening in the whole while. A fear inside her, and a feeling of helplessness about the things she wanted to protect but could not. Several miles to the north she saw the blaze of the fire engine's lights traveling down the highway to meet them.

"There's no way they'll be able to stop this thing, is there?" Hastings said.

"No," Kelly said. "This isn't the type of thing you can stop. It'll burn itself out soon enough. Until then it's just a matter of letting it go."

THROUGH THE DEPARTMENT WINDOWS, TOM heard a distant sound he couldn't quite figure. Something like a wrecking ball tearing through cement and rebar, metal on stone. Stepping close to the window, he stared out into the night, his reflection looking back at him out of the pane. The echo hanging in the air for a moment before all went silent again. He turned from the window, watching as his ghost turned away as well.

Upstairs he knew Claire was probably working. She'd be putting in a full day, trying to make up for what she missed. He thought about her now and what she'd offered, to simply drive back with him to his place, to leave all this behind. He'd

had his chance to say something to Tollville, to reveal everything, the bodies adding up, and the origins of it all. Only he
hadn't wanted to in that moment, knew now that perhaps
there would never be a perfect time. His own cousin, Ray, at
the heart of it all.

In the office Tom saw Tollville watching him where he
stood next to the windows. Tollville waited, his head half
turned, listening for anything more. Neither of them with any
idea what had happened until Deputy Pierce's voice sprang up
on the radio, fluttering between excitement and fear, followed
closely by the echo of gunfire reverberating up the street.

A LL SENSE OF CONTROL HAD LEFT RAY. WITH
a penny he'd taken the plates from the truck and then
scraped off the VIN, throwing the plates into a nearby
Dumpster with all of the paperwork from the glove. He'd tied
the wheel of his father's truck straight with his belt, securing
it all down, then depressed the accelerator with a spare piece
of timber he'd found in the bed. And then he'd just let the
truck go.

The big truck, weighing a half ton or more, sped out of
the side street, across the intersection, and rammed Dario's
bar headfirst, pitching forward on its front axle as if it were

a boat punching through the first big swell of surf, breaking through the spray. Glass and brick and metal, all of it suspended for a moment in the air. The back axle of the truck hanging for a moment before it rocked to the ground in a crush of metal. The deadening sound lingering, tactile and solid as he brought the shotgun around, his pace quickening as he crossed Main.

He came on toward the bar, two number-six shells in the belly of the gun and the Ruger loose in his waistband. The front of the bar now just a pile of rubble. The hood of the truck sitting about five feet inside the barroom with the front tires pushed over what remained of the outer wall. Brick dust everywhere and the sound of men coughing.

Ray climbed up over the rubble and entered the bar. The spark of an overhead electrical fixture cast a muted light everywhere about the place. Like lightning through a sandstorm. Dario's men now regaining their feet with nothing but the fine claylike brick dust all around them in the air.

Ray opened up with the barrel of the shotgun and took three men down in one blast, the birdshot playing heavy into all of them. Each number-six shell carrying with it a little over two hundred lead BBs. The men falling back against the wall, or landing full on the floor, guns still in hands. Blood beginning to show on their faces and clothes from every little ball that had found skin.

Ray pulled the trigger again. Firing into the clouded room.

Firing after the sound of men breathing. The echo of the gun swallowing anything that remained.

When Ray found cover near the broken remnants of the wood bar, they were firing at him out of the settling dust. Splintering up the bar as the bullets dug in. It was impossible to see anything through the brick smoke and the men went on firing blindly while Ray thought about what he needed to do.

He broke the shotgun open and fingered out the two shells, steaming and warm in his hand. He let them fall to the ground. With the Ruger he fired shots into the corners of the room until the magazine was spent and there was just the dull click of the hammer hitting against the empty chamber. The remaining guns opened up on him immediately. With the Ruger left behind him, he moved down around the back of the bar with the shotgun in both hands, keeping low.

Deep in his pocket he found two of the double-aught shells and played them into the barrel. Each one big enough to take down a mule deer.

He tried to steady himself there at the end of the bar with the taste of gun smoke bitter in his mouth and the chalk-dry smell of the brick dust billowing in through his nostrils. Up ahead the gunfire was still coming from somewhere in front of him. He marked the shooters and rose up and pulled the trigger, releasing both barrels. Ray heard the solid thump of the buck finding human contact. A man called out and then slowly whimpered to a stop.

IN THE BACK ROOM OF THE BAR DARIO TOOK OUT the .45 he kept in the drawer of his desk. The sound of gunfire coming in under the door as steady as smoke filling a room in a fire, creeping upward into the room until every bit could be felt crawling down his throat. He stood from the desk, watching the door. Every burst of gunfire rattling at the wood as the walls pulsed inward with every blast.

A crazed smile on his face, half-desperate in its making, thin and sharp as the first crease of skin beneath a knife blade. A shroud thrown over the air like death's own cloak come down on him. He crossed the room now, watching the door and anticipating every new shot before it came. His expectant gaze caught between where he wanted to be and where he knew he needed to be in the next minute or so. The steady kick of the shotgun outside his door and the jitter it sent rolling through his nerves like some sort of electric shock.

Not a single window in the room, and the door leading out into the main bar his only option. He took the vest from the file cabinet in the corner and strapped it to his chest beneath his suit jacket. Gunfire dying back till there was only the eeriness of the silence that followed.

THERE WAS A LONG PAUSE OVER THE RADIO AS Kelly and Hastings sat in the cruiser, the volume all the way up, and the rush of flame somewhere beyond them in the darkness. No sound but the hiss of the radio, speckled all over with static and the crush of their own breathing.

"Pierce," Kelly said, calling his name several more times, and then the sound of gunfire once more and the silence that followed.

"He's so fucking scared he's got his hand held down on the button and he's not letting up," Hastings said.

Kelly swore. She turned the ignition over and slammed the transmission down into reverse. The headlights in front of them still focused on the flames that licked out of the black smoke, popping as they snapped upright and then fell away.

She called Pierce's name once more before giving the car gas. The wheels spinning in the dust and the cruiser rocketing back over the dirt road, leading to the highway.

The town fire truck swerving out of their way as they came off the road, their tires dragging a cloud of dust onto the asphalt.

THERE WAS NO GOING BACK, AND RAY WENT from body to body, looking for any sign of life. Eight men total in the room, Ray turned each of them over as he came to them, searching for Dario. Two of the eight were still alive, one with his arm pinned beneath the truck tire, bone showing and the blood welling from an artery. Another winged by buckshot on his left side. The shallow breathing of a punctured lung, with a smear of blood peppered on his lips as he tried to suck more air than he had the strength to take. Neither of them able to form words when Ray knelt and asked them about Dario, the blood loss already showing in the paleness of their skin and the blue-tinged curve of their lips.

Ray shot both at close range. The sound of those two solitary shots hanging there in the air for a long time as he waited for the dust to clear. Sure at any moment he would hear the sound of sirens.

He dug out the steaming shells and loaded two more. Turning, he saw the door to the office. The door locked when he reached out a hand to try the knob.

Using the shotgun he took the lock out with one shell, then stood back around the cover of the wall. Nothing moved inside the office and he broke the rifle open and thumbed out the empty.

T HROUGH THE DEPARTMENT RADIO TOM AND Tollville were listening to the play-by-play description of what was going on outside the bar. Pierce's voice heard strong through the speakers. The loud cacophony of gunshots following close behind.

Tom standing close enough to the small four-inch speaker that he heard every gasp and breath the young deputy had made in those few short minutes, relaying the news to Kelly.

"Jesus, fuck, Jesus," Pierce kept saying, over and over again. Kelly trying to calm him, but the boy not listening. The sound of her sirens heard blaring overhead as she and Hastings rushed back toward town.

From what Tom had been able to glean from the frantic transmission, Pierce was a block up the street from the bar in his cruiser when the truck rolled through the intersection and took out the front wall of the bar.

Across the office Tollville had his jacket off. He was rummaging through one of the closets and when he found the sheriff's department vests, he strapped one down over his shoulders. The gun butt at his hip exposed against his white dress shirt. "How far away are we?" Tollville asked, the sound of gunfire snapping his head around as he tried to locate the source.

"Three blocks."

"How long will it take Edna to get back to town?"

Tom hesitated to answer. "Twenty, twenty-five minutes," he

said, watching Tollville kneel and remove a nine-millimeter Baby Eagle from the strap at his ankle.

"Are you up for this?" Tollville asked.

Again, Pierce's voice cut through them in a rush, his voice catching in the static.

"Stay there," Kelly said.

Pierce was talking so fast it was hard to hear him, saying something about a man and a shotgun, and the blasts of light that were appearing out of what was left of the bar.

"Stay in the car," Kelly said. "Just stay put."

Tollville tossed the Baby Eagle to Tom and told him to grab one of the vests. "You've been helping Kelly," he said, "and now I need you to help me."

Tom looked down at the nine-millimeter in his hand. He had come here to turn Ray in, he'd come here because it was the only thing he could do anymore. The only hope Ray had for some sort of salvation, but Tom could see even Ray was beyond salvation now. He knew already it was Ray who had crossed the street with a shotgun in his hands, walking straight on toward Dario's bar. No hope in the world for the men inside, for Ray, or even for the man Tom had always thought himself to be. He looked down at the gun in his hand, thinking about all that lay waiting for them three blocks away. And when he looked up, he said, "We're going to need more than just the two of us."

Tollville smiled now, looking at Tom as if something funny

had been said and Tollville had known the punch line all along. "For what?" Tollville asked. "You know something I don't know?" The smug tone of his voice telling Tom all he needed to know.

"I'll do my duty on this," Tom said. "I'll put on the vest and go down there with you, but I've got no clearance for the support you need right now. This whole department isn't enough for what's going on down there."

Tollville stared at him for only a moment before picking up the phone. A few seconds later he was on the line with the state police. Tom waited only long enough to see it was done before he pushed past Tollville and went up the stairs toward Main Street, Pierce, and the bar ahead. A sick feeling all the way through him.

With each step he felt himself moving faster and faster, until he was running. The vest heavy against his body as he moved, his lungs fighting the material with every breath and the thick weight of the straps as they shifted on his shoulders. Looking back, he couldn't see Tollville yet and he thought he'd bought himself a little time. To do what? He didn't know, and he focused again on the street ahead and the bar, and all that lay before him.

When he came to the cruiser he saw Pierce where he sat, his hands held tight in front of him on the dash, with his service weapon closed in his palms. A husk of fear papered thin across his face.

Down the block the truck sat buried halfway through the front wall of the bar. Even without the plates he knew it instantly. Bent and scraped, dinged and punched in all along its sides, the truck was Gus's.

Tom knocked at the passenger side of Pierce's cruiser, cautious not to startle him any further as he waited for the window to come down and Pierce's eyes to meet his own. "Tollville asked me to help out," Tom said. "I'm going to go around back and watch the lot there. You stay here and watch the front. Tollville is calling in the state police and we'll hold tight on this building for the time being."

Pierce looked shaken, his eyes skittering and coming up short as they rose and tried to focus.

"I need you on this, Pierce." The Baby Eagle grown slick in Tom's hand. Sweat felt hot in the creases of his palm. The first time he'd held a gun in almost ten years.

Pierce nodded. Down the street the sound of a single shotgun blast fell out of the bar and rolled past them. Both men ducked at the sound. No sign of Tollville or Kelly anywhere as Tom settled himself for the run across Main, his eyes already picking out the path he would take as he made his way toward the lot behind Dario's bar.

THE SHOTGUN BLAST HAD PLAYED DARIO'S office door back on its hinges. The lock completely gone from the wood and the door hanging open a foot into the small room. All around Dario the smell of cordite was suspended in the air, haunting him where he crouched with his back to the corner.

Dario held the .45 with two hands, his shoulders pressed tight together between the file cabinet and the wall. His skin gone clammy beneath the weight of the vest and a trail of sweat down the small of his back.

Outside he heard the shotgun shell fall to the ground and then the hollow sound of another sliding into place. He was watching the door and his shoulders were beginning to cramp. The ache of his muscles tense beneath the skin and a raw excitement as he pulled the slide back on the pistol and waited.

The shotgun barrel came through the door first, swinging wide to either side of the frame, pushing out the door on its hinges till the wood played back all the way to the wall. The shotgun searching the room like a snake, tasting the air.

Dario marked a point two feet above where the barrel of the shotgun showed, waiting for the singular tell of flesh. He held the gun straight out now. Sweat brimming his brow before falling into his eyes, where he blinked it away.

Come on now, he thought, watching the door, the gun held out and his eyes searching the empty space beyond. Come on.

RAY KNEW SOMEONE WAS INSIDE THE OFFICE but he couldn't tell where. He let the shotgun feel around for a moment, looking in through the door at what little he could see.

No way of telling where Dario was unless he stepped through the doorway. The only things he could see a desk at the center of the room with one buckshot brick wall behind and the two corners of the room to either side of the desk. Except for the wall behind, the office was penned in by cheap drywall on a wood frame. Taking a step back from the door, he cracked the shotgun open and looked in on the shells inside. Buckshot all the way through.

With the light leaking out of the office and falling onto the cement floor of the bar, Ray walked a few paces down the hall to where he judged the end of the office to be and pulled the trigger, blasting the wall open. Working quickly he walked back through the light coming from the office and blasted the other wall. Listening as a quick gasp escaped through the perforated holes in the drywall.

Dario lay wounded on the floor inside the office when Ray came in. He had one hand held to his neck, a creasing of red beginning to show between his fingers. His body flat on the office floor as he kicked out a leg, pushing through dust and pieces of wood with the pain of the shot. A tempering of buck all along his jacket, where the lead shot had bit through and caught against the metal plate of the vest. One shot finding Dario's neck.

Ray bent and picked the .45 from the floor, holding it loose in his hand. "Clever," Ray said, as he used the nose of the shotgun to open Dario's suit jacket and look in at the vest and the damage done. The man younger than Ray had expected, a sheen of sweat now glistening on his face, wetting the edges of his hair.

"I hoped for you," Dario said, his hand to the wound on his neck, his own red blood in the creases of his fingers, and his voice weak.

Dario worked himself up, his head pitched against the bottom of the desk and his chin forced against his sternum, pinching his windpipe and causing his breath to whistle in the silence of the room.

"I could have killed you," Ray said.

"You should have," Dario said. He was looking up at Ray from where he lay, the pain showing on his face.

Ray knelt and put the .45 in his waistband where his own Ruger had been. He took Dario's hand away from the wound, watching as a stream of blood erupted onto the office floor. "You're not in good shape," Ray said. "You could live through this but I doubt you will."

Dario grinned, his lips pulled tight toward their edges with the pain. "Funny how things turn out," he said. His hand back over the wound, slippery with blood, and his face a chalk-white color that Ray figured there was no returning from. "Nothing ever turns out the way you think it will."

"No it doesn't," Ray said. "But I hear that a lot in this line of work and the more I hear it the less I try to think about the outcome." Standing now, he toed at Dario's hand with his boot and watched the blood bubble up between Dario's fingers. The look in Dario's eyes like a gut-shot coyote, full of hate, cut down and lying broken in the dirt.

Ray had already been in the bar far too long and he looked around the room with wonderment, amazed he was still alive. The blood on Dario's hand unbelievably red against the whiteness of his skin.

"You're going to die," Ray said. He looked to the door and then he turned to leave.

"You can't," Dario said. His voice quickened and his eyes pleading with Ray to stop. "I made a deal with Memo. I deserve more than this. I shouldn't be the one lying here on this floor."

Ray stopped at the mention of his boss and looked to Dario.

"I told him where Burnham would be and at what time. I set him and Gil up."

Ray stared down at Dario where he lay. The blood now all over Dario's hand and glistening black and wet from the collar of his jacket.

Dario laughed. His face covered in sweat and a desperate

smile across his lips as he looked up at Ray. "Seems like Memo didn't mention that to you. Seems like there's a lot Memo didn't mention."

Ray looked down, trying to understand. Years ago, Memo had promised Ray everything. He had promised it would all work out, that all would be fine and that if Ray did the work he would be protected. None of that had come true and Ray had lost his wife and abandoned his son, believing somehow the cartel had found him, found his family—all of it unclear in his mind now. All of it turned upside down.

"Memo's guarantees aren't worth a thing," Dario said. "No one was supposed to die and none of what has happened should have happened." He was watching Ray where he stood, and he tried to push himself up higher on the desk, but he was too weak and his hand flopped loose on the floor, useless against his side. "It was a simple plan that went too far."

"My father is dead."

"I know," Dario said.

"He didn't know anything."

Dario kept his eyes focused on Ray's. "I can help you," Dario said. "You're not alone in this. Not anymore. You'll go after Memo but you'll never make it. I can help you. I can help you get there."

Ray laughed, the sound sudden and cruel in the silence of the office. He stared at Dario a moment longer before leaving him there on the floor.

Tom waited behind the bar. Not knowing what to do, thinking that Tollville must by now have met up with Pierce, and even at that moment, was probably making his move on the front of the bar.

Tom had been in the back for almost a minute. His legs stiff where he leaned against a small cinder-block wall, half his height, which allowed him a view toward the bar. His ears tuned now to all there was around him, listening to the night and the strange silence of the town sitting there with the absence of gunfire.

Two minutes passed before Ray came out the back door and stood in the moonlight. He was covered in dust, and he carried an old double-barreled shotgun in his hands.

"Aren't we a pair," Ray said when he saw Tom crouched at the wall, the Baby Eagle in his hand, resting over the top, barrel pointed toward Ray.

Tom stood, his arm shaky with the gun.

"I see you've been deputized," Ray said, nodding toward the sheriff's department vest Tom wore. "Was that what they gave you for turning me in?"

"I haven't said one thing against you," Tom said. "It's just me here, you don't have to worry about anyone else."

"Doesn't matter," Ray said. "Not anymore."

Tom looked from Ray to the back door. He didn't know where Tollville was. And he wasn't quite sure what he would do if the DEA agent found them there in the back lot of the bar, having a conversation like two men on a smoke break. "I'm not sure how this is supposed to work," Tom said. "I offered you a chance before and you didn't take it."

"You should have known it wasn't going to end that way for me."

"Yes, I should have," Tom said. "But somewhere along the way I hoped maybe it could."

Ray grinned. There was blood splattered on the front of his shirt and up beneath his chin. Tom was certain none of it was Ray's. "It doesn't have to end for us this way, either," Ray said.

"Ray," Tom said, and then stopped short, not knowing how to go on. But knowing he had to—that something had to be said and that Tom was perhaps the only one who could say it. "You've taken this too far, you've hurt yourself in the process, and I think you know the only thing—the best thing for you, is to turn yourself in."

"You didn't want any part of me before, why should you want any part now?"

"Don't force this, Ray," Tom said.

Ray took a step toward the street.

"Don't," Tom said, the Baby Eagle in his hand, held steady on his cousin. Tom's voice sharp in the stillness of the night, hanging there between them in the silence.

Ray took another step, watching Tom the whole way. He

never raised the shotgun more than a few inches from the ground, never pointed it toward Tom.

"Ray, don't force my hand," Tom said. But even he knew the tone of his voice had betrayed him. He knew he could never shoot Ray and that it was a mistake even being here, but that he'd had to come. He had to see it for himself to understand it all. His cousin and what he was capable of.

"You want to point that gun at someone," Ray said, "you'll go inside. You were never going to help me with what needed to be done. But you'll see that the job is finished and if you ever cared about my father, you'll understand why it needed to be done." He took another step and kept moving. His feet carrying him not toward Tom, but away. He was around the edge of the bar and crossing the street to the opposite side before Tom felt the Baby Eagle drop, hanging loose in his hand against his thigh. The back door to the bar partially open and only the bleakest of hopes for those inside as he ran across the lot.

The odor of spilled liquor and the metallic taste of blood came out of the bar to meet him, the door pulled wide, and a fog of clay dust suspended everywhere in the air all the way to the front. He let it all wash over him for a moment before stepping into the murk within. His eyes adjusting and the thin track of the hallway going on ahead of him for a space of fifteen feet before opening into the larger bar. As he went forward he crouched, listening for any sounds ahead.

A brief fall and clatter of masonry heard ahead of him and then the crush of brick underfoot. "Tollville?" he called, his voice weaker than he'd expected. He called the agent's name again and waited for a response as something electrical popped and fizzled out. The bar lit for a moment with a pale blue light, showing the haze of gunfire still in the air.

Tom waited, listening to what lay ahead. The thin scuffle of footsteps again and then Tollville's voice calling his name out of the haze.

Somewhere in between, down the hallway, Tom heard a choking cough rise out of the air, repeat several times, and then fall silent. The sound, Tom thought, of someone drowning.

WALKING QUICKLY UP MAIN, TRYING TO GET his thoughts in order, Ray dug the used shells from the shotgun, letting them fall warm to the street. With the empty sound of the plastic clattering up off the concrete behind him, he went on.

He'd come out of the bar thinking about all the years compounded behind him, built up solid as anything in his life. Where he'd been. What he'd done. And he realized that that road leading south—the one that had left his son mute and his wife dead—led north as well.

Marianne's car broadsided right off the road and the dark scar of those double tire tracks left there on the cement like some sort of calling card that Ray hadn't, until now, had any idea how to read. Though he'd tried. He'd given his heart to it all these years, hoping to replace something inside him that there was no replacement for.

All of it had been a setup. Marianne all those years before, all the way to Burnham where he lay on the ground three days ago, bleeding that pale watery blood from the side of his cheek, trying to speak the words Ray just wasn't ready to hear: Memo was playing crooked with all of them.

Jesus, Ray thought, the rules have changed and nothing is the same.

He'd been in the bar only a few minutes. Still, it had been too much, his thoughts now turned to what he would do and where he would go. He'd let it continue for too long, realized somewhere along the line that he'd even enjoyed it. He had to remind himself now that his father was dead. A man who— at his end—had known Ray only as a memory.

Ray had to think about that. Nothing else mattered, not the drugs or his life. A pressure in his chest he was all too familiar with, a white-hot pain carrying him forward.

All he had left was birdshot and he brought up a set of shells and played them down into the barrels. A car came to a stop a block off, its headlights on him. The driver sat there stunned, then pushed the car into reverse. Ray snapped the breach closed and moved away across the street, turning now to keep his eyes on the bar, not expecting to see Tom again, but not leaving anything to chance.

He hadn't expected to make it and the thought that he was alive seemed wondrous and strange. He kept moving away from the bar, the shotgun at the ready, with no real plan other than to get north to Las Cruces, to Memo, and to the office where he'd taken his first job.

T HEY WERE TOO FAR AWAY AND KELLY KNEW IT. Nothing from Pierce for five minutes and then his voice over the radio, bristling with panic, as he described for them what he was seeing before him on the street.

"Say again," Kelly said. The lights of Coronado only a few minutes ahead of them.

"He's just walking up the street."

"Who is?"

"The man with the shotgun."

"Stay there, Pierce," Kelly said. "Don't move from where you are, just stay right there." Beside her, Hastings had taken the Mossberg twelve-gauge off the stand and he was feeding shells into the body.

The night air outside her window rushed by, Coronado

ahead, and no way for her to be where she knew she needed to be at that moment.

"He's going to walk away," Pierce said, his voice diminished, as if coming from a distance, or in a rush. Then nothing and only Kelly left there on the radio feed calling Pierce's name.

A VOICE CAUGHT RAY MIDSTRIDE. RAY MOVED his head around slow till he could see the young deputy where he stood, holding his service weapon on Ray. The open door of the deputy's cruiser acting as a kind of shield to protect him, and almost no chance of using the shotgun at that distance. Perhaps the deputy would catch one, but most likely he'd just spray the car down with birdshot, all of it going into the metal.

The deputy calling for him to throw the shotgun down.

All Ray knew was that he wanted to get away, as far away from this town as he could get. With the deputy still yelling at him, Ray lowered himself to the ground, crouching low so that he could lay the shotgun flat out on the cement. It had been stupid to think that there was a possibility of making it out of Coronado alive. As he raised his hands up, he brought Dario's .45 with him.

The sound of the shot echoed out on the silent street, and Ray looked down at his side where the blood had begun to flow, and soak at the material of his shirt. The deputy still holding his gun on him, a look of shock and confusion painted on his face.

Ray put a hand over the wound and felt the warm blood on his skin. He dropped to one knee, the pain coming now, and the ache of the bullet's path through his skin.

With his eyes still on the deputy, Ray brought the .45 up and fired toward the deputy three times, aiming beneath the patrol car door, for the deputy's feet. The young deputy called out as one of the bullets hit, and he rolled out into the street.

Ray lurched to life. Pulling himself up, he limped forward. Warm blood now soaking down into Ray's jeans, the gun faced out on the deputy while the other hand held tight to the wound as his frayed muscles ground like sandpaper against his movements.

No time for the shotgun. Nothing left in Ray but the desire—pure as anything he'd felt in his life—for escape.

As Ray came closer, the deputy raised his own gun and Ray shot him once in the shoulder. The deputy's gun flying and Ray moving forward till he was standing over the young boy. The deputy sucking in hoarse breaths of air, his lungs gone shallow and the pain evident on his face.

Ray bent and whipped him across the temple with the butt of the .45, hard enough to knock him unconscious.

TOM WAS ALREADY ON THE OFFICE PHONE WITH the paramedics when he heard the single pistol shot outside. Tollville looking up from where he crouched, holding a handkerchief to Dario's neck. The white cloth beneath Tollville's hands a blood-red color and the thin glistening of liquid shimmering in the dim office light.

Dario long since gone unconscious and Tollville with his hands held to the man's neck as he looked up toward Tom. "You know I can't leave," Tollville said. "I can't leave him here."

Tom hadn't said a thing to Tollville about Ray. How could he? Every minute he was in there—every minute he didn't say something he fell a little farther down a rabbit hole of his own making. There was simply too much to explain now and he hoped with every second that he could somehow find his own way out.

Outside they heard three more shots, loud as the first but with a wild urgency. Tollville's eyes fixed on him till he couldn't take it anymore and he went running out of the office and through the bar. He had no plan but to get outside, away from Tollville and the stink of blood.

What he saw was worse than he expected, and he found himself moving fast, up the street and toward the receding taillights of the county cruiser as it went north. A body in the street that he hoped was not Ray's and in the same scope of time knew was Pierce's.

The boy there in the street with his gun fallen on the cement a few feet away. He was shot through the flesh of his shoulder and through the foot. The boy stiff where he lay on the street and a surge of fear through Tom that the boy might be dead. Guilt strong and fluid as it washed over him.

Kneeling, Tom felt Pierce's slow breathing. A welt on the boy's face that was now beginning to swell and that Tom knew must have been where Ray had hit him. Pierce was shot twice, but in places that Tom hoped would spare his life.

Up the street the taillights could only now be seen as a small blinking beacon of light far ahead. He looked behind him toward the bar, then farther still, south toward Mexico and all that lay along the highway. A blue and red shimmer of light he knew was Kelly.

In a little over a minute she would be there with him, asking questions Tom couldn't answer. So he left Pierce there in the road for Kelly. She would be there soon enough and in the meantime, Tom knew he would run, chasing after those taillights, Luis's truck keys in his hand, and no idea whatsoever of what was to come next.

K ELLY STOPPED HER CRUISER JUST A FEW FEET shy of the bar. A pickup truck with missing plates sitting there with its rear wheels on the sidewalk and the front hood and cab of the truck all the way through the wall of the bar. Her eyes lingered on this for only a moment. Hastings got up out of the cruiser with the wash of the lights now seen on his skin as he closed the door and Kelly searched ahead of them for Pierce's cruiser.

No sign of the bubble lights anywhere down the line of cars parked on Main and no radio contact from Pierce at all. Farther up, an ambulance rounded the corner, where the cross street for the hospital sat, with the wail of the sirens reverberating down the street.

Shielding her eyes from the red and white flash, she reached for the center console and brought up the radio again, repeating Pierce's name several more times and listening for a response.

It was only when the ambulance slowed several hundred feet ahead of her, its wheels turned sideways, that she saw the dark shape of a body lying in the street.

R AY PUSHED THE CRUISER PAST EIGHTY, THE speedometer climbing, the needle cresting ninety and still moving. All around him nothing but the empty desert. The lights of Coronado behind him, and the terrible pain in his side where the bullet had gone in. Blood soaking its way up through his shirt, and the sweat showing on his forehead as he drove.

In forty-five minutes he'd hit the interstate, and then, if he didn't pass out and roll the car, he'd get himself to Deming. Ditch the car and find a place to heal before he made his move on Las Cruces. Going after Dario had been a rash decision, he could see that now. Still, it hadn't been the cartel men who had shot him, but some deputy, half his age. There was some comfort in that, and he went on with the pain in his side pulsing beneath the skin every time he shifted in his seat.

Looking down at himself in the dim interior light of the cruiser he saw the dirty hole where the bullet had punched through the shirt. With his free hand he raised the cloth and surveyed the damage, a slick sparkle of blood high on his skin, like a fine, dark syrup over everything.

He was a mess and there was no way he would get past any motel clerks looking the way he did. Shirt stained with blood. Smelling of gunpowder, sweat, and murder. There was barely a chance he would make it to the interstate driving the way he was in a stolen county cruiser, swerving into the opposite lane to pass cars and the long semis heading north.

He just had to keep going. The cruiser feeling smooth and powerful beneath him. He hoped the deputy wouldn't die. The boy just a child really, probably one year out of high school. Too young for something like this. For this mess.

He swerved out into oncoming traffic, passing another big truck. Almost clipping an oncoming car as he swerved back into his lane and heard the semi's air brakes squeal behind him. Jesus, he thought. Stay focused. You still have a chance, just forty-five more minutes and you can put this all behind you.

WHEN KELLY MADE IT TO PIERCE, HIS SKIN was already brittle and flimsy as wax paper. His breathing gone shallow and labored. Blood all over the cement. But the paramedics were telling her there was someone down at the bar in far worse shape with a critical neck wound. They gave her a compress and moved on, leaving her there with Pierce.

She knelt next to him, pressing the compress to his shoulder, trying to wake him any way she could. Hastings, who had followed her at a run, had already gone back down the street, going for the patrol car, intending to bring it up the street so that they could get Pierce into the back and take him to the hospital.

There had been training for this type of thing, but all that just didn't seem to register. Raising her voice, Kelly realized she was yelling now, trying to get the boy to wake. Her voice carrying down the street with no one around.

Blindly, without thinking or really knowing what she was doing, she began to drag him up the street toward the hospital. A nasty-looking welt at the side of his temple and bullet wounds in his shoulder and foot. His shoes scraping on the cement as they went.

Where was Tom? Where was Tollville? Not a single person on the street, and Kelly dragging the boy beneath his armpits. Her own muscles beginning to ache with the effort. And Tollville now beside her, telling her to stop, to just put him down, that another ambulance was coming. He'd been on the phone to the state police, asking them to block the roads.

ONE HUNDRED MILES AN HOUR OVER THE blacktop and the bleeding hadn't stopped. Ray reached down and pushed his palm into the flat at the side of his ribs. Sudden pain and his vision drifting.

He didn't know if he would make it. Shot just above the gut like that. Blood all over him. Driving a stolen county cruiser right on into a major southwest city. He just couldn't see how it would play.

Up ahead the slight red and blue glimmer he knew was a state police cruiser, cresting the hill ten miles down the road. The highway leading on toward the Hermanos Mountains, no other roads to take, and a certainty the state police would block the highway off in the coming minutes, leaving Ray no way of making it to the north.

The turnoff for his father's place coming up fast, just two hundred yards away. He eased off the gas, taking the turn at a rough forty miles per hour, the back tires of the cruiser spinning in the gravel and the headlights sweeping the desert. A searing pain as he braced himself against the door.

He righted himself and went on.

T HE BRAKE LIGHTS WERE JUST BARELY VISIBLE in front of Tom as he followed the cruiser up the highway. No idea how fast he was going, his father's old pickup vibrating with the speed as the wind sloughed off and whistled past his mirrors. Even after five minutes the truck hadn't gotten any closer. The cruiser brake lights were barely visible in front of him. Then nothing.

Tom slowed the truck, rolling down his window as he came up on the spot he'd seen the brake lights go off the road. Cool air and a full moon above slipping through a series of dark clouds.

Nothing out there in the flatness but the dim shape of desert brush. Darkness beyond.

He drove on, taking it slow now, not wanting to miss anything. All around him the open blackness of the desert and a feeling of bewildered solitude. He had lost Ray and run from Kelly. There was little he could do now but go on and hope it would somehow turn out for him.

In the glove compartment he found a flashlight, and he pulled it out now and played it over the creosote and chuparosa growing off the bank of the road. Somewhere to the south the night air lit up bright with the flash of lightning, the thunder following a few seconds behind.

When he came to the intersection, he knew exactly where he was, and where the cruiser had gone. He pulled the truck down off the highway, feeling the tires leave the cement, and the dirt begin. The Lamar ranch just up the road.

THE ROOM HAD THE METALLIC TASTE OF BLOOD in the air. Kelly crept over the hood of the truck and slid into what was left of the barroom. Holding her gun out in front of her, she brought her flashlight up from her belt and flicked it on. The room was a complete mess. Chairs and tables upturned, walls broken up with gunfire—glass and wood splinters everywhere on the floor.

Behind her, she heard Tollville's feet touch down on the

brick rubble beside the truck tires. The crunch of his footfalls loud in the stillness of the bar. A light fog of dust still hanging there in the room. Pierce taken away to the hospital, while Hastings went north to help out with the state police roadblock. In the aftermath, a crowd of town people now gathered outside the bar waiting for news from inside.

Tollville came up beside her and motioned her on, the two of them moving around the bar on opposite sides. She recognized Medina where he lay on the floor, his eyes open, staring up at her, and a slick layer of blood everywhere on his face.

"I was just in this bar, I had a drink with Dario just a couple hours ago. I recognize every one of these men."

"I recognize some of these men, too," Tollville said, looking at the deep grooves of buckshot everywhere on the walls. "I think we can say this has officially become a federal investigation. The DEA office is sending a helicopter and we'll get up in the air as soon as we can."

Kelly looked around the bar, stopped, and with the foot of her boot, turned bodies over until their faces showed.

"Easy," Tollville said.

"I recognize every one of these men," she said again. Not raising her eyes to meet Tollville's, but simply standing there looking down at one of the dead men at her feet. Mexican like the others. It was amazing to her that in the three days since all this had started, she could feel so at home, almost casual, in a room full of dead bodies.

A S HE CAME DOWN THE ROAD TOWARD THE ranch, Tom turned his headlights off and navigated the slender dirt road in the overhead moonlight that remained, pale blue over everything. The bushes and fence posts, dulled in the light, seemed unfamiliar and ghostlike.

He crossed over the cattle guard and pulled in behind the sheriff's department cruiser. No sign of Ray. Lights on in the house and the pale trunks of the oaks up the valley just showing out of the darkness.

He turned the ignition off and the night came at him out of the dark in a million different sounds. The engine ticking, the call of insects, the wash of air over the surrounding brush. From the glove compartment he brought out the flashlight again and flicked it on, testing it against the palm of his hand.

Far out on the highway, he saw the line of cars building toward the red and blue pulse of a state police roadblock. A single cruiser going past—Hastings or Kelly heading north, flying down the highway toward the lights. Tom watched it go. A radio in the abandoned cruiser, but no intention of calling in anything till he found Ray, a slick shimmer of blood on the driver's seat as he moved past, Tollville's Baby Eagle held out in front of him.

He didn't know what was happening with Pierce, even if he was still alive. He wondered if Kelly or Hastings were looking for him now, trying to track him down. Everything

Tom had built for himself in the last ten years, the credibility he'd had to build back for himself in this small town, now worth nothing if they found out he'd been helping Ray all along.

Tom couldn't do anything about Gus's death. Perhaps those men down at the bar had it coming. Maybe they deserved every bit of Ray's revenge, but looking now at the stolen cruiser and the blood on the seat, he knew Pierce hadn't deserved any of it.

Taking care with his steps, Tom came to the porch. Darkness all around him and the soft light of a lamp somewhere toward the back through the screen door. A slight breeze working past, moving over the land and running on into the house, where Tom stood on the porch. The wind chime sounding in the darkness and the creak of the screen door's hinges, followed by a slight tremor of fear all down Tom's spine, the door bouncing light against its frame. Thunder and the wet-stone smell of rain from the south all around him in the desert.

One foot after the other he went forward across the porch until he was standing in front of the screen door looking in on the living room, where his father was waiting, and Billy sat across the room watching television on the small thirteen-inch black-and-white.

"He's not here," Luis said.

Tom stepped through the door and nodded to Billy where

he sat near the bloodstain on the wall, and where he could see Luis or someone had thrown a sheet over the chair in which Gus had died.

"Ray shot a deputy," Tom said, watching his father where he sat, wanting to know if his old man knew this already or if it was news to him.

"I figured as much," Luis said. He got up from the chair and walked to the window where they both could look out and see the cruiser sitting there. "Your cousin wasn't going to let this go and I think you knew it just as well as I did."

"You just let him go into town?" Tom lowered his voice. "Knowing what he was going to do?"

"I didn't know anything," Luis said. "I wanted to assume the best just like you did. But assuming the best doesn't mean that's how it will turn out. It rarely does."

"He's not here?"

"He was here just long enough to take his rifle and give the wound in his side a rough clean. In and out in less than four or five minutes, he didn't say much except that we should be expecting you and maybe some others. He said his good-byes to me and Billy and then he was gone."

"Where was he shot?"

"In the side. There was a lot of blood on his shirt. I can't say how bad it was but when he came out of the bathroom he made it sound like he wasn't going to be back."

Tom went through the house room by room. The dim light

he'd seen from the front of the house a mix of the living room lamps and the flicker of the television, and farther back a wall sconce left on in the bathroom. Nothing there except the remains of a roll of surgical tape, a large box of gauze, and some iodine left out on the bathroom floor.

KELLY LEFT TOLLVILLE INSIDE THE BAR AND stepped out the back. She was standing in the parking lot, the sound of the crowd out front now a low murmur of voices. From her belt she raised the radio and depressed the talk button. When Hastings came on she told him what they'd found.

"It's difficult," Hastings was saying. "None of these patrol-men have any idea who we're looking for up here."

"What do they have to go on?"

"Whatever we got out of Pierce before we lost contact."

"You're telling them to look for a man carrying a shotgun."

"Pretty much," Hastings answered. "What about the Mexican border?"

"Tollville put in a call to the Border Patrol and the Mexican authorities."

"We're going to catch him," Hastings said.

"We don't know anything about this guy. The border is

only ten miles away," Kelly said. "And if he's from the south he could have crossed already and gone on from there."

Nothing but silence for a moment, and then Hastings's voice on the radio. "The state police say they're sending two cars down your way to help. I'll bring them to the bar." His voice sounded cold and distant through the radio. "Edna," Hastings said a moment later, "have you heard anything about Pierce?"

"He's in surgery still, we won't hear for a while yet."

"And Dario?"

"The same," Kelly said. "There's nothing I can tell you."

"I hope we catch this guy," Hastings said, his voice lower now, and the sound of the state police in the background lessened. Kelly knew Hastings had walked off a ways and was talking to her in a place where he wouldn't be overheard.

"I know," Kelly said. "I know." They finished the conversation, Kelly telling him that the DEA was sending a helicopter back down for Tollville and then they'd get out and shine the spotlight around, but the hope of finding anything in the night was slim.

T OM CAME OUT OF THE HOUSE AND STOOD looking around at Gus's property. Nothing for him to see. He crossed from the house to the barn and found one of the horse stalls empty. If Ray had been there, he was gone now, and Tom came out of the barn looking for a sign in the sandy hardpack. The only bit of information his father had been able to tell him was that Ray had come out of the house and walked to the stables.

Working as quickly as he could, Tom found the indent of the horse's hooves in a little under five minutes. The hoofprints heading north up the valley toward the old Lamar oil station and possibly beyond to Deming. Luis waited on the porch as Tom searched.

For a moment Tom thought about Claire, that she might be more his family than even his father was. Luis and Billy all that were left to Tom now. Gus the only one in his life who had ever really been a father to either Billy or him, but Luis trying now, knowing that he had to at least for Billy's sake.

Tom knew Ray wouldn't come back, that he'd gone north and given them up. Whatever plan Ray was following, Tom knew it would end in disaster, just like the bar in Coronado, and that other people would be hurt.

Tom stood there looking at the cool blue light everywhere, enough light from the full moon above to make out the hoofprints ten feet in front of him in the night.

"Let him go," Luis said from the porch. "He's gone now. He's not coming back."

He didn't respond to his father and he knelt closer to the

ground, examining the cut of the hoofprints, the edges slowly slipping away in the wind. They headed away north in a low gallop. He didn't know what to do. The country ahead a flat wash all the way to the oil station and the mountains, then growing rougher as the land became steeper. It was horse country and he walked back inside the stables looking for a saddle.

K ELLY LET HERSELF INTO THE DEPARTMENT office and closed the door. Every one of the overhead lights had been left on. The room feeling foreign to her in the night with all five desks still arranged in rows through the office from when there'd been money to pay for the deputies who sat in them. Hastings down at the bar with the state police and no one inside the office now, though she'd hoped to see Tom sitting there waiting for her the way he had been that first day at the hospital, with his feet up, wanting to talk.

She went through to her office and looked in. From beneath the desk she heard a clink of metal on metal and she almost jumped when Jeanie popped her head around the edge of the desk and looked up at her. "Hello," Kelly said, bending down to put a hand out for Jeanie. "Where's Tom gotten to?" The dog simply looked up at Kelly where she knelt. "He's not giving you back, is he?"

Kelly left Jeanie in the office and sat at Pierce's desk. She put her head in her hands, taking three quick breaths, then holding the fourth, feeling it burn deep down in her chest.

She picked up the phone and dialed the hospital, watching Jeanie where she lay inside the office. The hospital had no update as she listened to the doctor give her the rundown again on Pierce. She didn't ask about Dario and she didn't care. It was out of her hands.

For a long time she just sat there. She wanted to pull the phone line right out of the wall, break the phone on the floor, and stomp on it till there was nothing left but bits of wire and plastic.

Outside she heard the whoop of the DEA helicopter move in off the desert. Tollville would be looking for her now, and soon they'd get out there to see what they could see. Tollville had said Tom had been in the bar with him, that Tom had even worn a sheriff's department vest and helped out. It was a lot to take in, and she ran her eyes around the room, searching for any sign, knowing that only an hour before, Tom and Tollville had been inside the office, along with Pierce.

She heard the helicopter circle once over the town, the spotlight moving past the office windows. And though Kelly knew she would go, she wasn't quite ready yet, and she picked up the phone again and dialed the old familiar number.

She let the phone ring five or six times, waiting as the

machine clicked over and she heard Tom's voice come on. She waited for the tone but at the last minute hung up.

Out in the parking lot she saw Tollville—through the light of the helicopter and the windblown dust the rotors were kicking up—moving toward the office. He was inside the office by the time she got Claire's answering machine, and he was at the desk by the time she remembered the crowd of people outside the bar and the faces she had seen there.

With one hand held up to quiet Tollville, she radioed down to Hastings and told him to ask Claire if she'd seen Tom anywhere.

When Hastings came back on he said Claire didn't know where Tom was, but she could identify the truck sticking through the front of the bar, that she'd seen it earlier that day, and it belonged to Gus Lamar.

DAY 4

TOM RODE THE BROWN MARE NORTH THROUGH the desert, a few minutes past midnight and the moon above at its midpoint.

As he rode the light shifted, blue to black, beneath what remained of the clouds. The trail lost and then found. The tall, spiked fingers of ocotillo rising in places and the brittle scrub everywhere on the plain like a dust across the darkened valley. After a while he saw it clear, the two burnished tire tracks left in the desert sand, where years before there'd been a road leading north. The hoofprints leading on.

He didn't know what he hoped for. Ray had shot a deputy, he'd murdered more than ten men, and he was out there still. All of it went against anything Tom could ever accept as a peace officer. But Ray was his cousin, a month older than him, and they'd been like twins once, growing up together and thinking for the longest time that they would always consider Coronado home. Now, Tom didn't know how he felt, and he rode north.

The old road leading on and the small dip to the north where the Hermanos Range slipped almost to the surface of the desert, before rising again in a series of endless hills, covered in a web of pinyon and locust. Then farther on, the white dusting of snow high up where last night's rainstorm had come across the peaks.

He saw jackrabbits stand on hind legs, then go skittering off through the desert at high speed. He surprised birds, bedded down beneath the creosote, sending them twittering into the night sky, circling until he was safely past. Behind, the desert went on in a roll of blue hills trailing away from the mountains all the way to the state police roadblock. The cars bunched up like a necklace of precious stones along the highway.

Not a single cloud above now as he came up the valley and saw the rusted tin roof of the old oil station sitting amid a hollow enclave of desert sand. The station only one room, the windows broken from their frames, and the old wood boards that made up the exterior looking worn and petrified by the desert sun. A place that had at one time offered a bit of protection for his father and the men he worked with. A memory now pulled loose from his childhood of riding north through the desert with Ray, carrying meals up from the ranch kitchen for the oilmen.

As they'd ridden north, they'd searched out snakeskins, cast away on rocks and bits of brush. They'd made games out of it all, chasing each other and turning up the dust. The road they'd used now nothing but two tracks of open land, no more than a foot in width in places, now often slipping completely from sight.

With the one-room building a hundred yards away, Tom dismounted and moved on foot toward the closest window. Ahead, he saw where the oil well once stood, now a heap of rusted scaffolding on the ground. The moon behind him as he went and his own dark silhouette stretched out in front of him, touching brush and sand seconds before he, too, passed the very same spot.

He went with the pistol raised on the shack, the road he'd followed through the night flush against the oil station. Peering in through the first window, Tom saw nothing in there but shadow, dark corners, and broken wood floors dusted with the fine sediment of time. No Ray. No horse. Not a sign that his cousin had set foot in the place.

Tom looked back the way he'd come, the horse standing there, tied into a growth of sagebrush. Nothing else around.

Just twenty paces farther on, he saw the water pump he'd once used as a child. The iron rusted and flaky to the touch. Kneeling, he examined the ground. The road ending here, not all at once, but drifting off little by little, the desert eating it with time. Ray's boot prints visible in the sand where he'd circled the pump trying for water. Tom's own hands stained with small bits of rust as he tried the pump, cold and brittle under his palms. The metal so eaten away it came off in his hand like scales.

For a minute or more he just stood there taking it all in. The hillside rising a thousand feet up out of the desert, through barren rock outcroppings and thick stands of pine and juniper. The high landscape above and a million different places to hide. The road ending and the bare horse track moving on, upward, over the crest of the mountain, and probably down again, on toward the towns and cities beyond.

Tom moved back toward his own horse and untied the reins. He mounted and pushed the horse on. He was about a hundred feet past the oil station, riding through a small grouping of rock, when the bullet buzzed by and hit the sand a few feet behind him. The horse skittered beneath him, sidestepping. The crack of a rifle somewhere high above on the hillside. And then the next bullet whizzed over the head of the horse, causing it to rise, legs clawing the cool night air. Tom trying for a hold on the horse, his hands gripped tight to the reins but nothing there as the horse bucked. No support, and the brief uncontrollable terror as he fell, hitting the ground hard.

He came up with one side of his face covered in the fine desert sediment, his gun out, and his eyes looking from one rock to the next. Looking for anything that would offer the least bit of protection.

The brown mare he'd been riding now far behind him, running, and the crack of the rifle again, the horse jumping, then surging off through the desert in the direction she'd come.

Up the hill nothing moved. He looked behind him at the

shack, and then he looked up the hill again. Nothing there to see. Dead if I do, dead if I don't, he thought. The sand still clinging to his face. Perspiration showing now on his brow. He got up and ran, straight on to the hill, the cover of locust before him, the green tufted tops of a thicket of pinyon up ahead.

The crack of a bullet three feet in front of him, the sand jumping, and Tom sliding to a stop and then turning again for cover. He was halfway to the protection of a large rock when another bullet hit just behind him, clipping a stone, the echo of the ricochet carrying past him down the valley.

K ELLY KNELT IN GUS'S LIVING ROOM EXAM-
ining the blood dried in a rough pool beneath the chair, and spattered up on the wall, the indentation of a single bullet hole in the frame of the door behind. Across the room Luis waited for her to say something, his hand up on Billy's shoulder keeping him from wandering. The boy dressed in his pajamas, his eyes turning from Kelly back over to Tollville, and then across the room to where the television sat on mute, showing an old movie on the screen.

Tollville stood a few feet away from the boy, near the door looking out through the wire on the white bulk of the DEA helicopter. It was a quarter past one in the morning and they'd come up the valley with the spot on and the pilot guiding them along the highway until Kelly herself had shown them where to turn to the west.

Pierce's cruiser sat in front of the house as if it had just been parked there for the night, looking just as it did in the department parking lot. The only difference a layer of blood soaked into the driver's seat.

"You should have called us," Kelly said, turning now toward Luis. There were a million different things she wanted to say to him, but not a one of them appropriate to the situation at hand. Just a few days ago she'd sat at a table with him and had a beer. The last couple days now feeling to her like some sort of layer built deep down into her skin, strong as mortar over brick, stopping her from saying all the things that might normally have come to her in that moment. "You say this is Gus's blood?"

Luis nodded, he was watching Tollville now, and Tollville was watching him.

"And the blood in the bathroom?" Kelly said. "The bandages on the floor?" She didn't want to come out and accuse anyone just yet. She knew time was a factor, that everything was a factor at this point. She hoped to God that Tom had been smarter than all this, but she knew, too, that he'd gone down this road before, and that she had probably been his only salvation. "If you want us to help," Kelly went on, "I need to know what happened here, I need you to tell me the truth, Luis."

Thirty seconds passed and no one said anything.

"You remember Raymond Lamar?" Tollville asked, his voice cutting through the silence. He walked over to the mantel and pulled one of the pictures down and handed it to Kelly.

Kelly stared down at the picture in her hand. It was an old photo of Ray, Luis, and Gus out at Gus's well up the valley. "Of course I do," Kelly said. "I was the one who brought the news about his wife."

Tollville walked past Kelly into the kitchen and saw the smattering of blood that dotted the linoleum floor. "Tom came by your office and he was looking to talk with you," Tollville said. "Right now I want to give him the benefit of the doubt. I want to say that he came by your office to tell you about whatever has been going on down here, and what happened to Gus." He turned and went into the bathroom, where the bandages had been left on the floor. Kelly and Luis exchanged a look.

"I'm not accusing Tom of anything, but I know how this looks for him," Tollville said from the bathroom. "Tom came into your office because he had something to say and for whatever reason, he wouldn't say it to me."

"I didn't know about any of this," Kelly said. She was looking to Luis with desperation in her eyes, urging the man to say something. To correct whatever it was that Tollville was implying.

"I'm not after Tom," Tollville said. He had come out of the bathroom and he was standing in the living room again, speaking to Luis. "I know all about Billy over there, I know what was done to him, and what that did to Ray. I know there's a lot this family has gone through, but I need to know anything you can tell me about Ray Lamar, and I need to know it now. You understand?"

Luis glanced toward the boy and then back to Tollville. "Tom always looked up to Ray," he said. His voice low in the room.

"Luis," Kelly said, but she didn't finish. She wanted to tell him to stop, but she knew she couldn't. She didn't want to go down this path with Tom again, she couldn't.

"Can you give us a moment, Edna?" Tollville asked. He was standing there just as he had been before, his eyes now on her, waiting for her to leave.

She looked to Luis and he met her gaze and nodded. "It's okay," Luis said. "Why don't you take Billy out back to my place and turn the television on for him."

She was going out the door with an arm around Billy's shoulder when she heard Tollville ask, "Tom and Ray pretty much grew up here, didn't they?"

THERE WAS A FINE SOOT OF DUST ON TOM'S FACE where he sat with his back to the large rock. Five minutes ago he'd heard the steady beat of the helicopter come up the valley toward Gus's place. Then watched the red and green navigation lights over the desert to the south. The helicopter circling the ranch, before drifting down in a slow descent.

A couple minutes before he heard the helicopter, he'd tried to look around the edge of the rock at the slope beyond. A bullet passed no more than a foot from his face and lodged in the ground near his feet. His body pulled back around the protection of the rock before he even heard the shot.

He was breathing hard, and when he had time to catch his breath, he yelled out, "Ray, goddamnit, stop shooting, it's Tom." He wanted to think that Ray was messing with him, that he wouldn't shoot him, and that all of this was just a way of trying to slow him down—bucking the horse like that and forcing him to the ground. Even if Ray didn't mean to shoot him, Tom knew Ray had been a good shot with a gun like that even when they were kids, and he could only assume he'd gotten better with his time in the army.

He waited, listening to the desert. The early-morning sounds of insects. The cold touch of the air on the skin of his face. He straightened his back on the rock. A miniature dust devil set loose at the heel of his boot, disappearing after a while as it moved off through the creosote.

"You hear me, Ray?" he yelled, listening for a response.

WHEN TOLLVILLE FOUND KELLY SHE WAS SIT-
ting on Luis's small cot with her back against the wall, the boy sitting beside her watching TV. The words almost sour in her mouth as she asked about Tom, Luis, and what Tollville had been able to find on Ray Lamar. Though she could guess already what had been said.

"I suppose I should explain myself," Tollville said.

"No," Kelly said. "You don't owe me that. You never did. I didn't mean to get in your way back there."

"I meant what I said in there. I'm not after Tom. I know he didn't do any of this."

"He helped though, didn't he?"

"He had some part, but I know going after Tom would only confuse this, it would put another layer between us and the men I really want to see go to trial."

"You're saying you're going to protect him?"

"Here," Tollville said, and he handed her a cloth he'd taken from his pocket with a metal slug inside. "It's a .45 round,"

Tollville said. "Other than the shotgun we found, everything else has been from a nine-millimeter, hasn't it?"

"Everything since Gil Suarez."

Tollville moved his eyes from where she sat to the boy beside her. "Come outside with me," he said.

After she'd risen and gone outside, she could see Luis out in front of the house, his truck doors open and a few things from the house gathered in the bed of the truck. "They're going to go up the hill to the neighbor's place for a while," Tollville said. "The call has already been made and they're expecting them."

"What's going to happen to Luis?"

"Nothing. I believe what he told me, and I'm going to keep him out of this if I can. I don't know if either Tom or Luis will come out of this untouched, but I gave Luis a promise to do all I can."

"You know where Tom is then?"

"Luis said he took one of the horses from the stable and went after Ray."

T OM WAITED FIVE MINUTES, COUNTING THE seconds, too nervous to move from behind the protection of the rock. An awareness growing in his mind that by allowing Ray his revenge, Tom was now responsible for what had happened to Pierce. It had been his decision to let Ray go, and now he knew he needed to bring Ray in, whatever that might mean for him.

Tom waited, building his confidence. Trying to find the courage to go forward with the things he needed to do. Any one of those seconds he expected a bullet to come whistling through the air, and when none came he slowly rose into the open. Waiting still for the bullet to come and spin him sideways as it had done Gil Suarez three days before. No shot. No sound of ricochet, or thump of sand.

Ray and he weren't family anymore, not in the way that Tom had always thought they'd be. They were something else now. Ray had put him in the sights of that rifle ten minutes before and pulled the trigger. He could have killed him, could have cut him down off that horse any time he wanted to. But he hadn't, and Tom had to believe there was still some good in Ray. Some small bit of humanity that wouldn't allow him to pull that trigger and kill him.

With the fear gradually dying back inside him, Tom went on up the hillside, following the trail left in the dusty soil, Ray's boot prints in the ground and the white scrape of the horse's hooves over rocks. The slope steep in front of him. Pinyon and aloe growing tight to the ground. Even without the horse, Tom thought he was making good time, the valley below, and the thin line of the highway that cut through its middle.

By the time he caught the first clank of a harness, the trees had thinned away in front of him and he could hear the rough mutterings of the horse up ahead and something else beneath—Ray's labored breathing.

RAY WAS AWARE THAT TOM HADN'T GIVEN UP. That he was still back there, behind him, following him up the hill. Down by the oil station he'd shot at Tom, meaning only to buck the horse, to scare Tom off, but Tom was still coming. He didn't want to shoot him, but he would. He'd do whatever it took to get away.

Somewhere along the way Ray's body began to fail him, the rasp and catch of spittle deep in his throat as he sucked at the air, searching for moisture. Hours since he'd shed a drop of sweat. And now a wheezing cough, a hand held to his mouth, and a thin speckling of blood on his hand. It was too steep to ride the horse, and all the effort he was putting into wrestling her up the hill was that much more of a strain against his weakened body.

Rounding a corner, he heard Tom's footsteps through the trees, close behind. Without even a look, Ray cut into the forest, leaving the horse. His feet slipping on a loose rock, he slid down the mountain for thirty feet before managing to stop. Searing pain in his gut and a collection of rocks scattering out beneath him, tumbling down along the slope toward the valley below. Ray lay there at the bottom of a steep chute, a protective hand held down over his stomach.

Low pine trees everywhere growing up out of the burned red soil. The sound of boots on rock above, and Tom's voice calling down the chute to him.

There was nothing left for Ray, the family he'd once planned to have, the fantasy of a happy life that just couldn't be. The realization of this felt deep within him where he lay against the rock, fired all the way through and dimming away like an ashen piece of coal, slowly burning toward its death.

All he'd wanted was to go home. But everything had changed and nothing was as he'd thought it would be. Up the hill Tom's voice calling down the chute to Ray. No hope left.

Ray brought up Dario's .45 and fired a shot in the direction of the voice. He heard the bullet hit rock, the echo caroming off over the valley below.

He was up and running before he heard the last reverberation fade away behind him.

K ELLY ROSE FROM WHERE SHE KNELT WITH Tollville over the hoofprints in the sand. The far-off sound of a gunshot opening up in the air to the north. Her shoulders squared already, looking toward the mountains, ready for anything.

Still night out there and the echo of the shot drifting through the air.

Tollville stood, examining the Hermanos. The eastern sky lightening in shades of violet and blue with the valley stretched on before them. "Handgun," Tollville said.

"Forty-five?" Kelly asked.

They were already moving back toward the helicopter as Tollville signaled the pilot.

THE BULLET HAD PASSED JUST OVER TOM'S HEAD, close enough that he'd felt the air move. Much closer than Tom would have thought Ray was willing to take it.

Below, out of sight down the chute, the loose rocks from the strike of the bullet were skittering away down the hill toward the valley. Lifting his head now, he could almost see to the bottom of the chute, a rush of wind moving through the pine trees. Then across the slope, thirty feet below, the brief glimpse of Ray's shirt flitting through a break in the trees. Tom up on his feet, gun raised—the back of Ray's shirt again—then gone again.

Tom slid down along the rocky chute to where he'd seen Ray last, following him into the stand of pine. A thin stream of dust still hanging in the air from Ray's movement. But no Ray, and the wind pushing the dust up along the slope and into the trees, where it too disappeared.

He followed, rounding a corner of the hillside, only to see Ray crouched on the slope between two pines with his gun drawn. Diving headfirst down the slope, Tom heard the bullet hit the earth where he'd been standing only a moment before.

He lay there listening. The heels of his hands scraped and bloodied from where he'd broken his fall. The feel of dirt all over him, and the painful sting from a cut on his head. No sound. Looking back up the slope, he kept his eyes on the forest above. When he thought himself safe, he looked down at his hands, each scraped pink with blood where the skin had come away. The blood beginning to collect and run down along the insides of his wrists, he pressed them to his pants, feeling the shriek of fresh nerves on his jeans.

No idea now where Ray was.

THERE WAS LITTLE TO BE SEEN OUT THE COCK-pit of the helicopter. The spotlight moving below as they went, skipping past rocks and trees, until they came up on the snow-topped ridge and ran along it for a time before dipping back down toward the valley below. For twenty minutes they cut back and forth, with only a small hope they would find something.

The first five minutes of the flight, Kelly had leaned out looking down at the flatness of the desert below them, then as they'd come to the hills and mountains farther on, she'd drawn herself up in the seat, picking what she could from the night. The sky to the east of them taking on the dull gray that came just before the dawn and the muted washed-out light that fell now along the slope over which they flew.

"Continue?" the pilot asked, turning to look back at Tollville.

Moving away from the rear window, Tollville told him to keep going, motioning with his hand for the pilot to make another pass. His voice, heard through the helmets they all wore, vibrating with the wash of the rotors. Like Kelly, he still wore the brown sheriff's department vest, his loose at the shoulders to allow for movement as he scanned the earth below. In his hand he carried his service weapon. His legs stretched wide for balance as the helicopter turned and moved back into a search pattern.

They were running a short grid of the area, and they hadn't seen anything yet but trees and rock. The sound of the blades fighting with the altitude as they climbed again, heading for the ridgeline.

ELOW HIM, RAY HEARD THE HELICOPTER ROTOR working up through the elevation. The sound of the blades still several miles off to the west.

Leaning into the hillside, he let his weight down and turned over on his back. With one hand on the .45 still, he unbuttoned his shirt to look at the wound. His stomach stained red with iodine where he'd cleaned the skin.

Minutes before he'd coughed up blood. None of it was a good sign. The bullet hole seemed too low on his body to have hit a lung, but his breath was definitely tougher to come by, and he tasted the alkaline flavor of his own blood now on his tongue.

Around him the pines were all but gone, and a mix of low grass and high desert rock was covered in places by a dusting of snow. Nothing ahead of him but the razed curve of the pass for a quarter mile or more, until at the end, the slope began its gradual decline toward the other side. In the distance to the north the thin ethereal light of the highway where it came through the mountains, and down below the larger swath of city light from Deming, another ten miles or so beyond.

Tom MOVED UP OUT OF THE RAVINE JUST AS
the DEA helicopter went past. The white underbelly of
the machine moving by along the ridge and the light splashing down everywhere.

Perhaps it had been a trick of the landscape, the sound
waves bouncing from one ridge to the next, or maybe just the
pulse of his own breathing and the scrape of his efforts up the
loose rock, but he hadn't heard the helicopter till then, thinking it was a mile or so more to the west.

He stood, watching it move away down the line of the pass,
suddenly there, then gone again, following the open track of
rock and grassland that separated the south slope of the mountain from the north. No sign of Ray.

Ray HEARD THE HELICOPTER BREAK FREE OVER
the top of the pass. Not there, then there in a sudden
shimmer of light, just a quarter mile to the west of him. The
shadow of his movements now falling before him on the rock
as he went. His gait crooked as he ran over the open, wind-
scraped ground toward the far protection at the other side of
the pass.

He went on, holding his stomach with one hand, the .45 in

the other. The rifle still strapped to his back and the blood from his wound dried coarse and brittle into the fabric of his shirt.

The helicopter moving toward him, with the spotlight beam now just a few hundred feet away. "Come on," he said, urging himself forward. His teeth clenched and the air pushed up out of his mouth tasting metallic and sour.

He ran, scrambling over rocks and into hummocks of dirt and sedge. His face contorted with pain, the top of his stomach tight beneath his hand. The strain evident in the rigid gait of his movements and the warmth of the wound felt on his bare palm.

He ran with difficulty, the climb behind him and the strength gone from his legs. Snow everywhere now on the rocks and in the shallow indentations between. He slipped, one leg going out from under him while he reached a hand out to catch himself. He gasped with pain as he came down, the shock of his movements cutting through him.

The light moved across him for a moment and then came back, wavering above him like a celestial body, floating there a hundred feet above. The sound of the machinery and the rush of wind suddenly all around him.

Looking ahead, there was still a chance of making the tree line a hundred yards away. He brought the rifle off his back, desperate with the idea of escape. The beat of the helicopter's rotor splashing down everywhere along the bare rock. Pain echoing up out of his stomach, and the ever-present thirst in the back of his throat.

THEY WERE TAKING SHOTS TO THE BODY OF THE helicopter. Kelly could hear them digging through the metal. Something sparked and the lights on several of the onboard displays blinked red, then faded, a warning signal sounding as the helicopter began to list.

"Move!" Tollville yelled, his voice more frantic now, telling the pilot to drop, to pull the helicopter down to the east and get beneath the ridgeline. Another bullet hit, breaking through the underside and ricocheting off the ceiling of the cabin.

Kelly turned to see if Tollville was hit but they were falling now, faster than Kelly thought possible, the pilot pulling the helicopter hard to the left and the nose dropping toward the protection beyond the ridge.

TOM BEGAN TO RUN. SCRAMBLING FROM ONE rock to the next over the gradual rise of the pass, then cresting the top, he saw Ray out in front of him running down the slope toward the line of squat trees farther on.

Tom had heard the shots, watching helplessly as the helicopter wavered there in the air for a second, then dipped hard to the left and fell away.

Running, he followed after Ray till his cousin was lost from sight in the low pines and stunted juniper that clung to the wind-worn ridgeline. With fifty yards still to go, he couldn't hear the helicopter anymore and he went on, knowing that if he was going to catch up to Ray it would have to be now.

Breaking past the first couple trees, Tom slowed, listening to the air around him. Shadows thick within the trees. He stood in a deepening stand of pine. The sedge that had covered the pass appeared in sparse pathways between the trees, poking its grasslike stalks from the snow.

Ahead, on the ground, the heel of a boot print in the snow one place, then the toe of another five feet on. No telling where Ray had gone and Tom following, trying to make sense of what little trail he could take from the snow before it, too, disappeared.

Tom went on, his gun held out in front of him as he took his steps carefully, pausing to sweep the undergrowth and watch where he put his feet. Ray's footprints visible ahead of him for maybe thirty feet, disappearing into the gloom. The sun just beginning to rise, and the air filled everywhere with the stark contrasts of light and dark.

"Stop there, Tom."

Tom stiffened. Ray's voice close behind.

"Throw the gun out and then step away."

Tom did as he was told, throwing the gun toward one of the small clumps of grass, where the metal took up the light from the dawning sky above. Tom watched Ray move out from behind him, limping from beneath the shadow of a juniper, his side held tight in one hand. A .45 in the other hand. When he reached Tom's gun, he knelt and picked it up, examining it for a second in his bloodstained palm before slipping it into his waistband. "Come on," he said. Waving Tom on with the .45. "I'm not going to be here when that helicopter comes back. And I'm not leaving you here to signal them."

"How do you know it'll come back?" Tom said.

"Listen."

Tom looked back toward the ridge. He could just see to the first part of the pass through the trees, scraped to the soil in places by the winds that rushed across the mountain range. Then, listening, he heard the beat of the helicopter again, down low on the other side of the mountain, working up through the altitude, the sound intensifying even as he stood there. "How long?" Tom asked.

"A couple minutes at most," Ray said, waving the gun again, gesturing for Tom to keep moving. "I winged them, though not good enough to take them down."

"You could have killed them," Tom said.

"I could have, but I didn't. Now, let's keep moving."

"You nearly killed Pierce," Tom said. "You didn't need to do that."

"Who?"

"The young deputy outside the bar."

"He'll live," Ray said. "I did what I had to." He turned his head over his shoulder as the sound of the rotor intensified behind. The helicopter rising on the other side of the ridge, the first glimmer of light from the spot reaching up into the sky. "I can shoot you in the leg right here or you can come with me," Ray said. "I don't have any better options for you at the moment."

Tom watched Ray where he stood. No idea what to do and any hope he had of bringing Ray in now gone. He didn't want to go on with Ray, but he didn't want to get shot either. Tom was sorry about the whole damn business and he stood watching Ray, trying to figure if he would have done anything differently, and knowing without a doubt that he would be right here on this ridge, all the same.

The sound of the helicopter again and Ray motioning for Tom to follow.

THE PILOT THUMBED OFF THE WARNING LIGHTS, there was a smell of burned wires and blown fuses, but they were still in the air. Dropped almost a thousand feet and working their way back up the mountain, with Tollville urging the pilot on. Telling him to climb and get them back up there.

Composing herself, Kelly looked behind her to find Tollville braced in his seat, one hand held out against the wall for support and the other wrapped into the webbing overhead, the gun he'd been holding loose on the floor, jittering back and forth across the metal as the cabin of the helicopter shook.

A slight ticking now heard from the tail rotor, the pilot pulling at the stick, trying for control. Every tick a new adjustment for the pilot to make as Kelly felt the helicopter shift ever so slightly to the left, then back to the right, climbing still but not completely under their control.

THE RAVINE LED NORTH, CLOSING IN AROUND them on both sides. Nowhere to go but down, Tom leading the way with Ray following behind, still holding the .45 on Tom.

"Would you really have shot me?" Tom asked, walking. "Up there on the ridge?" He paused to look at Ray where his cousin had stopped, holding his side as he rested against one of the rock walls.

Ray took his hand back from where he'd kept it against his side, the blood grown in a wet circle against the material. "Who says I'm not still thinking about it?" he said, pushing himself off the wall and motioning Tom on with the muzzle of the gun.

Tom kept walking. Overhead, the sun was up in the sky and the top of the walls showed the orange slant of light. Every echo of their movements caught between those two walls as they moved down toward the plain. "Why keep me alive if you think I betrayed you?" Tom said.

"Let's just say we're even now."

"I didn't tell them anything about you. I wanted to but I never got to."

Ray laughed. "I'd have loved to have heard that conversation."

They walked on for a while. Behind, Tom heard the beat of the helicopter as it ran along the ridge, once even skimming across the narrow opening of the ravine above. There and then gone in less than a second.

"So you're just going to run now?" Tom asked. "Just like you did before. Leave Billy again?"

"You know that's not how it is," Ray said. "I wanted to come back. I've always wanted to. But I see it's just not for me."

"I don't know," Tom said. "I don't know anything about you anymore."

"I've tried to be the same as I was ten years ago, before Marianne died. But it's never worked," Ray said. "Every day I try to hold on to my past it just seems to fall farther away."

Tom went on, he could see the city before them. A sliver showed through the ravine opening ahead, the blue-yellow lights of a city at dawn.

"I've been getting played this whole time," Ray said. "I've been getting played for over ten years and never knew it. After everything I did back there, it turns out it wasn't the cartel I needed to be worried about at all."

"HERE," TOLLVILLE SAID. "PUT IT DOWN HERE." His voice heard loud through Kelly's helmet. The helicopter wavering over the open, rock-strewn pass and the pilot fighting to bring the skids even. "You ready?" Tollville asked. His hand held out on Kelly's shoulder as he leaned forward checking the pilot's progress.

Kelly felt the skids hit ground. The pilot cut the engine, going down through the switches, as the blades wound to a stop above. Tollville opened the side door and got out onto the ground, urging Kelly to follow.

"Can you get your deputy on that radio?" Tollville asked once they were away from the rotor wash.

Kelly took the radio from her belt and as soon as Hastings's voice came through Tollville was telling her what to say. Relaying their location and asking Hastings to talk with the state police. "You ready?" Tollville asked as soon as she'd put the radio back on her hip.

"You making this up as you go along?" she said.

"WHAT WILL IT TAKE?" TOM ASKED. HE WAS watching Ray where they'd stopped to sit for a moment. Ray's breath ragged in his chest, his back to one side of the wall, while Tom sat opposite. Ray had laid everything out now—getting the job from Memo, Sanchez, Gil Suarez, Burnham—all of it, going all the way back to the death of his wife and leaving Billy with Gus.

"To stop all this?" Ray said. "I don't know, I thought I'd finished all this years ago, but I can see it was never done."

"You're going after your boss then? You think it was him this whole time, setting you up against the cartel?"

"I don't know," Ray said. "I don't know anything anymore. I've done a lot of bad things in my life. Things that I can't take back, but at one time thought were for a good reason. I don't think that anymore. I don't know if I ever will again."

"Whatever you do, Ray, none of it will bring back Marianne or the life you had."

"A lot of people have been hurt by me," Ray said. "There's a lot I need to make up for, even if it is in my own way." Ray coughed and looked down at his hand, where there was a speckling of blood on his palm. He coughed again and spit into the dirt at his feet. "Come on," he said, looking to Tom and waving him on with the gun. Another thousand feet before they would come out onto the plain below.

Tom just sat there, unsure now where he was in all this. Why he'd come. Had he ever really intended to take Ray back with him, give him over to Kelly like any other criminal on the run?

Deputy Pierce would be okay, Tom had known it all along. Chasing after Ray had never really been about Pierce, never about anyone but himself and the person he'd once been. No idea now where he belonged in all this. He'd wanted back in with the department, meeting Kelly that evening outside the hospital, he'd wanted a small piece of a life he could no longer have. Claire calling him every ten minutes because of a past he no longer wanted any part of. It was his fault and he knew it. There was no avoiding that now, though he'd tried.

Where had it led him? Just hours before he'd felt just as sure about wanting Dario dead as Ray was about going through with it. Now, Tom didn't know where he stood. Dario laying there on his office floor, white in the face, with blood leaking from the wound in his neck at an alarming pace. Tom hadn't wanted that. Had he?

Shouldn't Tom want to see Memo get the same punishment he'd been so certain Dario deserved? Pierce had been shot because of him, because Tom had looked the other way.

"Ray," Tom said. "I can't go any farther with you."

The look on Ray's face washed away slowly, then solidified. A blank expression Tom didn't know how to read. Would he be murdered right there or set free?

"I know I should want to go with you," Tom said. "Gus meant a lot to me. I should want what you want on this, but I can't just stand by for this one, pretending that other people won't be hurt in the process."

Ray stood five feet away, the gun in his hand still, offering nothing but a blank, unreadable stare.

"You're not going to make it," Tom said.

"I can't let you go."

"Shoot me if you have to, but I'm not going any farther."

Ray took Tollville's Baby Eagle from where he'd stashed it in the waist of his pants. Replacing his own .45 in his waistband, he slid the magazine into his hand and then put it into his pocket. "You asked me to do the right thing once," Ray said.

"I wanted you to turn yourself in."

"I don't have much left," Ray said. "I'm not going to turn

340

myself in, not anymore. I'm past that now. But I can try for once to do a good thing."

"Killing your boss?"

"No," Ray said. "It doesn't matter much now, but maybe it will mean something down the road. If you go back to the Sullivan house, you'll find what this has all been about, buried twenty paces straight out from the back stairs."

"You're talking about the drugs?"

"It's not much," Ray said. "But maybe it will help you get clear of all this." From where they stood, five feet apart, Ray underhanded the Baby Eagle to Tom. "I hope it works out for you," Ray said. "In everything."

"Don't do this, Ray. You need medical attention. You need to come back with me at least."

"I've already come this far."

"You're not going to make it."

Ray grinned. "Tell Billy I'm sorry and say hi to Luis for me."

"You tell Gus the same," Tom said.

The flash of a smile from Ray. "This it, then?"

"I think so."

"Good-bye, Ray."

"Good-bye, Tom."

Tom watched Ray turn and leave, heading down the ravine, the rock tight around him on both sides, and the city lights from Deming shining below across the desert.

Tom turned and walked up the ravine, feeling every step

now and questioning whether he'd made the right decision leaving Ray like that. Perhaps he could have talked him out of it. Perhaps he could have helped Ray in some small way, trying to get him to let this go. There was no way now of knowing something like that.

Pausing to catch his breath, he sat on a rock, the ravine walls not as tall as they'd been below. Those walls now seeming more like a canyon than any kind of ravine, and he imagined Ray now, heading down, taking his steps with care as he went on between the two sharp-faced walls.

He waited, sweat cooling on his skin, until Kelly and Tollville showed a few hundred feet above him, working their way down.

"Are you okay?" Kelly asked when she'd drawn even with Tom. A crescent of sweat under each of her arms, just like he remembered from their meeting on the road four days before.

"Tired, but fine," Tom said.

Tollville stood behind Kelly, checking his watch and looking down the ravine. "Where's Ray, Tom?"

"How's Pierce?" Tom asked. "Is he stable?"

"He lost a lot of blood," Tollville said, his gray hair matted with sweat at the sides of his temples. "I've seen people live through worse."

Tom nodded. He wanted to ask about Dario, but he didn't want to hear the answer. Nothing mattered anymore and Tom knew now he would never wear the star again. His own hopes

DEAD IF I DON'T

already given up and a certainty he would do time for what he'd done already to help out his cousin.

"This has gone too far, Tom," Kelly said. "We already talked to Luis. We know about Gus and everything else. You need to help us here."

"I know that, now," Tom said. "He's headed down this ravine, working his way toward the valley."

"I'm going on," Tollville said. "Call us in to Hastings and tell them I'm going to drive him out onto the plain below."

Kelly turned to look at him, but he was already moving. When she turned back, Tom didn't have anything to say. "You trusted him, didn't you?" Kelly said.

"Yes," Tom said. "I always have."

Kelly watched him for a moment longer, then raised the radio to her lips and told Hastings their location, then where to set up the patrolmen below.

RAY BROKE OUT ONTO THE PLAIN. HE WAS LIMPing badly now, still holding his side where the bullet had gone in. But he felt strong, stronger than he'd felt in a long time, and he knew all his training had been for this. There was a surety there, a certainty he couldn't just give up on. He needed to believe all that had come before counted toward

343

where he was now, crossing the plain in the early-morning light, with the low-lying shape of the city before him.

All of it had led him to this—this moment, no one but him and the plain and the pulse of the wound beneath his hand, driving him forward. His training, all those years he'd worked for Memo, trying to be as quiet as possible, letting that life take him over, and grow around him like a vine.

He stumbled over a rise and then went down into the depression beyond, his thighs surging with the weight of his body, pulling him up one rise, then easing him down into the shallow before the next. No thought other than to move forward. His stomach long since locked up into itself. Layer upon layer built into his skin, thick as any armor.

He stopped when he came up the next rise. The sun glowing there on the horizon, the light just enough to see the black figure. Looking close he saw it was not one figure but a whole group of them. The dark shapes of men out there in front of him. Who they were and how they'd found him, he didn't know. He took a step, heard them call out to him, heard their voices carried on the air like something from another realm.

He looked down at the wound in his side. With one hand he raised his shirt. No blood now, only the slick, clear ooze of plasma running down the skin of his stomach. He was okay, he was just fine, and he knew nothing could stop him, not these men or their words. He felt beyond himself, far out, already coasting down city streets toward his last victim.

Someone called his name, a voice much louder than the others, amplified in his mind. He was glad to have left Tom behind. Tom telling him he wouldn't make it, trying to get Ray to stop, to just slow down and look at where he was. But Ray knew he couldn't do that. He couldn't let that happen. He was stronger than this, feeling it now as he took one step, then another, the voice there again, loud as it was before. Telling him to stop, to just stay where he was.

THEY HEARD ONE SHOT FAR BELOW. TOM RAISED his eyes from where he sat then stood and listened. They'd waited forty-five minutes already, the wind in the short pines all around them. Low, slanted light falling everywhere through the trees with the motes of dust embedded in the ground like fallen spears. All around the early-morning calls of birds as they came awake in the surrounding pines.

It had been a single shot. Something loud, a .45 Tom knew was Ray's. Then close behind the volley from the patrolmen. They waited still longer, Tom still standing, still listening as the echo of gunfire died away in the valley below. Then, only a few seconds later the hiss of Kelly's radio as it came back on, and Hastings gave her the news.

DAY 365

DARIO ARRIVED ON THE SIX O'CLOCK BUS FROM
El Paso. A scar on his neck and a history marred with
violence now visible to anyone. In the trial that followed he'd
been cleared of any indiscretions. The only men willing to testify against him, Ray's cousin Tom, and Tom's father Luis.
Both easily discredited by Dario's lawyer. Tom for his own
troubled past and Luis for his constant drinking. The judge
even going as far as to say Dario was the victim. Singled out
for being an outsider in a closed-off town. Dario's own .45
found in Ray Lamar's hands, and the death of his father, Gus
Lamar, still inconclusive.

As he stepped down off the bus he could feel the heat in the
air. The linen suit he wore blowing open for a second in the
wind, and a small leather case carried in his hand. The case
was as wide and tall as a ream of paper, with a zipper running
along one edge.

His first time north of the border in almost ten months,
and as he'd remembered from his years in the state, the air
tasted dry and clear as the surrounding desert. The weather
unseasonably hot for that area of New Mexico and a thin
veneer of dust hanging over the plain in a haze.

As he got down off the bus Dario wiped at his forehead

with a handkerchief. The small white cloth was still in his hand as he looked around at the empty lot he'd been let off in. Nothing around except a small diner across the street and a gas station.

The big man he was there to see was waiting for him under the shade of the gas station awning, a black Chevrolet two-tone parked in one of the spaces close by.

When they were seated in the car, the man, six feet tall, dark skinned, with acne scarring around his neck and a week's stubble, turned and looked at Dario. "You're not what I was expecting."

Dario unzipped the top of the case, reached in and took out four stacks of bills—ten thousand dollars in each—and handed them over. "Think of me as an extension of the man I work for," he said. His voice darker in tone than it had ever been in Coronado, a result of the surgery that removed a sliver of his vocal cord. "When you look at me, you're looking at him," Dario went on. "I'm just here to see the work is done."

The man was examining the money in his hand, more money, Dario thought, than he'd seen in one place at one time. "And the rest?" the man said.

"When the work is done."

They drove across the flatlands, watching the scrub pass by a mile at a time. The lines of the road rarely veering left or right, but rather just going on toward the mountains some two hours away across the flat *bajada*.

An hour passed before they turned down off the road and wallowed through a small creek running low with the season's first snowfall far away in the mountains. They came up out of the creek bed, Dario listening to the headers sucking up air as the engine pulled the car forward over the small rise.

They went on for another thirty minutes, the sun fading down in the west, the light slanting away into cross-sections of pale pink and purple stratifications.

The house, when it appeared, was built in the old style of the Spanish missionaries who had populated the land a hundred years before, but had now abandoned it. One room in all, walled with mud and hay, a series of long wood beams over the top as a sort of roof. The wood grayed from age, missing in places, and worn and dried by years of sun. Getting out of the car, Dario could smell mesquite and sage. As at the bus stop an hour before, there was little to greet them but the dry wind.

Dario stood looking at the small house for a minute or more and then asked, "You said on the phone his sister in Las Cruces turned him over?"

"That's how I found him, yes."

"And the sister?"

"She said she didn't want to know."

Dario stood there now, listening to the desert. Not a sound. The pink light everywhere, and all of it bound up together somehow as if they were all part of the same being. "You use this place often?" Dario asked.

"Your boss wanted it discreet," the man said.

"Yes," Dario said.

"Ready?" the man asked.

"Yes."

They went on inside. Roof beams half down into the room, no light anywhere but what managed to reach down from above, hanging there before them like a thin filament. The interior nothing but shadow, cut up in places by the fall of the light.

On the dirt floor before them, a man's head was faced away from them, so that he couldn't see them enter.

"You dug him into the ground?"

The big man beside him nodded. "Wanted to make sure he'd be here when we got back."

Dario breathed in. The smell of urine everywhere, so strong he had to blink it away.

Noticing Dario's nostrils flare, the big man said, "Before, when I was holding him for you, before I put him in the ground, I gave him a bucket, but he tried to throw it at me whenever I brought his food, so I took it away."

Dario walked around the room keeping an arm's length from the wall as he went. The man buried up to his neck in the ground, a savage open cut along his cheek, running below his eye. The pus in a line down along his face crusted to the underside of his jaw. His eyes closed, and his skin sunburned so bad it was peeling away from his face. "Is he alive?" Dario asked.

The big man walked over and kicked sand at the head there on the ground. He groaned, blinking away the sand. His mouth bound with a piece of cloth.

"Has he said anything since you picked him up?"

"I was told you wanted his mouth bound."

"Even when he eats?"

The big man smiled, looking down at the welts that showed everywhere on the man's face. "He learned quick enough."

"Would you mind going out to the car?" Dario asked. He waited while the man left, giving the big man time to walk away from the building before squatting down. "Memo?" Dario said. "It's been a long time."

Memo tried to focus his eyes, one lid drooping much lower than the other.

"You caused a lot of trouble for me in Coronado," Dario said, removing the cloth from Memo's mouth so that they could talk.

"Just go on and do it," Memo said. "Get it over with."

"After the trial it was pretty hard tracking you down. What type of deal was it you made? Didn't seem to take them long to make up their minds in your favor. We were wondering what you might have said."

353

Memo slanted his eyes upward till Dario could see the irises. "You know the offer I made you is still good," Memo said. "I can still help you. I can still get you out from under them."

"Raymond Lamar trusted you, too, didn't he? Trusted you right up until the end."

"It's different," Memo said. "You're different. Can't you see I can help you?"

"No," Dario said. "I don't think that's what you're going to do."

"I never said anything about you. I wouldn't have done that."

"Is that right?"

"I'm telling you the truth."

"In the end it didn't seem like I needed you at all, did it? No drugs in my bar, and Ray Lamar's fingerprints on my .45," Dario said, then held his voice for a time. "Whatever you might have told them, it didn't matter in the end."

"I wouldn't say anything to anyone about you."

"I know," Dario said, "but you've already said too much as it is. A lot has changed since we talked last year, a lot of water under the bridge. Many different experiences to draw from." Standing, he looked down at Memo there on the ground.

With the case still in his hand, Dario unzipped the top and brought out a small scalpel he'd bought in El Paso, just after crossing the border out of Juarez. Seeing the blade, Memo began to work his head back and forth, desperately trying to defend himself.

"I don't enjoy this work," Dario said. "But I've gotten used to it. And you're going to be our messenger." With one hand Dario reached down and pinched Memo's nose closed, waiting as his face reddened. When Memo's mouth opened, Dario inserted the blade and drew it across the tongue, letting the sharpness of the blade do the work.

ACKNOWLEDGMENTS

Sometime in 2008, when I still lived in Boston and worked in a restaurant in Kenmore Square, I took my friend James Ferguson up on his offer of a ride home. A week before, James had been to an auto auction in New Hampshire. The car he'd bought was a late-model Jeep Cherokee. We'd just finished up one of the long brunch shifts where we would sit in the back and read the Sunday papers or play dice games in the little drawer beneath the Micros screen. Needless to say we were feeling a little dispirited from a long day of work that didn't really involve any work, and therefore didn't really involve any money. Plus James had won all the dice games, so I wasn't feeling all that lucky.

When we got into the Jeep, James told me to flip open the glove and look inside. He pulled out into traffic and by the time we were headed down Commonwealth Avenue I held a little black box in my hands with a single red button on the top and wires leading back into the glove. It was the type of box that made me think that maybe if we got the Jeep up to eighty-eight miles per hour something truly special might happen. So of course I pressed the button and for about a block the headlights flashed like we had somewhere we really needed to be, and everyone on Comm Ave. got out of our way. It was a flasher box and it was going to take me into the future just like Marty McFly and Doc Brown. (Oh, and if anyone's wondering, the bet I lost on that dice game was that I had to work *Back to the Future* into my acknowledgments.)

The real truth to this story is that the ideas for a novel come from a variety of different places and owe thanks to a variety of different sources. James gave me the beginning of a novel that I didn't know existed until many years later. Thanks, James.

For a long time these ideas feel like they run in place inside your head, waiting for the light to change so that they can sprint across the street and continue. For that I want to thank people like Reed and Tina Waite, Paul Sullivan, and Lizzie Stark, people who gave me a place to write for a week, two weeks, or even a few months. That time helped me get my thoughts in order and, more important, get those thoughts down on paper.

I also want to thank and apologize to everyone who went out for a drink with me after I finished up a long day of writing. This means you Dan Coxon, Mitch Cunanan, Carter Sickels, and Zachary Watterson. James Scott, thanks for always being there for a bourbon and a talk. Chip Cheek, thanks for letting me run ideas past you and thanks for sharing your ideas with me. Thanks to both of you for putting up with my grumpiness and overall bad behavior, and helping me on many nights find my way.

To Debby DiDomenico, thanks for encouraging me to get out there into the woods and thanks, as always, for being my reader. To Tony Matson, Victoria Wang, Jan Turecek, and Hal-Bear, thanks for camping out in the deserts of New Mexico, waking up in an ice-covered tent, and enjoying every minute of our adventure (even if Hal-Bear's badge didn't open as many doors as we'd hoped).

From start to finish I owe a huge debt to everyone at Sobel Weber and the Abner Stein Literary Agency. In London, Caspian Dennis, Arabella Stein, and Sandy Violette, and in New York, Julie Stevenson, Adia Wright, Kirsten Carleton, and especially Nat and Judith, who read too many drafts of this project for me to count. Thanks so much to the two of you for everything. Your advice has been invaluable.

This book took me two years to write, about a year past my due date, and for that I want to thank Simon & Schuster U.K. for their continued support and faith in my work. Ian Chapman, Francesca Main, Maxine Hitchcock, and Clare Hey, thank you for simply being the best and always encouraging me on. To Peter Hammans in Germany, Takahiro Wakai in Japan, Manuel Tricoteaux in France, Susan Sandérus in Holland, and all my foreign publishers, thank you so much for the e-mails, conversations, and support these last couple years.

In the States I want to thank my editor David Highfill of William Morrow for always being honest with me, for asking questions, and for being in general a very down-to-earth guy. The world is a better place now that I know you're out there doing literary good. I also want to thank Jessica Williams for keeping me on track these last couple months. To Laura Cherkas and her team of copyeditors, thanks for making my bad grammar seem not so bad, and for letting me keep some of my comma splices.

I spent a lot of time on the road in the last few years and I owe something of this book to the places I went and the people I met. To my friend Justin St. Germain, whom I met years ago when we were waiters at Bread Loaf, thanks for recommending Oakley Hall's *Warlock*. And then thanks for yelling at me a few years later when I still hadn't read it but you knew I should. You were right. It's one fine book. Thanks to everyone at Sewanee, especially Kevin Wilson, who took some time away from his busy schedule to talk to me about second books. Thanks, I needed that more than you knew.

I learned a lot while I was away, listening to people, talking, and sharing stories. I don't think I would have this book without that time. So thank you to the Theakston Old Peculier Crime Writing Festival in Harrogate; to Sewanee; to the Cuyahoga County Library, which flew me out and put me up; and to the state of New Mexico and everyone there. But the person to whom I owe the biggest debt and the greatest thanks is my wife, Karen, who puts up with me and everything that entails. Which, in her words, seems to be a lot.

Penny Hancock

The Darkening Hour

Dora on Mona

'Mona is, I guess, a few years older than me. Crooked teeth. Poorly nourished, pale brown skin. Health care is expensive where she comes from. I'm helping her, I think. I'll improve her life.

A fair exchange – after all, she's here to improve mine.'

When Theodora Gentleman employs Moroccan immigrant Mona, she has little choice but to invite this perfect stranger into her home.

But when two women are forced to make their home under the same roof, power struggles are quick to occur.

And Theodora soon begins to suspect that Mona is not all she seems.

Mona on Dora

'When I arrived, Theodora opened the door herself. She smiled, though I know from experience that looks can lie. I could see straightaway that Dora needed me.

This is good. Need creates opportunity.

It gives me power.'

Mona knows that this job is the only hope left of supporting her elderly mother and daughter living back home in Rabat.

But with each passing day, Mona begins to realise that Dora might not be the kindly employer she had hoped for . . .

Hardback ISBN 978-1-47111-124-2
Ebook ISBN 978-0-85720-626-8

Chris Carter

One by One

Detective Robert Hunter of the LAPD's Homicide Special
Section receives an anonymous call asking him to go to a
specific web address – a private broadcast. Hunter logs on
and a show devised for his eyes only immediately begins.

But the caller doesn't want Detective Hunter to just watch,
he wants him to participate, and refusal is simply not
an option. Forced to make a sickening choice, Hunter must
sit and watch as an unidentified victim is tortured and
murdered live over the Internet.

The LAPD, together with the FBI, use everything at their
disposal to electronically track the transmission down, but this
killer is no amateur, and he was more than prepared for it.
Before Hunter and his partner Garcia are even able to get
their investigation going, Hunter receives a new phone call.

A new website address. A new victim. But this time the killer
has upgraded his game into a live murder reality show,
where anyone can cast the deciding vote.

Hardback ISBN 978-0-85720-305-2
Ebook ISBN 978-0-85720-309-0

Craig Robertson

Witness the Dead

Scottish Police are called to a murder scene in Glasgow's Northern Necropolis. The body of a young woman lies stretched out over a tomb in what looks like a ritualistic murder. Her body bears a three letter message from her killer, daubed in lurid red lipstick.

In the 1970s, Danny Neilson was the detective working on the infamous Red Silk murders. Still haunted by the memory of the unsolved investigation, he spots a link between the new murders and those carried out by Red Silk - details that no copycat killer could have known about. But Archibald Atto, the man suspected of the killings all those years ago, is rotting in jail, so Danny has to face up to his fear that they never caught their man.

Neilson goes with police photographer Tony Winter, to visit Archibald Atto in prison. But Atto will not speak to them unless it is on his terms. As clues begin to surface, they learn that they are dealing with a killer whose agenda is so terrifying and history so twisted that it will take the combined efforts of police forces past and present to make an arrest.

Paperback ISBN 978-0-85720-420-2
Ebook ISBN 978-0-85720-421-9

Camilla Grebe & Åsa Träff

More Bitter Than Death

Sometimes reliving the past revives old demons ...

In a Stockholm apartment, five-year-old Tilde watches from under the kitchen table as her mother is brutally kicked to death.

Meanwhile, in another part of town, psychotherapist Siri Bergman and her colleague Aina meet their new patients - a group of women, all of whom are victims of domestic violence.

From Kattis, who was beaten by her boyfriend and lives under the constant threat of his return, to Malin, the promising young athlete who was attacked by a man she met online, and from Sofi, the teenager abused by her stepfather, to Sirkka, an older woman who had a troubled marriage – each woman takes her turn to share her story in the safety of the sessions.

But as the group gets closer, it is not long before the dangers lurking in the women's lives outside invade the peace with shattering consequences. And somehow, the fate of five-year-old Tilde is intertwined with that of Siri and the other women, so that what started out as the search for peace will swiftly turn into a tense hunt for a murderer.

Trade Paperback ISBN 978-0-85720-949-8
Ebook ISBN 978-0-85720-951-1

Lynda La Plante

Wrongful Death

Six months after the body of Josh Reynolds, a London nightclub owner, was found and determined by police and coroner to be a suicide, DCS James Langton tasks DCI Anna Travis to review the case. Reynolds died from a single gunshot wound to the head, the gun held in his right hand.

But details are emerging that suggest someone else may have fired the gun ...

As soon as she wraps up the case, Langton tells Anna, she can join him at the FBI Academy in Virginia for training. Meanwhile, a Senior FBI Agent, Jessie Dewar, crime scene expert, is seconded to Anna's team as part of her research and immediately the competence of the original investigation team is questioned ...

Hardback ISBN 978-1-47112-582-9
Ebook ISBN 978-1-47112-586-7

Robert Ryan

Dead Man's Land

Deep in the trenches of Flanders Fields, men are dying in their thousands every day. So one more death shouldn't be a surprise.

But then a body turns up with bizarre injuries, and Sherlock Holmes' former sidekick Dr John Watson – unable to fight for his country due to injury but able to serve it through his medical expertise – finds his suspicions raised. The face has a blue-ish tinge, the jaw is clamped shut in a terrible rictus and the eyes are almost popping out of his head, as if the man had seen unimaginable horror. Something is terribly wrong.

But this is just the beginning. Soon more bodies appear, and Watson must discover who is the killer in the trenches. Who can he trust? Who is the enemy? And can he find the perpetrator before he kills again?

Surrounded by unimaginable carnage, amidst a conflict that's ripping the world apart, Watson must for once step out of the shadows and into the limelight if he's to solve the mystery behind the inexplicable deaths.

Paperback ISBN 978-1-84983-957-0
Ebook ISBN 978-1-84983-958-7

Sean Slater

The Guilty

When Homicide Detective Jacob Striker discovers a torture
chamber in a steel barn down by the river, he is propelled
into an investigation that leads to two mysterious bombers.
Every few hours, another victim is targeted, located -
and then blown to smithereens.

Very quickly, Striker realizes the attacks are not random. But
one obvious question remains: Why? With people dying at an
alarming rate, Striker desperately searches for an answer to this
question. When he discovers it, a stark coldness fills him. For he
begins to understand. The reason leads back to a police file that is
now ten years old. To a dark and dangerous place across the seas.
And to one of Striker's oldest mentors and dearest friends.

With time running out, Striker must catch the two bombers before
they finish the job and complete their kill list. Otherwise there
will be little left for Jacob Striker to save.

Little left, but dust and bones.

Paperback ISBN 978-1-47110-137-3
Ebook ISBN 978-1-47110-138-0

Casey Hill

Hidden

A Fallen Angel. A Devil on the Loose.

When a young girl is discovered dead on an isolated Irish country road, it seems at first glance to be a simple hit and run. Then the cops see the tattoo on her back – a pair of beautifully wrought angel wings that lend the victim a sense of ethereal innocence. Forensic investigator Reilly Steel is soon on the scene and her highly tuned sixth sense tells her there is more to this case than a straightforward murder.

But with almost zero evidence and no way to trace the girl's origin, Reilly and the police are at a loss. Then the angel tattoo is traced to other children – both dead and alive – who are similarly marked, and Reilly starts to suspect they have all been abducted by the same person. But why? And will Reilly get to the bottom of the mystery and uncover what links these children together before tragedy strikes again?

Paperback ISBN 978-0-85720-985-6
Ebook ISBN 978-0-85720-986-3